THE CRITICS LOVE
THE MANDY DYER MYSTERY SERIES

WASH, FOLD, AND DIE

"[A] tightly plotted who-done-it."—*Publishers Weekly*

"A DELIGHTFUL ROMP WITH AN IRREPRESSIBLE HEROINE."—*Romantic Times*

"If you love to laugh while you work through a mystery, you'll love *Wash, Fold, and Die.*"—*Rendezvous*

A DRESS TO DIE FOR

"A FUN READING EXPERIENCE, starring a delightful sleuth."—*Midwest Book Review*

"A WITTY, STYLISH MYSTERY with plenty of provocative twists and turns."—*Rendezvous*

"Johnson enlivens her plot with a quiet wit and a polished writing style."—*The Denver Post*

Please turn the page for more extraordinary acclaim. . .

HUNG UP TO DIE

"A HIGHLY ENTERTAINING BOOK . . . A good, fast-moving mystery with a lot of subtle humor . . . A fun read . . . you're going to like this one."
—*Rendezvous*

"Johnson's chatty dialogue and believable characters make for a lively story . . . skillful plotting and characterization."
—*Ft. Lauderdale Sun-Times*

"Johnson's own quick wit is the best reason to read *Hung Up to Die* . . . a strong straightforward mystery . . . I read it in one evening."
—*The Mystery Review*

TAKEN TO THE CLEANERS

"DELIGHTFUL. Good, clean fun."—Dorothy Cannell, author of *How to Murder the Man of Your Dreams*

"This book is definitely a lot of fun."
—*The Armchair Detective*

"Fast-paced and filled with good humor . . . *Taken to the Cleaners* is a delight."
—*I Love a Mystery*

Dell Books by Dolores Johnson

TAKEN TO THE CLEANERS
HUNG UP TO DIE
A DRESS TO DIE FOR
WASH, FOLD, AND DIE
HOMICIDE AND OLD LACE

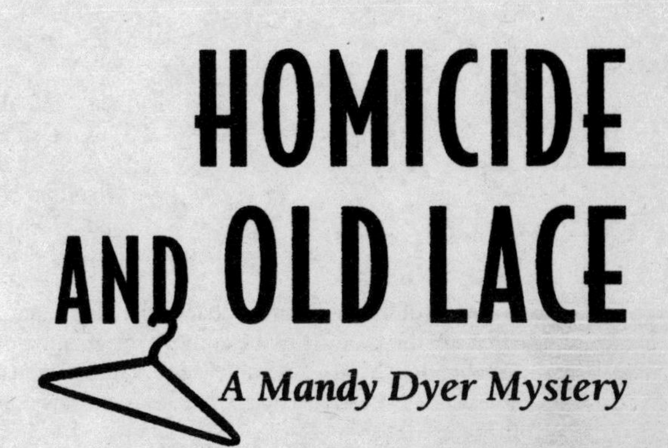

DOLORES JOHNSON

A DELL BOOK

Published by
Dell Publishing
a division of
Random House, Inc.
1540 Broadway
New York, New York 10036

Cover art by Ellis Chappell

ISBN 0-440-23524-3

Printed in the United States of America

Published simultaneously in Canada

September 2000

10 9 8 7 6 5 4 3 2 1
OPM

To my friends
Marilyn Higginbotham
Gayle Barnas
and
Barbara Freeman

ACKNOWLEDGMENTS

I wish to thank Detective Gary Hoffman of the Denver Police Department, Loren Ryerson of the Aspen Police Department, and Deputy Sheriff Roger Ryan at the Pitkin County Jail for answering my questions. Any errors in this book are mine and not the fault of the people I interviewed.

A special thanks for their help to members of my two critique groups—Rebecca Bates, Thora Chinnery, Diane Coffelt, Cindy Goff, Donna Schaper, and Barbara Snook; and to Lee Karr, Kay Bergstrom, Carol Caverly, Diane Davidson, Christine Jorgensen, Leslie O'Kane, and Peggy Swager. Also a debt of gratitude to my agents, Ruth Kagle and Meg Ruley, and to my editor, Laura Hoguet.

Finally, I want to thank Rose Keating for helping me move into the 21st Century with a new computer system.

CHAPTER 1

I didn't realize I was being set up when Olivia Torkelson brought me the wedding gown to be cleaned. Why would I? I'm a dry cleaner, and customers bring me wedding gowns all the time.

By the time I did catch on, I decided poor Olivia was even more of a victim than I was, and I didn't have the heart to tell her about it.

She came into Dyer's Cleaners one day in April with the satin and lace gown that had been worn, I found out later, by two earlier generations of Torkelson women.

"I would like to talk to the owner," she said, shoving a strand of long blonde hair back over her shoulder. It was a gesture she would repeat throughout our first meeting, and at one point I almost offered her a rubber band so she could pull her hair back from her face in a ponytail.

She was sweet-looking rather than beautiful, with gray eyes and eyebrows that were dark enough to make me wonder if she might originally have been a brunette like me. I couldn't see any dark roots, however, and so I gave her the benefit of the doubt.

"I'm Mandy Dyer, the owner," I said, only slightly irritated that new customers always seem to expect a man to be the proprietor of the business. However, in this case, I was wrong.

"I'm sorry," she said. "I was expecting someone older."

Okay, I could accept that kind of misunderstanding. I'm thirty-five, and the woman across the counter from me looked to be in her mid-twenties. There was a vulnerable quality about her that made me feel as if I were the one who should apologize. I was sure that same quality made men want to protect her.

"You were recommended as an excellent dry cleaner, and I'm getting married here in Denver in June," she said as she gave her hair another flick, then introduced herself. "I'd like to wear my grandmother's wedding gown, but it needs to be cleaned and taken in."

That was an understatement. The gown had yellowed through the years, and when she held it up, it was apparent that her grandmother had been a much larger woman. Olivia was maybe five feet two inches tall and thin. I didn't think the heavy gown with its sweetheart neckline, gathered skirt, and long train was going to do a thing for her. It would swallow her up. She needed a sheath or a princess-style gown with her slender figure, but I certainly wasn't going to be the one to tell a bride what to wear at her own wedding.

"You know, it might be cheaper to buy a new wedding gown," I said, realizing that the whole thing was going to have to be torn apart and reassembled, even the long, lace-covered sleeves. "It's going to be expensive to get the dress cleaned and altered, maybe as much as seven-hundred-and-fifty or a thousand dollars."

"Oh, that's okay. Mother said it wouldn't be cheap."

Since money appeared to be no object, I told her we'd have to clean the gown before we did the alterations. Then our seamstress, Katerina, would call her for the first of several fittings, after which we would clean the dress a final time. Olivia agreed, gave me the veil that went with the dress, and left. The veil was no problem to clean but getting the dress ready for the wedding was a different matter.

We cleaned it in what's known as a wet-clean process. This is a method favored by cleaners because it works beautifully on satin and cuts down on the use of chemicals. It's really just water with the temperature and agitation carefully controlled to protect against shrinkage.

After that, the gown was lifted overhead on a hoist my Uncle Chet had installed to air-dry long garments. It hung there for several days like a huge panel the artist Christo might have used when he once draped a Colorado canyon or wrapped the Reichstag in Germany in some tightly woven nylon fabric.

Katerina set up an appointment with Olivia for an initial fitting, but unfortunately, she forgot to mention it to me when she called in sick that day. So when Olivia showed up, it was up to either me or Betty from our laundry department to do the fitting. Betty's a reformed bag lady who was filling in for Katerina with the minor repairs that called for immediate attention. She swore she'd been a dressmaker in a previous life, but I wasn't ready to trust her with anything complicated.

I decided to handle the pinning and tucking myself. It was just that Katerina, our Russian-born seamstress, had a way with the customers that I couldn't begin to duplicate. I showed Olivia to our spacious fitting room, which had a couple of yellow chairs and a glass-topped table with a bouquet of artificial flowers, a bowl of potpourri, and a box of tissues. I told her to put on the gown while I went to get the pins and measuring tape from Katerina's worktable back in the plant.

"I'm sorry I'm late," Olivia apologized. "I'm a little upset this morning."

"That's okay," I said, since I hadn't been expecting her in the first place. I pointed to the tissues. "Be sure to blot your lipstick before you put on the gown, and on the day of the wedding, put on the gown before you do your makeup." After those words of wisdom, I promised to return in a minute.

When I reached the repair and alterations department, Betty looked up from sewing a button on the sleeve of a man's jacket. "Want me to do that for you?" she asked.

Betty was working out better at her job than I'd hoped, despite the dire predictions of Mack Rivers, my plant manager, but I still didn't trust her with the customers. You never knew what she was going to say at any given moment. She probably would have told Olivia that she had no business wearing a dress that looked like a lace-covered tent and was as heavy as the mast on a sailing ship.

"No, I can handle it, Betty," I said. "You just keep working on the orders back here."

She finished sewing on the button, and snipped off the thread. "You know, I was watching an old rerun of *Cheers* the other night . . ."

Well, if she wanted to watch a sitcom about a bar, that was fine with me. Just as long as she didn't start patronizing one herself. She'd had a drinking problem when she was on the street, but since she came to work for me, she'd stayed away from the bottle.

"Anyway," she said, "Cliff, the mailman, asked if anyone in Cheers knew why men have buttons on the sleeves of their jackets. Any fool can see they don't button a damn thing—so do you know why they have 'em?"

I put the little watermelon-looking pincushion on my wrist so I would look like a bona fide seamstress. "I have no idea."

"Napoleon ordered buttons sewn on his soldiers' jackets—" Betty paused for dramatic effect. "—so the men wouldn't rub their runny noses on their sleeves when they had a cold."

I grimaced, and Betty gave a loud guffaw as I left. Yep, I'd made the right decision to do the fitting myself.

When I reached the changing room, Olivia was on her cell phone. I heard her just as I reached the door.

". . . but why would someone send me a weird note like that?" she was asking a person on the other end of the line.

"Oh, excuse me." I started to withdraw.

"No, I'm not going to tell Mom." She shook her head as she glanced up at me. "Look, I gotta go." She put the phone away and rose from the chair, still in the jeans and blue sweater she'd had on when I left her. "I'm sorry," she said. "It just isn't a good day."

It didn't get any better when I helped her into the wedding gown. I hadn't realized just how thin she was, and the dress with its low-cut bodice and gathered skirt almost slipped right on down to the floor.

"I don't think Nana's dress does a thing for me," she said. My sentiments exactly. "But Mother has her heart set on my wearing the dress, and I don't want to disappoint her." She puckered up her lips in a delicate little pout, and it made me think that maybe I'd been wrong about her age. She sounded younger than twenty-five.

I tried hard not to say anything, but I couldn't help myself. "You know, it's your wedding, and you really should pick out the dress you want."

"Oh, but Mother wore the dress herself, and she would be so disappointed if I didn't wear it, too."

Now I was convinced that she was younger than she looked. Either that or she had a serious problem with Mom, and the man she married was going to be in for a rough time with Mumsy always in the picture.

"When I got married," I said, venturing into an area I seldom discussed with customers, "my mother would have liked me to wear something with ruffles and a hooped skirt that looked as if it were straight out of *Gone with the Wind*.

She's the frilly type, but I'm not, and I had to put my foot down."

Olivia looked down at my hand with the pincushion bracelet on it. "You're not wearing a wedding ring, and I just assumed you were single. I'm sorry." She apologized a lot.

"I'm divorced." I stuck one of the pins in my mouth so I wouldn't have to talk about it anymore. Katerina did that all the time, but I was always afraid I would inhale at the wrong time and swallow one of the tools of the trade. It's the same reason I wouldn't want to be a glass blower. I removed the pin, and then I felt as if a further explanation was necessary. "My husband was a womanizer, so the marriage didn't work out."

"I hope my marriage works out." Olivia showed me her engagement ring, which was so large it looked like an ice cube on her hand. "Isn't it beautiful? But my fiancé has been married twice before and that worries me."

The poor kid. She sounded as if she needed a friend more than she did a seamstress, and I wondered whom she'd been talking to on the phone. Obviously, it wasn't her mother. Mom sounded as if she were more interested in the bridal-gown tradition than seeing that her daughter was happy and had the kind of wedding she wanted.

"So what'd you wear to your wedding?" Olivia asked.

"Something simple," I said as I grabbed a clump of material at her waist. I didn't add that the gown had been a short cream-colored dress and that I'd been married to Larry Landry, alias Larry the Lustful Law Student, by a judge he knew through his law school connections. It wasn't something that a customer needed to know, especially one who would soon be wearing a gown that would swallow her up.

"I would have liked something simple, too, but Mother has her heart set on a big wedding since I'm the only girl in the family."

I stopped pinning and tucking. "Maybe you should bring

your mother with you for the next fitting." I didn't want to come right out and say that seeing Olivia in the dress might make Mom realize that her daughter would look better in a different style.

Olivia shook her head. "No, let's just go ahead with it."

I grabbed a handful of material at the waist. "Okay, see, when we take it in, it's going to look a lot different."

"Okay, anything you say, Mandy."

It seemed sad when she called me Mandy—as if I were her best buddy.

"What does your fiancé think about the dress?" I asked.

"Oh, you can't show the groom your dress before the wedding. That would be bad luck."

Oh, yeah, that's right. Maybe that's what jinxed my marriage—the fact that Larry saw me in my wedding dress in the car on the way to the ceremony. After all, we had to get to the judge's chambers some way.

"What does your fiancé do?" I asked. I was just making conversation as I pinned huge clumps of material together at the seams.

"Oh, he works for my father, and he has an excellent future with the firm," she said, tipping her head to one side as if hoping that would make the dress look better.

Big surprise. Obviously he had an excellent future, I thought, if he were marrying the boss's daughter.

"It just doesn't look good on me, does it?" She sounded as if she might start to cry.

"It's going to look a whole lot better when we get it altered," I said, trying to make her feel better. "My seamstress will baste it up, and we'll call you in for a second fitting. It'll be fine. Just wait and see."

She sniffed, and I handed her a tissue and tried to change the subject.

"Do you think you're going to want such a long train? It's pretty heavy." She seemed so fragile I wasn't sure she could march down the aisle without a whole crew of people to hold it up. Heck, it might even take a couple of diesel engines to move it.

"Mom wants the train." She gave a half-sob and stood up straighter as if trying to resign herself to living with Mom's desires. "By the way, would you be able to bring the gown to the hotel the day of the wedding?"

"Sure, if that's what you want. We can deliver it as long as it's in the Denver area."

"That would be great. That way the dress won't get wrinkled—with the long train and all."

I stopped to grab the notepad where I was writing down her measurements. "What day is it?"

"It's a Saturday. Is that a problem?"

"No, Saturday is fine." It meant I'd have to make the delivery myself, but I usually worked Saturdays anyway.

She gave me the date and time and the name of the hotel where the wedding and reception were to be held. It wasn't far south on Colorado Boulevard and would only take ten minutes or so to get there from the Cherry Creek Mall area where our cleaners is located.

"What time do you want me to be there?" I asked before I began to pin another seam in the bodice of the dress. Unfortunately, this time I did venture to put a couple of pins in my mouth, a la Katerina.

"The wedding's at two, so noon should be fine, and just in case there's another wedding at the hotel that day—" She paused for just a beat. "—it's for the Torkelson-Landry wedding."

I spat out the pins and ran the one I was using into my middle finger.

"Ow." I yanked my finger away from the dress before blood squirted on the bodice. Even if it had, we remove stains, after all—even blood, and right now, I was feeling like drawing some more if my worst fears were confirmed.

"What happened? Are you okay?" Olivia tried to look

around at me as I grabbed for a tissue in lieu of a bandage and wrapped it around my finger. Her voice was filled with a concern that seemed out of proportion to what had happened.

"I just stabbed my finger with a pin," I said, trying to reassure her. "It's nothing." I watched as blood soaked through the tissue. Thank goodness, I hadn't jabbed the pin into Olivia or it might have gone clear through her rib cage.

"I'm sorry," she said, still sounding uneasy. "Do you want us to do this another day?"

"No, it'll stop bleeding in a minute, and I'm just about through." With my finger wrapped in tissue and sticking out at an angle as if I were making an obscene gesture, I finished pinning the bodice of the dress. Then I got down on my knees and surveyed the hem. "Are you planning to wear heels?" I asked. When she said yes, I told her that she should wear them the next time she came in. If the skirt was too long, Katerina was probably going to have to take it up at the waist because of the lace sections sewn around the bottom.

My voice was shaking as I spoke, and I cleared my throat and tried to sound nonchalant. "Is your fiancé's first name—uh—Sam, by any chance? I think we have a customer by that name, and I wondered if he recommended us."

I knew she was going to say no, because we had no customer named Sam Landry.

"No," she said, "it's Lawrence Landry, but everyone calls him Larry."

Damn his lustful, lecherous hide. I reached down on the floor, picked up the pins I'd spit out of my mouth and jammed them into the pincushion as if it were Larry's heart. My ex-husband apparently wanted me to know he was getting remarried, but why would he do it in such a nasty way?

I wished the pincushion were a Larry-the-Lustful-Law-Student Voodoo doll so I could have stuck the pins in his private parts.

"Are you sure you're all right?" Olivia asked.

I looked up at her and gave her what I hoped was a reassuring smile. There was no sense taking my anger out on her or making her more nervous than she already seemed.

"I hope this isn't some kind of omen," she said.

"Oh, of course not, Olivia. I'm fine."

"Can I tell you something?" Her voice was almost a whisper.

I nodded.

"Well, I got a note in the mail this morning. It said if I decided to marry Larry I'd be *really* sorry. It sounded like a threat."

CHAPTER 2

I tried to comfort Olivia, but I didn't know how. She might indeed be sorry if she married Larry, but it wouldn't have anything to do with a prediction in a letter.

"Don't worry about it," I said finally. "It sounds as if someone's just trying to play a joke on you."

Olivia seemed to take comfort from my words, but as soon as she left, I went tromping off to the dry-cleaning department, holding the tons of Torkelson satin in my arms.

"That unethical, evil bastard," I said as I reached Mack, my plant manager, at his spotting board where he was removing a stain from a suit jacket. "Of all the unmitigated gall."

Mack looked at me accusingly. "You're dragging the gown on the floor, and we'll have to clean it again."

I didn't bother to tell him that the gown was being altered, and we'd have to clean it anyway. It wouldn't have made any difference to him.

Mack had always seen himself as an artist with a steam gun and bottles of spotting solutions, able to work his magic on the most difficult stains and the most fragile fabrics. To deface the garment after he'd cleaned it to perfection was a sacrilege in his eyes. I, on the other hand, saw this gown as the symbol of some sort of gigantic plot, designed and planned by Larry to embarrass and humiliate me. And had he even considered how it would make Olivia feel?

"Just guess the name of the man who will soon be seeing his bride in this monstrosity of material," I said.

"The way you're acting, I would say it was Larry."

"How'd you know that?"

Mack shrugged and took the gown from me. "I figure no one else would make you this upset." He went up front and hung it on our rail for long gowns.

"You're right," I said, trailing after him and trying to explain how I'd discovered that the gown, which had already been in our cleaners for a week, belonged to Larry's bride-to-be. "The nerve of him sending his poor fiancée here to get her gown cleaned and altered."

"But how do you know Larry's the one who recommended that she come to Dyer's Cleaners?" Mack asked, heading back to the dry-cleaning department.

That stopped me for a moment. It had never occurred to me that anyone but Larry could have perpetrated this dastardly deed.

"Maybe it was someone else," he suggested.

That's the way Mack is. Always able to provide a different perspective when I go off on an emotional tangent. A big black man, Mack had worked for my Uncle Chet for years and had been one of the constants in my life. He'd always been the voice of reason when I had problems with my much-married mother, my ever-changing stepfathers, and even my uncle who, for the sake of in-law relationships, had been required to walk a diplomatic tightrope between Mom and me. Mack had also been my support when Uncle Chet died and left me the cleaners. That was shortly after my break-up with Larry, and I don't think I could have gotten through the turmoil of those months without him.

Despite Mack's logic, I couldn't quite give up on the idea that Larry had suggested Olivia bring the gown to us.

I continued to rant and rave until Mack suggested that we take a break and go over to Tico Taco's for a cup of coffee.

Once we were tucked away with our drinks—actually a coke for me and a beer for Mack—in a back booth of the restaurant, I continued to vent. "Doesn't Larry know that this will be an embarrassment to his fiancée, even more than it is to me?"

"What about Larry? I can't see him wanting to embarrass himself by having the two of you get together."

"Good point," I admitted. "You know, I should have told her about Larry right there in the fitting room, but frankly, I was too dumbfounded." I lifted my middle finger, still wrapped in a tissue. "I even stabbed myself with a pin."

"I wondered how you did that."

I told him the whole story, punctuating each point by jabbing my finger at him. Finally, I decided that the gesture was best left for Larry, and I put my hand back in my lap.

"So, should I call her and suggest that she take the gown someplace else?" I was wishing that I'd gotten a beer, too, or maybe a shot of whiskey, but I still had to work on the counter this afternoon, and besides, I didn't want to set a bad example for Betty. "Maybe I could just call his fiancée and say we can't clean the gown. She'd look better in a gown with less material, anyway."

Mack shook his head and took a drink of his beer. Mack was through for the day and had left his assistant to take the last load of clothes out of one of the dry-cleaning machines. "No, Mandy, we're in the business to clean clothes no matter who the customer is, and that's what we should do."

"I suppose," I said reluctantly. "She actually did seem like a nice person, even if she's really naive. But maybe she should be forewarned about Larry."

Actually, maybe she already had been. Maybe the note was from Larry's second wife, Patricia, the lady lawyer he'd left me for. That marriage hadn't lasted long either.

"Nope." Mack interrupted my thoughts. "You don't need to get involved in that, and besides, you'd only feel bad about it after you told her." He always did take the high road.

"Okay, but listen to this," I continued, "Olivia—that's the fiancée's name—she wants us to bring the wedding gown to the hotel where she's getting married."

"Have Phil do it," Mack said, referring to our route driver.

"It's on a Saturday so I was planning to do it myself, but what if I run into her and Larry? That'll be a whole lot worse than if I'd told her right now."

Mack was the epitome of calm and reason. "Look," he said. " 'The world is what you make of it. If it doesn't fit, make alterations.' "

I gave him a puzzled look. Wasn't that what we were doing already with the gown?

"I bet you don't know who said that."

Sometimes his philosophizing irritated me. "I have no idea. I suppose the same person who said, 'If life hands you a lemon, make lemonade.' "

Mack chuckled. "No, it's from a movie."

I figured he was trying to get my mind off Larry with our ongoing game to try to fool each other with film quotes. I had to admit I was stumped.

He looked pleased with himself. "Linda Hunt said it in *Silverado*, but it really fits here."

So it did. After all, I was the boss, and I could order Mack to make the delivery. But Mack and I didn't operate that way. "Please, would you do it for me?" I asked.

Mack grinned. "Thought you'd never ask."

I felt an overwhelming sense of relief. "Okay, I'll really owe you for this. But maybe when Olivia comes in for her next fitting with Katerina, I can at least ask her who recommended Dyer's Cleaners to her."

Mack shrugged. "I guess—if you really have to find out, and knowing you, you won't rest until you do."

"If it's someone other than Larry," I said, "then it has to be Olivia's worst enemy in the world."

"Or," Mack suggested, "someone who doesn't even know the connection and happens to think we're the best cleaners in town."

The gown was a constant reminder of Larry for the next month. Katerina took out huge clumps of material from the seams, and all I could think was that hopefully any daughter Olivia and Larry had from the upcoming union might not have to wear the gown again—unless she, too, was thin as a porch rail.

When Olivia returned to the cleaners for her final fitting with Katerina and later for her inspection of the finished gown, I wasn't around. On the first occasion, Phil had called in sick and I was out running the route to our business customers at their offices. The second time I was at lunch, something I seldom did off-premises, and I took that as a good sign. Maybe I didn't really need to know who had sent her to us.

Better just to let it go and collect the money we would make off the gown, which was charged out as billable hours to Katerina and Mack. I might have felt more kindly to Larry if I found out he wasn't the one who recommended Dyer's Cleaners. But who cared? He was out of my life now.

All the plans for Mack to deliver the gown to the hotel had been made on the Friday before the wedding. He would pick up the gown from the cleaners Saturday morning, using the company's panel truck to haul it to the hotel without wrinkling it.

The trouble was that Mack got called out of town Saturday morning. His brother had suffered a heart attack in Alabama, and Mack needed to leave immediately to be with him. I could hardly refuse to let him go, but I think the thing that bothered me the most was that it reminded me that Mack was getting old himself. He was in his early sixties, and he'd be retiring soon. If I couldn't get along without him for a few days, I didn't know what I'd do without him for the long haul.

I tried calling Phil, our regular driver, but he'd gone camping for the weekend. In desperation, I even called Harry, one of the pressers who sometimes doubled as a driver, but his daughter said her parents had gone shopping and wouldn't be back until five. There was nothing to do but take the gown to the hotel myself.

It was an overcast day, unusually cool for June, and I prayed it wouldn't begin to rain before I made the delivery. I was in jeans and a T-shirt and wearing running shoes, the better to get in and out of the hotel in a hurry so I wouldn't run into Larry.

I never thought about bumping into his friends until I got to the hotel. I made it across the lobby to the registration desk without seeing anyone familiar. So far, so good. I had the top of the gown lifted high in the air and was holding the bottom with its runaway train as far off the floor as I could get it. The dress was in a long poly-garment bag, but I was trying to avoid as many wrinkles as possible. In case there were any, I had a small iron tucked in my shoulder bag so I could do some touch-up pressing.

I told the desk clerk I was here for the Torkelson-Landry wedding, and although the words sort of stuck in my throat, the woman said the bride was waiting for me in room 421. She directed me to a bank of elevators, but I asked hopefully if there was a freight elevator I could use, the better to avoid Larry or his entourage.

"No, the passenger elevator will be more convenient," the woman said.

I was tempted to go for the stairs, but with my luck, I'd trip on an errant piece of plastic or the train and fall all the way to the basement with the gown, ripping and soiling it as I went. I decided the elevator was best after all, and I was almost sure there was no one inside when I climbed aboard.

Trouble was I couldn't figure out how to punch the button for the fourth floor. I tried to hit it with my elbow, and the doors started to close. Lord knows where I'd wind up.

Someone pushed the door open just as it was almost shut. "You going up?" a man asked. Oh, swell, the voice sounded vaguely familiar.

"Yes," I mumbled into the plastic that hid me from view.

"Looks like you have your hands full," the voice said. "None of the buttons are lit. What floor do you want?"

By then I recognized the voice, and with the obvious exception of Larry, it was the one person in the world I would like least to share an elevator ride with.

"Four," I said, more loudly now. If I got this over quickly, maybe I could escape without being recognized.

The elevator door closed, and we started our ascent. My stomach dropped to the basement when the man spoke again.

"Mandy, is that you?"

I peeked around the gown. "Oh, hi, Brad," I said with as much bravado as I could muster. "Fancy meeting you here."

But why wouldn't he be here? He was Larry's best friend, after all, and the person who'd dragged Larry into all those singles' bars when we were married. Not with a great deal of protest from Larry, I'm sure. And that's where Larry had found bachelorette number two, Patricia, who'd become wife number two and could have sent the note that Olivia had told me about.

I'd always thought of Larry's buddy as Brad the Cad. He was a criminal lawyer now, but he still reminded me of Woody Allen with a weight problem. Right now he looked like Woody Allen masquerading as a chubby penguin in his black tuxedo. When I managed to peer around the bridal gown, he was staring at me through his horn-rimmed glasses with a look of pure delight on his face. Could he have been the one who recommended Dyer's Cleaners to poor Olivia? After all, he was a practical joker without peer.

"What are you doing here?" he asked. "Don't tell me you're delivering the wedding gown for Larry's bride-to-be?"

"How did you even know it was me?" But of course, he would know it was me. Even with my face hidden from view, our Dyer's Cleaners logo was emblazoned all over the plastic bag that covered the gown.

Brad snickered as the elevator stopped and the doors opened. "Fourth floor," he said. "Lingerie, nightgowns—everything for a perfect honeymoon, including the ex-wife."

I hoped Brad realized I was giving him a look that could kill from behind the yards of lace and satin that hid my face.

"Seriously, can I help you with the dress?" he asked.

"No," I said haughtily. "Just keep this to yourself, okay?" But I came to a stop outside the elevator, unable to see which way to go. "Well, maybe you could point me toward room 421."

"It's to the right, chief." The elevator door closed in front of what I was sure was Brad's gloating face. I would bet he was on his way to spread the news that Larry's ex-wife was the delivery person, bearing the bride-to-be's wedding gown.

Oh, well, as long as I didn't see Larry it was okay. He would probably see the cleaning bag at some point, anyway, and then he would know I'd been here. Maybe it would even give him a ghostly feeling that his ex-wives were haunting his wedding.

I was halfway down the hall when someone yelled in a commanding voice. "It's about time you got here. We've been waiting for the gown."

I went toward the sound of the voice, and when I managed to lower the top of the dress, I saw a stout, broad-shouldered woman with steel-gray hair who must be Olivia's mom.

Olivia confirmed it when I entered the room. "Mother was starting to get upset that you wouldn't be here in time.

She's anxious to see the gown." Olivia was the one who sounded upset.

So why didn't Mom come to the final fitting for a dress rehearsal? I hooked the gown on a knob on a storage compartment above the closet so that the hem wouldn't touch the floor. Then I prepared to make a quick getaway. No tip necessary, and to heck with the touch-up pressing.

"No, no," Mrs. Torkelson said. "We'll need you here to make sure everything is satisfactory with the gown."

Okay, so I was going to have to stay at least until Olivia was safely tucked into her gown with the train from hell.

Olivia's blonde hair was piled high on her head, which only served to emphasize the thinness of her face. It had a washed-out look, but that was because she'd taken my suggestion not to apply her makeup until she had put on the gown. I suggested that she protect the hairdo with her hands until Mom and I got the gown over her head.

Once she was zipped into the gown, I stepped back to check the overall effect. Frankly, the gown looked better than I expected now that it had been cut down to size.

I put our garment bag back on the hanger so Olivia could use it for the gown once the ceremony was over. Then I got out the iron, plugged it in, and did a little touch-up pressing. It was mainly for show; the gown had survived the trip remarkably well.

I started to make my exit, but Mrs. Torkelson began to shake her head. "No, no, no," she said again. "That won't do. There's a loose thread there at the waistline. You'll need to snip it off."

Short of biting it with my teeth, I didn't know how I was going to do it. "Okay," I said finally, "but I'll need a pair of scissors."

Mrs. Torkelson went to the door, and in the voice of a general commanding her troops, she yelled down the hall. "Charlotte. Yes, you, Charlotte. We need a pair of scissors in here. On the double."

Where Mrs. Torkelson expected the unseen Charlotte to get scissors I didn't know, but there was a knock on the door a few minutes later.

"Come in," Mrs. Torkelson shouted.

"The door's locked," someone said from the hallway.

Mrs. Torkelson went over and opened it to a young woman wearing a street-length blue dress with shoes to match. She was carrying the largest pair of scissors I'd ever seen. They looked almost like gardening shears, and snipping off a thread with them was like using an Uzi to kill a spider. I clipped off the offending thread, put the scissors on a dresser, and prepared to leave.

"You'll need to make sure there aren't any more loose ends that need to be cut off," Olivia's mother continued.

I felt like telling her that I was the only loose end left in the room, and frankly I needed to get out of here before my "ex" tied the knot with her daughter. Otherwise, things might really unravel.

It wouldn't have done any good because Mrs. Torkelson wasn't listening. "While you do that, I need to check on the flowers for the reception," she said, then turned to the young woman. "And Charlotte, I want you to see if there's anything the bridesmaids need before you go down to attend to the guest book." Even though Charlotte was a part of the wedding, she must be the "gofer" girl like they always have on movie sets—someone designated to run all the errands.

Charlotte nodded, pushing back a lock of her light brown hair which lacked the shine and curl of Olivia's salon set.

Olivia's mother grabbed the gofer girl's arm and led her out into the hallway. A quiet settled over the room. I checked the other seams. Nope, no other loose ends except me.

I was suddenly overcome with guilt. I wondered if I should tell Olivia who I was before she found out from someone else, but I knew I couldn't do it at this late date.

"I'm so nervous," she said right then. "Were you nervous before you got married, Mandy?"

Oh, please, just get me out of here. "Sure," I said, "everyone's nervous at a time like this." If she only knew. My stomach felt like a corroded, rusted-out engine right now about to spill its fuel all over her wedding gown. I got up and started to leave. "Just try to enjoy it, okay?" I wondered what Emily Post would suggest one say in way of a farewell to the future bride of one's ex-husband. "It'll be fine," I added. "Just wait and see."

"Thanks, Mandy."

Olivia's words trailed after me as I slammed the door shut. I was now in full retreat. I started to the elevator, then thought better of it. I finally found a stairway, yanked open the door, snuck down the three flights of steps and out a side entrance of the building. I unlocked the truck and breathed a sigh of relief once I was behind its tinted windows where I could hide my nervous breakdown from view. Then I looked around and realized I hadn't taken the veil with its elaborate headdress up to the room when I took the dress. Damn, damn, damn.

I was amazed Olivia's mother hadn't missed the veil, but I guess she was too busy giving Charlotte and me orders. I'd have to run the gauntlet one last time, but it took me a few minutes to work up the courage. Maybe I could cover my head with the veil; that way no one would recognize me.

I forced myself to return to the side entrance of the hotel, the long veil dangling out behind me like a sail on a windless day, and trudged back up the stairs to the fourth floor.

When I got to Room 421, I knocked on the door, which was open a crack. "Olivia, I forgot the veil to your wedding gown." I pushed inside.

The first person I saw was Olivia. She was on the floor with the scissors I'd just used embedded in her back. The second person I saw was Larry, ex-husband and the groom-to-be. He was bent over Olivia's body.

CHAPTER 3

"She—she's dead," Larry said in a voice so choked I hardly recognized it. He was feeling for a pulse at Olivia's wrist, but he suddenly glanced up at me as if I were part of some surrealistic nightmare. "What are you doing here?"

I shook my head in horror. I couldn't even speak, but behind me, someone let out a high-pitched scream and rushed past me. The woman was a blur of blue taffeta, and her voice seemed to rise in decibels as she got closer to the body.

"OhmyGod, ohmyGod," she screamed, her words running together in her panic.

Larry was still staring at me as if he knew I wasn't supposed to be in this particular nightmare.

I started to move out of the way of his accusing eyes, but I was nearly knocked over by Olivia's mother as she rushed into the room. Mrs. Torkelson let out a shriek and fell to the floor beside her daughter where she tried to yank the scissors from Olivia's back. I could see where blood had run down across the white satin from another puncture wound and pooled on the carpet.

Other people ran into the room behind Olivia's mother. I knew they shouldn't be tromping all over the crime scene. I just didn't know what to do about it. Mrs. Torkelson shouldn't be touching the murder weapon, either, but I couldn't help thinking that maybe she would cover up my fingerprints. My prints were sure to be on the scissors from when I'd snipped the loose threads off the bridal gown. I hoped the killer's prints would be there, too, but as I glanced at the crowd now swarming toward the body, I saw that all the bridesmaids were wearing elbow-length gloves. Nobody seemed to have blood on them the way they should have if they'd jammed the scissors into Olivia's body.

Soon I couldn't see the body or Olivia's mother. The full-skirted blue bridesmaids' dresses and the black tuxedo legs of the groomsmen blocked my view. As the whole bridal party flooded the room, someone ripped the fragile lace of the veil I trailed across the floor. All I could hear were the moans from Olivia's mother and the screams of other people as they drew near her.

"Everyone should get out of here," I yelled, but no one paid any attention to me.

"He did it." The voice came from the circle around the body, and as a few people shrank back from the speaker, I saw that it was another bridesmaid—this one with short, dark hair. She waved her hand at Larry. "I saw him leaving the room just a few minutes ago."

Larry's normally tanned face turned almost as white as the shirt and vest underneath his tuxedo jacket. "No," he said as he shook his head in denial. "I just wanted to see how she was doing. I knocked on the door and called her name, but no one answered so I left."

Other members of the bridal party retreated from the groom-to-be. A few left the room, apparently unable to look at the body of Olivia in her once-pristine white wedding gown. Mrs. Torkelson was on her knees sobbing.

"Larry must have come back after he killed her so he could pretend to find the body," the bridesmaid continued, still shaking her finger at Larry.

He was no longer the neatly-groomed man who always

reminded me of a young George Hamilton with his dark hair, tanned skin, and dazzling smile. He was on the defensive now, and his lips seemed gray and drawn as if he could hardly open his mouth to speak.

"I came back because I began to wonder why I hadn't heard anyone inside the room," he said in a strained voice. "It scared me when I saw that the door was open a crack."

Thank God I wasn't the focus of his attention anymore, but why would Larry kill his bride-to-be?

"Larry's right." This time I could see Charlotte, the gofer girl who'd brought me the scissors in the first place. "I saw him go toward her room and then come back down the hall again. He wouldn't have had time to go inside."

Larry gave her a grateful look, just as I spotted a bellhop at the door. I went over to him, still clutching the veil in my hands. "Please, call the police right away," I whispered. "Someone has been murdered in here."

The words were barely out of my mouth when I heard Larry. "Don't let her get away." He was trying to push himself through the crowd toward me. His buddy, Brad, whom I'd already seen on the elevator, was right behind him.

"What the hell are you doing here?" Larry yelled, grabbing my shoulders and shaking me. "Did you do this?"

I tried to pull out of his grasp. "Of course not. You were the one bent over her body when I came in the room."

"Calm down, both of you." Brad wedged himself between us, and for once I was grateful to the short, chubby guy and his legal know-how. "Go back to your room, Larry, and wait for me. I'll see that Mandy doesn't leave, but right now, we need to get out of here."

Larry gave a shake of his head toward me. "First, I want to know why she's here."

"She was delivering Olivia's wedding gown when I saw her on the elevator," Brad said.

"Why were you doing that, for Christ's sakes?" Larry practically spat out the words.

"Olivia came to me and wanted her grandmother's wedding gown cleaned. I didn't know she was marrying you."

Brad was trying to push Larry out of the room, but Larry resisted. "But why would Olivia come to you?"

"Someone recommended me to her."

"Go back to your room, Larry." Brad glared at him and turned to the rest of the horrified spectators. "And everyone else, get out of here, but don't leave the hotel. The police are going to want to talk to all of you."

Finally, Larry left in the company of a groomsman I didn't know. Thank God for Brad the Cad. I never thought I'd say that. After all, I'd always held him and his singles' bar antics partially responsible for my divorce.

The rest of the bridal party followed, giving me curious looks and a wide berth as they left. But the first bridesmaid who'd rushed into the room was still standing by the body, her scream having turned into a whimper. She was tall with long, blonde hair piled high on her head the way Olivia's had been, and she look vaguely familiar. I wondered where I'd seen her.

Brad went back and grabbed her as a slender man with graying hair pushed his way through the departing crowd. Despite his slight build, he had a commanding presence which came partly from his ramrod posture and partly from his orator's voice. "What's going on here?"

People parted to let him enter, and then he saw Olivia.

"Oh, dear Lord," he said, and he seemed to shrink before my eyes. "Olivia." He dropped to the floor beside Mrs. Torkelson, and I could only assume it was Olivia's father.

As I hurried out of the room, I noticed that the Dyer's Cleaners' bag was crumpled on the floor by the door. I stepped around it and wondered why it wasn't over the hanger where I'd left it so Olivia could return the gown to the bag once the ceremony was over. It didn't matter now.

"I'll sit over there, Brad." I motioned to a chair in an alcove a short distance from Olivia's room as Brad led the last bridesmaid down the hall.

He nodded, and I dragged the bridal veil with me to the chair as if it were some sort of security blanket. I was grateful for the fact that the chair was far enough away from Olivia's room that I didn't have to look at her body.

I should never have agreed to clean Olivia's bridal gown. I should have followed my own instincts and not listened to Mack with his the-customer-is-always-right attitude. But I couldn't really fault Mack for that. Nope, it was my own cowardice for not telling Olivia that I couldn't clean the gown once I'd already accepted it. Could I help it if I didn't know the name of the groom until we were almost through the first fitting?

I wasn't sure I could sell my innocence to the police, not with Larry raising questions about my presence. And maybe I should even be thankful that it hadn't been Mack who'd delivered the gown. Larry could just as easily have made the accusation against him since Mack, in his role as my surrogate father, had been almost as angry at Larry as I had been when the lustful law student dumped me. I'd rather be the one under suspicion than to have it be Mack. Besides, the thing that was wrong with the Mack scenario was that he probably would have had the good sense to bring the veil up to Olivia's room at the same time he delivered the wedding gown and would have been long gone from the scene by the time she was killed.

I soon realized that, even if I'd gotten away before this happened, I would have been a suspect, anyway. Brad would have told the cops about running into me in the elevator, and the police would have seen the garment bag with the Dyer's Cleaners' logo on it inside the room. If those things weren't bad enough, Olivia's mother and the hapless Charlotte had left the room by the time I finished checking for loose ends.

I was sure I'd shut the door behind me when I left that first time, and it should have locked automatically. It had been locked when Charlotte came to the room. Whoever came in next would have had to gain entry with a key or else Olivia would have had to let them in. And that person must have been her killer.

But why had Larry and I found the door ajar when we returned? All I could figure out was that the door must not close by itself the way most hotel doors do and the killer hadn't taken time to slam it shut as he fled the room. Neither had Larry when he saw Olivia's body and rushed inside.

Suddenly I felt like crying, but just as I started to tear up, I heard someone knocking on the door across the hall from me. My eyes shot open, and I saw Brad.

"Where's Ryan?" he asked when one of the tuxedoed men inside opened the door.

"Beats me," the guy said. "Knowing Ryan, he's probably drowning his sorrows at a bar somewhere after that big blow-up awhile ago."

Who was Ryan? And what had the fight been about? At least this new development got my mind off Olivia for a moment. I didn't really want to start bawling in the hallway of a Denver hotel.

I was especially glad I didn't embarrass myself right then. The police arrived along with the paramedics as I was pondering the unanswerable questions about Ryan. At first, there were just uniformed cops and the ambulance unit. A short time later, the plainclothes crew arrived. I presumed they included a couple of homicide officers, someone from the medical examiner's office, a lab tech or two, and probably even the house detective.

I wasn't sure whether to be relieved or upset that my own personal homicide detective, Stan Foster, wasn't among the group. We'd been having a great relationship the last few months, once we'd cleared the air about a lot of things that had been bothering us. One of them had to do with his opinion that I'd had entirely too much involvement in some other murder cases, but that had nothing to do with why I neglected to tell him I was cleaning the wedding gown for my former husband's bride-to-be. I'd thought Stan would tell me it was a stupid thing to do, and as it turned out, he would have been right. But how did I know it was going to land me smack in the middle of another homicide investigation?

Even if Stan had been assigned to the case, I supposed he would have withdrawn when he found out Larry was the fiancé of the victim and that I was apt to be a suspect in her murder.

I lost all track of time, and I don't know how long I'd been sitting there when I realized someone was standing in front of me. "Excuse me, ma'am," a man said. "I'm Officer Sampson, and I need to get a statement from you."

I made it as brief as possible. As soon as I signed it, he left but returned almost immediately. "Detective Perrelli wants to speak to you."

He led me to a room and introduced me to Perrelli, who looked nicer than the detective I'd crossed paths with when my friend Kate Boslow died the previous summer. He was short and thin with dark hair to match, and he had sad, droopy brown eyes that reminded me of a basset hound.

"I understand you were here to deliver the wedding gown to the bride," he said after I was seated across from him at a desk.

"Yes, I was," I said in my most businesslike voice.

"I also see from your statement that you are the ex-wife of the groom." He gave me a puzzled hang-dog look. "Now why would you undertake to clean and deliver the wedding gown for your former husband's new bride?"

"Well, actually, I didn't know Olivia was marrying Larry when she came in with the gown."

"Tell me more."

And so I did. I must have talked for twenty minutes with only an occasional nod from the detective, even when I mentioned that I'd used the scissors to clip off a loose thread on the bridal gown.

"And let me get this straight," he said finally. "You planned to have someone else make the delivery, but at the last minute, that person was called out of town."

"That's right. Bringing the gown here to the hotel is the last thing in the world I wanted to do, and I was so flustered by the whole thing that I forgot to bring the bridal veil up to the room when I delivered the gown. That's why I had to come back."

"And you're sure the door locked behind you when you left the first time?"

"Almost sure. I heard a click."

"Did you run into anyone on the stairs when you returned?"

"No," I said, which was too bad because that could have meant the murderer was an outsider.

"Is there anything else?"

Much as I hated to help Larry's case, I told Perrelli about a thought that had just occurred to me. "Olivia was superstitious about letting the groom see her in her wedding gown before the ceremony, so I don't think she would have let Larry in the room. I know one of the witnesses claimed she saw him coming out of the room, but he said he'd gone to the door and called her name and when she didn't answer, he left."

Perrelli made no comment about this, but I thought I could see a gleam in his sad eyes, like a hound about to be fed. Oh, damn, he was probably thinking I still had a "thing" for Larry and that explained why I was trying to protect him. And from there, it might not be such a giant leap for the detective to conclude that I could have killed Olivia because I still wanted Larry for myself.

I probably never should have volunteered my opinion about Olivia's superstitions, but fortunately I'd saved my coup de grace for last. I leaned over toward the detective. "One other thing that I wanted to mention. When Olivia came to the cleaners for that first fitting, she told me she'd received an anonymous note from someone who said she'd be sorry if she married Larry. She said it sounded like a threat."

Perrelli seemed surprised at the information. I saw him put a little star by the notation in his notebook, which made me think that no one else had mentioned it earlier. Perrelli must be wondering why Olivia had told a dry cleaner about it instead of telling one of her friends.

"I know she told someone else about it," I said, trying to undo the harm the revelation might have cost me. "She was talking on her cell phone about it when I got to the fitting room. I think she mentioned it to me because she was so upset and was spilling her feelings the way you do sometimes with a stranger."

Perrelli looked at me as if I were speaking a foreign language, perhaps one only understood by women, and I decided it was time for me to shut up. I was afraid he was sitting there thinking that I might have written the note myself and was telling him about it now so that, in case it turned up later, he wouldn't think I was the author. After all, who better than an ex-wife to write a threatening, anonymous note to a poor hapless fiancée?

Perrelli asked me a few more questions and then said the police needed to take me downtown to headquarters for a videotaped interview. It lasted two more hours and covered information I'd already given, plus a lot of questions about my relationship with Larry, which I said was nonexistent at this point.

When an officer finally brought me back to the hotel to get my panel truck, his parting words were "Don't leave town."

"I won't," I promised. In fact, as shaky and drained as I felt, I'd be lucky even to get home.

The parking lot had fewer police cars than had been there earlier, which I was sure the hotel was happy about. Management always wants to keep a low profile when it comes to crimes in their establishments. I wanted to keep a low profile, too, but I did consider having myself a good, long cry once I was hidden away from view behind the protective tinted windows of the truck. Then I thought about the Dyer's Cleaners' logo on the sides and decided the best thing I could do was get out of the parking lot as fast as possible.

I had to stop and identify myself at the entrance to the hotel. A policeman glanced in the back of the truck, then asked to see my driver's license and took down my name and address before he let me leave. I pulled out on Colorado Boulevard, but I had to head south because of a traffic island in the middle of the street. I would have to circle around to get to either the cleaners or my apartment, but I decided to forget about returning to the cleaners for my car. All I wanted was to get to my apartment, barricade myself inside, and hide there forever.

Only trouble was I had a date with Stan that night, and I'd have to tell him about Olivia's murder. I tried to comfort myself by thinking that maybe talking to him would help, but I was afraid it wouldn't, and that seemed to prove the point I'd been trying to make with Detective Perrelli. Sometimes it's easier to unload your problems on a stranger who has no emotional investment in you than it is to dump on a friend, especially if he's another homicide detective.

I decided to get in the left lane and make a U-turn at the next intersection, but just as I started to check my rearview mirror to switch lanes, I heard a rustling sound from the back of the truck. A second later, I felt something hard and metallic jam into my shoulder blade.

"Keep your hands on the wheel," a male voice said from just behind the driver's seat. "You won't get hurt as long as you do exactly what I say."

CHAPTER 4

I don't think I could have pried my hands off the steering wheel if I'd wanted to. My whole body seemed to clench up in a giant cramp as I realized I was being held prisoner by a carnapper I couldn't even see.

"Dammit, put on the brakes or you'll hit that car," the man behind me said.

I moved my foot to the brake pedal and slowed the delivery truck. The driver in front of me didn't seem to notice the near-collision. I wished there were some police officers around. They'd been in the parking lot of the hotel only moments before, but now there wasn't a single one in sight.

Surely the cops had searched the vehicles in the parking lot. If so, why hadn't they found the guy in my truck? Or why hadn't the cop at the entrance noticed him as I left?

More importantly, would he want me to drop him off as soon as we were away from the hotel, or was he planning to shoot me and commandeer the truck? My whole body began to shake and I broke out in sweat despite the coolness of the day.

Why hadn't I had the good sense to lock the truck when I rushed the veil up to the room? I already knew the answer to that: I hadn't taken the time because I'd planned a quick getaway as soon as I dropped off the veil that I'd forgotten on my first trip with the dress.

I wiggled nervously in my seat.

"Don't turn around, and don't pull any smart-ass tricks," the man said. "If you do what I say, I won't have to hurt you."

This time he was near enough that I could smell the sourness of alcohol on his breath. Could this be the guy who'd stabbed poor Olivia with the scissors? Perhaps a jealous ex-lover who'd had a fight with her earlier in the day. Maybe a guy who'd decided if he couldn't have her, no one could. A man like that wouldn't think twice about killing the hapless driver of a delivery truck.

"Get on the freeway up ahead," the man said. "Go north toward downtown."

"Okay." It was all I could do to give a one-word response.

I checked the mirror to see if it was clear to get in the turn lane. I couldn't see my abductor. He must have ducked down to avoid being in my line of rearview sight.

"If you take your hands off the wheel, you're dead meat."

My hands were listening to him, but my foot was jerking up and down on the accelerator as if it had a mind of its own.

I felt the cold metal against my back move as the guy shifted his weight behind me and as I glanced in the rearview mirror again, I saw him staring at me through blood-shot blue eyes.

"Keep your eyes on the road," he ordered.

I swung right to the entrance ramp to Interstate-25 and glanced at the side mirror as I merged into freeway traffic.

"Get into the middle lane," he said.

I eased to the left. Too bad there were no windows on the side of the truck behind the driver's seat. Even the ones on the sliding door behind the passenger seat and in the double doors at the rear were tinted. That made it unlikely that someone in one of the cars to either side of us would spot the guy and the gun rammed into my back.

At first, my mind was blank with fear, and then ideas began to slough off from my brain like earth crumbling away from a mountainside. What about driving into a concrete abutment or starting a traffic jam?

"No fancy stuff, understand? No speeding or calling attention to yourself."

That eliminated the other idea I had of weaving in and out of traffic until some good citizen got on his cell phone and called the police. At one point, a patrol car passed the truck in the outer lane, and the man behind me shrank back even though I didn't think he could be seen. I felt the metal object move away from my shoulder blade, and while the gunman wasn't looking, I tried blinking my lights.

"Shut off the damn lights," the man yelled.

It hadn't done any good, anyway. The police car whizzed past us, and no one else seemed to notice.

What about road rage? Maybe I could make some other driver mad enough to follow us to whatever destination the gunman had in mind.

"Don't try anything crazy," the man said, seeming to read my every thought. "I have a gun, and I'll use it if you make a wrong move."

The part of my brain that was still working argued the point. If he shot me, we'd careen out of control amid the high-speed traffic.

"All right, but where do you want to go?" My voice was so tight it didn't even sound like me asking the question.

"I'll tell you when we get there." He pulled himself up, saw that the police car was gone, and resumed his earlier position with the gun jammed into my shoulder.

I could see the high-rises of Denver silhouetted against overcast sky up ahead of us, and we would soon be skirting the heart of the city. I wondered if he were planning to make me drive him out of town to some remote area where he'd kill me and leave my body in a ditch. I had to do something before that happened, but I couldn't think what.

"Get off here," he said as we saw the sign for Sixth Avenue.

I exited the freeway, maneuvering the panel truck over the viaduct above the railroad tracks onto a one-way street going east. I didn't know whether to be relieved or afraid that he would now order me off on a side street so he could force me out of the driver's seat, shoot me, and then steal the truck.

I tried to summon up another shot of courage to speak, but my words came out in a half-sob. "Look, just take the truck, but let me go. I won't say anything."

Obviously, he knew I was lying. "Just shut up, will you?" His voice seemed to crack in fear or as if he were going through puberty. "I gotta figure out what to do."

We passed the Denver Health Medical Center complex, speeding along as if we were still on the freeway. This was not the time to be catching all the lights.

"Turn left on Broadway," he said.

"That's the wrong way on a one-way street." I cursed myself for pointing that out. What better way to draw attention to my plight than to head into oncoming traffic.

"Okay, take the next street."

I turned on Lincoln, going north again. If the carnapper didn't have a plan, I wondered if he were going to make me drive aimlessly around the city until I ran out of gas. I looked at the gauge. The tank was still half-full.

"When you get to Eighteenth, head down to Lodo."

That was the newly Yuppified area of downtown near the baseball stadium, formerly Skid Row, where a lot of young people hung out. Did he think he could blend into the crowd there?

I moved to the left-hand lane, ready to turn when we reached Eighteenth. We were surrounded on three sides by other drivers as I came to a stop for a red light at Colfax, just past the State Capitol and not far from my apartment.

This might be my only opportunity to jump out and run for my life. I made a movement toward the door, but his hand reached out to stop me and I saw the flash of a dark sleeve on my shoulder. "Don't even think about it." His words were tough, but his voice cracked again. "Look, I'm sorry I had to scare you. I didn't mean for any of this to happen."

The thought gave me a tiny ray of hope. "Look," I said, "I don't think you really want to hurt me, Ryan, and if you'll tell me . . ."

I heard a shuffling behind me and glanced around. I got one quick glance of his face before he opened the double doors at the back of the van. He had scraggly blond hair and a thin face with wide-set eyes that I didn't think I could ever forget from seeing them in the rearview mirror.

"Hey, I didn't even have a gun," he yelled as he swiped a long strand of hair away from his eyes and bailed out of the truck. "It was just a lighter." He slammed the doors shut and ran.

The light turned green up ahead, and the traffic started to move. All I could do was watch as he raced through two lanes of traffic to the right of me, wearing a tuxedo and holding the lighter aloft like a torch.

Anger replaced my fear. I couldn't believe it. I'd been held hostage by a Bic.

He darted through the cars, which had to slam to a stop, and raced east on Colfax past the wide expanse of Capitol grounds. He had to be Ryan who'd had a fight with someone earlier in the day and had been missing from the wedding party. Otherwise, why would he have fled when I mentioned the name?

Relief won out over my anger. I wanted to pull over to the curb and collapse, but it wasn't an option. Irate drivers honked at me from behind to let me know they were mad at me for holding up traffic. One guy in a truck whipped around me, yelling out an obscenity. I stepped on the gas. By the time I got to Nineteenth, I managed to squeeze over to the right-hand lane and turn east. When I worked my way back down to Colfax, there was no sign of the "gunman." But how far could he get? On East Colfax, known for its casual—even scuzzy—attire, a guy in a tuxedo was sure to stand out.

I raced home and called 911. Two officers showed up almost immediately to take a statement from me and tell me that the police were conducting a search of the area. They promised to return, but just in case they didn't find him, I got out my sketch pad as soon as they left and tried to recreate my abductor's face: Straight hair the color of straw, a long greasy strand of which fell into his eyes from a high forehead. I'd always fancied myself as an artist, and in my Bohemian phase, I'd even drawn sketches of people at street fairs, but I no longer seemed to be able to get it right. His face seemed too wide, but I knew I had the eyes right. Blue, wide-set, and bloodshot.

I kept working on the sketch until the cops returned about an hour later. They told me there was no sign of the guy, but they would put out an APB on him. I figured he was miles away by now, but I gave them my sketch anyway. I had finally decided it was as close to a likeness as I was going to get. I also let the officers go through my van looking for clues.

I told them, as I'd also told the police dispatcher, that I thought my abductor's name was Ryan, the missing member of the wedding party when Olivia Torkelson had been murdered earlier in the day.

I'd been looking forward to my date with Stan when I got up that morning, but after everything that had happened that day, my enthusiasm had turned to dread. I hated to tell him I was involved in yet another police matter. That's the one thing that drove him nuts, but there was no way to hide the truth from a homicide detective.

Some years ago his fiancée, a policewoman, had been shot

and killed when she'd answered a call of a robbery in progress. Because Stan had taken off that day, she'd pulled his shift at work, and he'd never gotten over feeling responsible for her death. I sometimes wondered if he'd been attracted to me because I was in what he perceived as a low-risk job of cleaning other people's clothes, and it drove him nuts when I became involved in their problems as well.

I tried to pull myself together for our date. I put on a long black skirt with a swirl of coral running through it and a matching coral silk blouse. I took extra time with my hair and makeup, but as my late Uncle Chet used to say, I still looked as if I'd been wrung through the wringer.

It was as good as it was going to get, though, and when Stan knocked at my third-floor apartment door, I was ready for him. I grabbed a small clutch purse rather than the shoulder bag I normally carried and opened the door.

"Let's go," I said, trying to put on a smile.

I'd decided to wait until we were in his car or maybe even in the restaurant to unload on him. As soon as I saw the concerned look on his face, I realized he'd already heard about the murder.

"Are you all right?" he asked, giving me a long hug.

"You heard about it, huh?"

He let me go. "Just a few minutes ago. Rick Perrelli called me about it."

That's what I got for dating a cop. I didn't even know what I saw in him, considering the fact that he always got so upset about my propensity to get into trouble. I guess it was his blond hair and the off-center cleft in his chin that was out of line with his straight-arrow personality. He was a young Clint Eastwood but without any of the Dirty Harry mentality about taking the law into his own hands.

But was I interested in just the superficial things about him? I didn't think so. I also liked the fact that I could count on his inherent decency and concern about people when the chips were down, not to mention that I could usually wheedle, cajole, and tease him into forgiving my transgressions. I was hoping I could do it this time.

"So are you okay?" Stan asked. "Rick told me you cleaned and delivered the wedding gown to Larry's fiancée this afternoon just before she was stabbed. How'd you happen to get involved in that?" He seemed to be having trouble keeping his voice under control.

I obviously wasn't going to be able to delay the conversation until we got to the restaurant. "Come on over and sit down." I motioned him to the table that was in front of a counter that divided my tiny kitchen from the rest of my studio apartment. "It may take awhile to explain."

At six feet four inches tall, he dominated the room, and I always liked it better when he was sitting down. His height didn't intimidate Spot, however. My grouchy yellow tabby was a perfect foil for the tall thin detective, and one time the cat had shredded his shirt and slashed his back when Stan inadvertently sat on him.

The cat twitched his tail and went over to my sofa that doubles as a bed when it's open. He settled down on the sofa and gave Stan the evil eye as if to say "I dare you to try sitting on me again." Who says cats don't have long-term memories?

"Okay." Stan glanced nervously at Spot and sat in one of the chairs at the table. "I don't know quite how to say this other than to come right out and say it. Why did you take on a dry-cleaning job for the bride-to-be of your ex-husband?"

I guess he knew I'd be defensive about it. "Okay, if you must know," I said. "We'd already cleaned her grandmother's gown in preparation for doing the alterations on it. I was almost through the first fitting when I discovered that she was going to marry Larry. I didn't know what to do—admit who I was, say we couldn't finish the gown and comp her for what we'd already done, or go ahead with the work. Mack calmed me down and said he would make the delivery. Then last night his brother had a heart attack in Alabama, and Mack flew down there to be with him. I tried my best to find someone else to make the delivery, but no one was available, and I had to get the gown to the hotel or it was going to be late for the ceremony."

I paused for breath. Despite my run-on sentences and the fact that my words had been bubbling up like too much soap in a load of wash, Stan seemed to be handling my explanation. Yep, that's what I liked about him.

Still, he ran his hands through his curly hair, messing it up as if we'd been having some serious pillow talk. "You have a habit of attracting trouble like a magnet. You know that, don't you?" He shook his head.

I shrugged. "How could I have known that something like this would happen? Olivia—that was Larry's fiancée—seemed like such a naive young thing that I would never have dreamed someone might want to kill her."

Stan squinted his eyes in Eastwood make-my-day fashion. "No one except maybe a jealous ex-wife."

I jumped up from my chair. "Stan, you know I'm not jealous of Larry."

"Yes, I know, but I'm not sure Rick agrees."

I didn't want to think about Detective Perrelli and his skeptical reaction to my explanation for why I'd been at the hotel.

"Look, can we just go now?" I got up and started to pace. "I haven't had anything to eat all day."

"Calm down. We'll go in a few minutes. First, tell me exactly what happened."

So I sat back down at the table and told him every gory detail—from the embarrassing encounter with the best man Brad in the elevator, to the scene in the room with Olivia and her tyrannical mother, who demanded that Charlotte, the gofer girl, find a pair of scissors so I could snip off a few loose threads.

"They both left, and I finished checking out the gown. Then I took off, too, going down the back stairs to avoid seeing anyone else I knew. If I hadn't forgotten the veil, I'd have been gone by the time Olivia was killed. As it was, I found Larry bending over the body when I returned to the room."

"So you were alone with Olivia for a few minutes?" Stan shook his head, and I could see how upset he was.

"But she was alive when I left the room."

"How long were you gone?"

"Maybe ten minutes by the time I got to the van and then came back up to the room."

"And then somebody hijacked you and your van . . ."

I had to tell him all about that, too, but at least I was glad to hear that the message about my abduction and its possible connection to the murder had been transmitted to Perrelli.

"Did they find the guy yet?" I asked.

Stan shook his head, and when he finally got up, he hugged me again. "I'm sorry about all this, Mandy, but please stay out of it from now on. You could be in real trouble with Perrelli if you don't."

I was afraid I could be in real trouble, even if I did, but I didn't say that to Stan. Instead I asked, "Can we please go now? And let's try to talk about something else. Okay?"

Stan nodded, but when we got to his car, his police radio squawked a reminder that crime was never far away. I thought about asking him to turn it off, but it filled a void. Neither one of us seemed to be able to think of anything to say.

"So where do you want to eat, Mandy?" Stan asked, after he'd driven several blocks.

"I don't know. Where do you want to eat, Stan?"

"I don't know . . ."

Suddenly, I began to giggle. He looked at me as if I'd lost it, and I probably had. Our conversation reminded me of one of Mack's favorite movies, which he'd taped and loaned to me one time. Mack said Ernest Borgnine won an Oscar in the title role of *Marty*, a guy who hung out with his pals because none of them could find dates.

I tried to explain to Stan how our exchange reminded me of the movie. "Marty says, 'What do you want to do, Angie?' and Angie says, 'I don't know, what do you want to do, Marty?' " Stan didn't seem to find it amusing. "Well, I guess you had to see the movie yourself." I was no longer laughing.

Stan had crossed Colfax and was up on Seventeenth by then. There were a lot of restaurants in the area, and it was as good a place as any to eat.

Suddenly, the police radio came to life with a lot of code words and copspeak that I didn't understand. What I did pick out of the message was the single word *tuxedo*.

Stan translated for me: A possible tuxedo-clad suspect in an abduction earlier in the day had just been spotted coming out of a bar on Colfax only a few blocks east of where we were.

CHAPTER 5

Let's go check on the guy," I said, tugging on Stan's jacket sleeve.

"No." The vehemence of his answer surprised me. "It might compromise the arrest."

"Yeah, but he held me up with a Bic."

I still hadn't gotten over my anger about that. It really burned me up. When they said cigarettes were hazardous to your health, nobody ever said anything about lighters. I wanted to punch out the guy's lights for scaring me with a stupid lighter.

Stan pulled to the curb and started to get out of the car.

I climbed out the other side before he had a chance to come around and open my door. "But aren't we going to do something about this? I'm the one who can identify him."

Stan seemed preoccupied with one of the store fronts on the street. I looked over and saw that it was a German restaurant.

"Here's a place called Greta's," Stan said. "Why don't we try that?"

I shook my head. "No, I want to find out about the guy in the tuxedo. I'm going to walk over there if you won't go."

Stan grabbed my arm. "Please, Mandy, go along with me

on this. You need to be able to pick the guy out of a line-up in order to make the charges stick."

I began to calm down.

"Why don't you go in the restaurant and get a table for us," he said. "I'll check it out. Okay?" He'd already pulled out his cell phone.

I knew Stan wasn't going to budge on this. "All right," I said, "but be sure to point out that he's a suspect in a murder."

As soon as I got inside the restaurant, a hostess came up to me. "Only one for dinner?" she asked.

I hated it when people phrased it that way—like dining alone was something to be pitied. Eating by myself might even be preferable the way I felt right now, but I said, "No, there'll be two of us. The other person will be here soon."

She led me to a table in the back of the room, which was like a travel brochure for a vacation in the Alps. The walls were covered with murals of mountains dotted with castles and colorful chalets along with a lot of cuckoo clocks. It felt more like Switzerland than Germany, but at least it was cheerful.

"Are you alone?" a waitress with a real German accent asked as soon as I was seated. I wondered if she was Greta, the owner for whom the restaurant was named. She had blonde braids across the top of her head, and she was wearing a red dirndl skirt, a blue apron, and a white blouse with puffed sleeves—the kind we dry cleaners hate because they're so hard to press.

"I'm expecting someone else in a minute," I said, "but I'll have coffee while I wait."

After the waitress's third trip to the table to see if I was ready to order yet, I went to the front window to check on Stan. He was no longer there. Neither was his car. He'd snuck off without me, and I could hardly suppress my anger as I returned to the table and hailed the waitress.

I ordered the most expensive thing on the menu,

Wienerschnitzel but with pork instead of veal, and said my dinner companion had been delayed. "But you can serve me now. I don't want to wait for him."

"Good for you," the waitress said.

So there, Stan.

The woman had just returned with my salad and a bowl of soup when I saw Stan come in the door.

He grinned at me when he reached the table. "I was going to say to start without me, but I see you already have." He didn't sit down, and I was suspicious of that. "Look," he continued, "I have to go downtown, but it shouldn't take long. Just wait for me here. All right?"

No wonder he'd been happy to see that I'd already ordered. Now it was difficult for me to insist on going with him.

I wasn't about to let it go at that, however. "Did you arrest the guy? Was his name Ryan?"

"We'll talk about it as soon as I get back." Stan didn't wait for my blistering response.

Just then, the cuckoo clocks on the walls began to sound the hour of nine. First one—then a whole chorus of cuckoos. It was enough to drive a person nuts.

I stabbed my lettuce and watched Stan leave as I sizzled with anger. When he returned, he better tell me what he'd learned about the guy in the tuxedo.

The waitress brought my entree, and she gave me a sympathetic look. "Is he coming back?"

"Yes, but he has to do something first." It irritated me that I felt I needed to explain.

While I ate the Wienerschnitzel, potato dumplings, and red cabbage, I wondered about the guy in the tuxedo. My first thought had been that he'd been a former lover of Olivia's who'd killed her in a fit of passion. But would a former lover be a member of the wedding party? And if he'd killed her, why had he spent the rest of the day drinking at a bar on Colfax? But if he hadn't killed her, why force me at gunpoint—okay, Bic-point—to drive him away from the hotel? None of it made sense.

And it really popped my buttons, as Uncle Chet used to say, that Stan hadn't wanted me along when the guy had been handcuffed and hauled off to jail. It aggravated me even more that I was in so much hot water with the police already that I didn't dare risk losing perhaps my only ally on the force. I might need Stan later to give me a character reference.

"It's been nearly an hour. Your friend doesn't seem to be coming back," the waitress said, jolting me out of my funk. "Would you like me to bring you the check now, or do you want to wait a little longer?"

"I'll wait," I said, which seemed like the only logical thing to do when I realized I probably didn't have enough money to pay the bill. I looked in the little clutch purse, and I was right. Three dollars and change. No credit cards. I should never leave home without my big old shoulder bag.

What's more, I hadn't realized how long it had been since Stan left. I glanced at my watch and saw that it was nearly ten o'clock. I looked up at one of the cuckoo clocks to confirm the time, and a little bird came out and cuckooed the hour. A few seconds later, there was the whole cacophony of cuckoos from the other clocks. I wanted to cover my ears and scream.

More than an hour, and the worst thing about it was that I'd eaten the whole meal without even enjoying it. So where was Stan? Why hadn't he come back by now?

I got up and disrupted a few other diners when I squeezed between tables to look out the window again. No Stan. No car.

I should have at least asked for a window table when the hostess seated me so I could have watched for him. I had a more immediate problem, and I thought of making a quick escape out the door while I was at the front of the restaurant. It was either that or wash dishes. No, there was another solution. I went back to the table and ordered some apple strudel with a dollop of whipped cream on top and another cup of coffee. Maybe by the time I finished, Stan would be here. If not, I might as well make it worth my time to wash dishes.

I dawdled over dessert. "I have to make a phone call," I said to the waitress as she passed my table. "Don't take the strudel away."

I went to the telephone in a hallway by the bathrooms at the back of the restaurant. I tried calling Stan at police headquarters and on his cell phone. No answer at either place.

By then, I noticed that the restaurant was clearing out. Greta's must be getting ready to close. It was pay-up time, and I didn't have the cash. I went back and played with my food.

I stared at a chalet painted on the wall opposite me. It had red shutters with bluebirds on them. I felt like Hansel without Gretel. No, it would be the other way around since Hansel was the boy, but maybe I could skip out without paying and leave a trail of strudel crumbs so that Stan could find me if he ever showed up. Except right now I didn't care if I ever saw him again, so the crumbs were out.

The waitress went past me to another table, and a moment later she returned with a stack of dirty dishes. "Let's face it, fraulein, you been stood up," she said. "The guy isn't coming back."

This was a humbling experience, but I had to deal with it anyway. "When you have a minute, I need to talk to you."

"I'll be right back," she said, halfway across the dining room by then.

Yeah, sure, that's what Stan had told me, too.

But of course the waitress came back. You can always trust a woman. Not only that, but she had the bill with the strudel added to the total.

"This is rather embarrassing," I said, motioning for her to lean down toward me while I whispered. "But I don't have enough money with me to pay for the meal. I was wondering if I could leave my watch with you as collateral until I can go home and get some cash."

She shook her head sympathetically at the fickleness of men. "Look, I been there myself. I'll loan you the money, and you can pay me back later."

I don't know what came over me at that point. I guess maybe the whole day's events hit me all at once—the small kindness of this stranger, the enormous cruelties of friends and family that had apparently led to the killing of a young bride-to-be. Other than the death of a child, I couldn't think of anything more tragic than the death of a bride on her wedding day. I began to cry.

The waitress didn't know about the bad stuff that had happened to me earlier that day, but she sat down in the chair beside me and patted my hand. "It's okay, honey, you don't have to pay me back right away. I got a lot of tips today. I can afford to cover you."

"Thanks," I said, "but it's not just that."

"I know." She patted my hand some more. "I know. Men are scum."

"No, it's—" I sniffed to try to get myself under control.

Stan chose that moment to appear. That made me even madder than I'd already been. I slipped my hand out from under the waitress's and tried to wipe my eyes.

"What's the matter?" he asked.

"It's you men," the waitress said, getting up from the chair. "You're all alike." With that, she turned on the heels of her Birkenstocks and headed for the kitchen.

"Damn it," I said as I fumbled in my purse for a tissue. "From now on, we're going dutch."

Stan paid the tab, and we waited while the hostess unlocked the door so we could go out to Stan's car.

"Just a minute," I said and went back to the table. I added all my cash to the tip Stan had already left. Greta deserved it.

"I'm sorry it took so long," Stan tried to apologize as the hostess held the door for us.

"Never mind." I hurried over to the car, opened the door, and climbed inside. As soon as he went around to the driver's side and got behind the wheel, I continued, "Just tell me what happened."

"I'm not going to say anything until I take you down to headquarters to see if you can make an ID."

Even though I was happy about the opportunity to finger the guy in the tuxedo, I was still mad at Stan.

We didn't say anything on the trip to the central police station which was just as well. I didn't feel like small talk.

He escorted me to the adjacent pre-arraignment detention facility—in other words, a jail—and turned me over to another detective with the promise that he'd wait for me. I wasn't even sure I cared.

The ID turned out to be from a physical lineup, not a photo lineup of driver's license pictures, and according to my escort, the whole thing would be videotaped from both inside and outside a one-way glass.

Six men filed in behind the glass. All were approximately the same height and coloring as my abductor, and they were dressed in a mix of blue and green short-sleeved, V-necked shirts and draw-string pants that I assumed were regular prison garb. They were instructed to turn to the left, turn to the right, and answer a few questions. Each one had to say "Keep your hands on the wheel. You won't get hurt if you do exactly what I say."

Even before he spoke, I knew which one was the guy who'd put the Bic to my back. He looked even younger than I'd thought he was, and his words didn't seem as threatening now that he was behind a glass and couldn't see me.

"He's the second one from the left," I said.

I was pleased with myself. My sketch hadn't been as far off as I'd thought, but I'd been right that his face was a little thinner than the one I'd drawn. I probably could have gotten it right if I'd had more time.

"You sure?" my escort asked.

"Positive. Can you tell me his name?" I figured I might have a better chance of getting it from a stranger than I would from Stan.

"He didn't have any ID on him when he was arrested." The man led me out to another room where he had me sign documents indicating I'd made an identification.

He told me I was free to go, and Stan got up from a chair where he'd been waiting for me. The two men exchanged a few words, and then Stan escorted me down to his car.

"Would you mind stopping at some all-night place so I can grab something to eat," he said once he started the car.

"Only if you'll tell me everything that happened," I said.

"I really can't do it right now."

I felt as if I were about to explode, but I tried to contain myself. "Can you at least tell me what he'll be charged with?"

"Probably felony kidnapping and felony carnapping. That's all I can say right now."

"Fine. Then take me home."

"Hey, I'm really sorry about all this."

"Me, too," I said, "but it's been a really bad day, and I just want to go home."

If this was what being married to a policeman would be like, I could understand why there were so many divorces among cops and their spouses.

Stan drove me the short distance from police headquarters to my apartment.

"You don't have to escort me upstairs," I said, taking off the seatbelt and opening the door before the car was even stopped. "I'll be fine."

"All right. I'll call you tomorrow."

"Swell."

I was out of the car, up the sidewalk, and through the front door before Stan even had time to pull away from the curb. Actually, I suppose he was waiting to make sure I got safely inside before he left, but that irritated me, too.

I was so tired as I trudged up the steps to my apartment that it seemed difficult to put one foot in front of the other. I rounded the second-floor landing to the final set of stairs and saw someone sitting on the steps in front of my door. Damn. I didn't want company tonight unless it was Mack, and he was in Alabama.

I labored upward, but it wasn't until I was halfway up to the third floor that I recognized my visitor. It was definitely the last person in the world I wanted to see right then.

"What the devil are you doing here?" I asked when I was almost at the top of the stairs. "You must be out of your mind, Larry."

CHAPTER 6

"I didn't know where else to turn," my ex-husband said, getting up from the steps and brushing off his dark pants. "The police had me downtown, but they finally let me go. I went home, but I decided I needed to talk to you."

At least that explained why he was wearing the slacks and a knit shirt instead of the tux, but it didn't explain what he was doing here.

"Look, you practically accused me of killing your fianceé," I said. "Why come to me?"

Larry seemed as if he'd aged ten years, and his tan, which usually set off his dazzling white teeth, now gave him a muddy, sick look as he winced at my words. "I was in shock. I'm still in shock. And I was so stunned to see you at the hotel that I just said the first thing that came into my mind."

"And the first thing that came into your mind was that I might have done something like that?" I had my keys in my hand, but I wasn't about to let Larry inside my apartment. "I'm really sorry about what happened to your fiancée, but I don't think it's a good idea for us to talk to each other right now. Why don't you go visit your friend Brad? He's a criminal lawyer, and remember how you tried to get me to go to him for advice when that man was killed in the cleaners? He's the one you need to discuss this with."

Larry gave me a pleading look. "But I have to talk to you. I have a confession to make."

My blood started pounding in my ears. Surely Larry wasn't going to tell me he'd killed Olivia? I couldn't have misjudged him that badly. He was a chicken-hearted wimp who had never seen a woman he didn't like, but he wasn't a killer. Ambitious, maybe, and he saw each new wife as a stepping stone on his rise up the corporate ladder, but why would a chicken kill the goose that laid the golden egg? Olivia's father would probably have made him a partner in the Torkelson law firm, but not before the marriage was consummated. Well, I assumed it had already been consummated—so maybe the word I wanted was "official." Not until the marriage became official. But what if Olivia had decided to call off the wedding? Oh, God. Could Larry have been so angry at his missed opportunity for making partner that he'd killed her?

"Look, I'm not letting you in," I said, as my heart pumped overtime and I twisted my keys around in my hand in case I had to use them as brass knuckles. "If you have something to confess, do it to the police."

"No, no, not that kind of confession." Larry ran his hands through his dark hair with the hint of gray at the sides, but it still stayed neatly in place from all the gel he put on it.

I wished now that I'd asked Stan to come upstairs with me. "Then what kind of confession is it?" I demanded.

"It's about your mother."

My mother? The blood running through my veins turned to ice. I felt as if I might start to hyperventilate. I unlocked the door. "All right, come in."

What did any of this have to do with my mother, the much-married Cecilia, now living happily (I hoped) with her sixth husband in Phoenix? My mom and stepfather had been in the midst of a lovers' spat the last time she'd come up here, and Mom had almost driven me nuts.

I went over and slammed my tiny purse on the table where Larry and I had once shared TV dinners while I worked two jobs to put him through law school. "Okay, what about my mother?" I asked. "What does she have to do with this?"

Larry collapsed in a chair across from where I was standing. "Oh, God, Mandy. How can this be happening?" He put his head down on the table and began to sob.

I stood awkwardly for a moment, then went over and gave him a tentative pat on the shoulder and sat down beside him. "I'm really sorry, Larry."

He continued to sob, which was something I'd never seen him do before. When he finally stopped, he grabbed my hand as if it were a lifeline and the only thing that was keeping him from falling into the abyss. A little voice in my head told me this was not a good idea—not for me, not for Larry, and especially not for the police perception of us.

Before I did something dumb like give him a comfort hug, I jumped up, rounded the table and grabbed a tissue from a box on the counter. I handed it to him.

"I really loved her, Mandy," Larry said, wiping his eyes. "She was so sweet and gentle. Not like you and Patricia."

That brought me back to reality. Thanks a lot, fella, I thought, and there was this little part of me that was glad to hear that his second wife, Pat, the lawyer he'd dumped me for, was feisty, too.

But to show that I had a gentle side myself I gave him a few more minutes to recover before I asked again about my mother—which was, after all, the reason I let him in.

"Well, she called and left a message on my answering machine," he said. "I found it when I finally got home from the police station." Larry hung his head. "I guess the mur—what happened to Olivia made the nightly news down in Phoenix and she was upset when she heard I was the groom."

I sat down at the table across from him and willed him to

look me in the eye. "Please don't tell me you called her back."

Larry looked up, then glanced away. "I needed someone to talk to, and Cilia and I always got along so well."

Oh, yeah, she'd always thought Larry was such a wonderful catch for her daughter that she was devastated when we broke up. "Okay," I conceded, "just as long as you didn't tell her I was anywhere near the hotel when it happened."

Spot the cat had jumped down from my folded-up sofa-bed and was looking questioningly at Larry. I'd have sworn he recognized my ex-husband, who had been one of the few people he'd tolerated on Larry's infrequent visits to the cleaners. That's where Spot had lived when my uncle was alive, before I inherited the cleaners and the cat and decided Spot might be happier here with me.

I don't always make wise decisions, and Spot's transfer was one of them. He wasn't much happier here than Larry had been, and now the cat had the audacity to waltz over and rub up against Larry's leg as if trying to console him.

Larry reached down and patted Spot lightly on the head, but he didn't answer me.

"You didn't tell my mother, did you?"

Larry looked sheepish, which was unusual for him. "I'm afraid the cat's out of the bag," he said.

I like to think it was because he was staring down at Spot that he used such a hackneyed expression. I might even have thought it was funny coming from someone else and under a whole different set of circumstances. Now it made me furious.

"You told her? Are you out of your mind?"

Larry refused to make eye contact with me all this time. Instead, he continued to watch Spot as the cat curled around him and rubbed against his other leg. I always did think the cat was a bad judge of character, and this confirmed it. He liked Larry, barely tolerated me, and hated Stan.

"I'm sorry," Larry said. "It just slipped out. She's coming up here to be with us as soon as she can make arrangements."

"Us?" I got up and started to pace. "There is no *us*, and you know it as well as I do."

He was looking toward me now, somewhere over my right shoulder. "I'm only quoting what Cilia said, and I didn't know what to do about it, so I thought I better tell you."

"You're damned right you should tell me. I only hope it isn't too late to stop her."

I went over to the phone that was on the counter between the kitchen and the rest of my apartment. Four messages on my answering machine. I punched the "play" button and continued to the sink where I ran some water in a mug and zapped it in the microwave. I needed a double shot of instant coffee.

"You wouldn't happen to have something alcoholic to drink, would you?" Larry asked.

"No, I wouldn't." I had a beer in the refrigerator, but I wasn't about to offer him a can. He was the white wine and martini-with-a-twist type of guy, anyway.

"Yo, Mandy." The first message on the machine started to play. I knew the voice wasn't Mom's, but it belonged to another person I didn't particularly want to see right now—my longtime friend, Nat Wilcox, the newshound from hell.

"Did you hear about Larry's fiancée getting killed today just before the wedding ceremony?" Nat asked. "It blew me away. I thought you might want to talk about it and hear what I found out."

Well, okay, maybe I might want to hear what, if anything, he'd uncovered, but chances were he was merely pretending to know something because he wanted to find out if I had any information. He couldn't have discovered very much, however, if he didn't know that I'd been at the hotel.

"Give me a call ASAP. Sooner, if possible. Ciao." Nat's the

king of clichés and slang, so I would have understood if Larry's cat-out-of-the-bag remark had come from him.

The next call was from Mack, and hearing his familiar voice from faraway Alabama made me want to start crying again the way I had in the restaurant. My father had died when I was a baby, and I'd always thought of Mack as a father substitute. That's because Mom's husbands number two, three, four, five, and even six had never quite filled the bill, although I thought Mom's current spouse, Herb, was the best of the bunch. He was just a little too slap-on-the-back hearty for my taste—like a used-car pitchman, but that's exactly what he'd been before he retired. God, I hoped they both weren't planning to come to Denver.

"This is Mack," Mack said as if I didn't recognize him by his deep resonant voice. "I just wanted to let you know that my brother is out of ICU."

That was certainly the best news I'd had all day.

"They put a stent in one of his arteries, but the rest of his heart looks good. The doctors are optimistic he'll have a full recovery. Anyway, I'm staying at a hotel near the hospital, and I just wanted to let you know." He left the phone number where I could reach him.

I glanced at my watch, which luckily I hadn't had to pawn to get out of the restaurant. It was probably too late to call him now, at least with bad news.

The third call was it. "Amanda." Oh, yep, that was the call I'd been afraid would be on the machine. No one else called me Amanda. "This is your mother. I just talked to Larry, the poor dear. He said you were at the hotel, too, delivering the wedding gown. Now do you think that was a wise thing to have done?" She paused as if waiting for me to respond. "Anyway, I'm coming up to Denver as soon as I can get a flight out of Phoenix, and I won't let you talk me out of it so don't even try. I'll call you as soon as I know my arrival time. Goodbye, dear."

There was one more call, and it was from Mom again. "I'm worried about you. Where are you? I tried calling Larry back to find out if they'd taken you down to the police station, too, but he's not home. Please call me the moment you get in."

The microwave had already buzzed so I pulled the mug out and started to dump the instant coffee in it.

"Maybe I'll take a cup of coffee, too, if that's all you have," Larry said.

I slammed a spoonful of coffee crystals in the mug, shoved it across the counter for him to doctor with milk and sugar, actually Creamola and Sweet 'n Low, and poured water in another mug.

As long as he was going to persist in staying here until I threw him out, I might as well find out what else he knew. "Who do you think might have wanted Olivia dead?"

He shrugged, then looked dejectedly into the mug and stirred the substitute sugar and cream around in it, clanking the spoon against the sides. It had always been a habit that annoyed me.

"Okay, what about a guy named Ryan?" I suggested.

Larry blinked at me. "Ryan Torkelson?"

I had a sinking feeling about this. "Yes, if that's his name? Who is he?"

"He's Olivia's brother."

The information blew me away. He'd been my only real suspect, and now I find out he's Olivia's brother. Hard as I tried, I couldn't really imagine one sibling killing another one, but I wasn't ready to let it go. "I heard he'd had a big blow-up with someone this morning and had disappeared. Do you think he could have killed Olivia?"

"No way." Larry shook his head. "He's kind of the black sheep of the family, but he would never have killed her. She's the only one who tolerated him."

The microwave beeped again, and I pulled out the second mug and loaded it with caffeine. "So what was the fight about?"

"It wasn't with Olivia, if that's what you're thinking. It was with his father, who was furious when Ryan showed up for the wedding. He hadn't even bothered to get a haircut, and he was already half-snockered."

Ryan sure had a lot of staying power if he could drink all day and still be out bar-hopping tonight. Maybe the guy I'd identified wasn't Ryan after all.

I came over to the table and sat down across from Larry. "Describe him to me."

"Thin build, straight blond hair that's always hanging down in his face." Yep, that sounded like my abductor.

"So what did his father say to him? That Ryan couldn't be in the wedding party?"

Larry nodded.

"Why would her brother care about being excluded from the ceremony? It doesn't sound as if he wanted to be there, anyway, if he'd already been drinking before he arrived." And even though I didn't say it, being excluded from the festivities didn't seem like enough of a motivation for Ryan to cower in my delivery truck and force me to drive him away from the hotel.

"No, it escalated from there," Larry said. "It was the last straw for Mr. Torkelson."

I couldn't help wondering if Larry would have been permitted to call his father-in-law by his first name once he was elevated to partner. "Go on," I prodded.

"His father told Ryan to get out, and if he showed his face at the wedding, Mr. Torkelson said he would call the police and have him thrown out of the hotel. That was after Ryan tried to throw a punch at him."

My God, was it possible that Ryan—in his alcohol-induced state—had seen the police and decided to hide out in my delivery truck, not because he'd murdered Olivia, but because his dad had threatened to call them?

"Mr. Torkelson disowned Ryan right then and there," Larry continued. "Swore he was going to write his son out of the will first thing Monday morning."

I'd had my mug halfway to my lips, but I slammed it down. "Well, there you are. That's a motive."

Actually, it was only a motive for Ryan to kill his father before the elder Torkelson changed the will, but maybe the drunken Ryan had decided he'd be the only one left to inherit anything if he killed Olivia.

"No, I don't think Ryan could have done it." Larry shook his head. "He took off before Olivia was—was . . ."

I considered telling Larry that Olivia's brother hadn't left until he put a Bic to my back, but I rejected the idea. Instead, I stood up. "Look, Larry, I'm going to have to kick you out. I have to call my mother, and I want you to leave before I do."

If I couldn't talk her out of coming, I might do some serious bodily harm to Larry if he were still here.

He looked dejected, but the puppy-dog expression on his handsome face no longer had the power over me it once had.

"Maybe we can talk later," he said.

"Sure, Larry." Yeah, I thought, when you're appointed to the Supreme Court or donkeys fly, whichever comes first.

He went to the door and let himself out as he had so many times when he went to the law library to study. Only problem was that he and Brad had actually been going to a singles' bar where he'd met wife number two.

I took a deep breath and went over to the phone. I punched in Mom's number in Arizona. It was already past midnight, but I never could remember what time it was in Phoenix. Arizona stayed on standard time the whole year so sometimes it was on Rocky Mountain Time with us in Colorado and the rest of the year the state was on Pacific Time with California. But the time didn't really matter; Mom had said to call her whenever I got home.

Besides, the only thing I seemed to have inherited from my mother was my propensity to stay up late. Sadly, I was a night person with a day-person's job while Mom was a night person who'd never worked, except for a short stint at the cleaners in the afternoons right after my father died. Otherwise, she'd let her various husbands take care of her while she slept until noon.

Don't get me wrong. I love my mother. I just don't understand her. She's a frilly person who had a "Fascinating Womanhood" attitude even before there was the book on the subject of how to keep your husband happy. Obviously, it hadn't done the same for Mom, or she wouldn't have run through all those husbands in search of the perfect man. I, on the other hand, am a no-frills/no-fuss person with a feminist take on life.

Our differences aside, my mother is a meddler who always complicates things. Last time she was here she kept trying to reunite me with Larry, partly because she thought I needed his legal advice. That brought out the worst in me, and the worst can be pretty mean-spirited.

Furthermore, she can't stand to be alone and yet she refuses to stay on my rollaway bed because she's allergic to Spot. On her previous visit, I wound up staying in a hotel with her, which I absolutely refuse to do again.

The phone kept ringing until the answering machine came on. I hung up and dialed again. Still no answer. If she were so worried about me, why didn't she pick up?

I was punching in the numbers for the third time, when someone knocked on my door. My finger stopped on number eight, and I couldn't seem to lift my hand from the phone.

Why weren't Mom and Herb answering in Arizona? They had to be in Phoenix; they couldn't be here already. I unblocked the signal from my brain to my hand, lifted my finger, and kept on dialing. Someone kept knocking at my door.

I waited until the answering machine came on again and finally hung up, but I was in serious denial about the person or persons at my door. I was considering a fourth call to Arizona when I came to my senses. Answer the door, damn it, and please don't let it be Mom and Herb.

CHAPTER 7

Be careful what you ask for. Sometimes your prayers are answered and the alternative is almost as bad. It wasn't my mother and stepfather at the door, but Nat. He's my best friend under normal circumstances, but this wasn't one of them and he knew it. That's why he tricked me by not giving me his usual Morse-code SOS knock.

"What are you doing here, Nat?" I asked.

He tried to push his way into the room, using his motorcycle helmet as a battering ram. "I just heard that you were at the wedding when Larry's fiancée was killed. I came over for a first-hand account."

Nat is skinny and only three inches taller than me, and I planted my feet and blocked his way. "Where did you hear that?" I couldn't believe the police had released that information, but Nat had a lot of contacts that the rest of the press didn't have.

"The best source of all," he said, grinning wickedly. "Your mother."

Oh, swell, she wasn't even here yet, and look at the trouble she was causing. "What do you mean—my m-m-mother?" I was actually stuttering.

"She called me because she said Larry told her what

happened. When she couldn't reach you, she called Larry again, but he wasn't home. That's when she called me and told me you'd been at the hotel when they found Larry's fiancée. She was worried that the police might have arrested you."

I let my guard down for an instant, and Nat slipped around me into the apartment.

"What did you tell her?" I trailed him into the room, but what I wanted to do was tackle him and pull him feet-first out of my apartment.

Nat went to the refrigerator as if he owned the place and grabbed the last beer. Too bad I hadn't offered it to Larry. "I told her it was news to me," he said, which must have cost him dearly, since he didn't like to think there wasn't anything he didn't know. "Then I checked out a few people, called her back, and reassured her that you weren't in the slammer."

I sat down at the table and drank the last cold dregs of my coffee. "Why would she call you? She doesn't even like you."

But, of course, I knew the answer. She had never approved of Nat from the time I met him in junior high, but she was no fool. She knew he was the police reporter on the *Denver Tribune* and would be able to find out if I were in jail.

"I hate to tell you this." Nat came back over to the table, popping the top on his beer. "She said to tell you she's on her way up here *right now*."

I gripped the edge of the table. "Right now? Didn't you try to stop her?"

He plopped down across from me and took a swig of beer. "Of course I did, but she wouldn't listen."

So that explained why she wasn't picking up the phone. "When—when will she be here?" Now my voice was shaking as I tried to speak. "Please don't tell me she's on a red-eye and will be here any second."

"No, she couldn't get a flight out of Phoenix so she's driving. She was starting out tonight, but she said she probably won't get here 'til Monday."

Relief that I had a two-day reprieve almost overcame my dread. The dread won out. "And Herb—is he coming with her?"

"No, he's out-of-town with some of his old buddies at a golf tournament for used-car dealers, and she didn't want to bother him."

But yet she didn't mind bothering me. I felt as if I were at some personal point of no return with no way to stop her imminent arrival.

"So tell me what happened at the hotel?" Nat said, looking at me from above his granny glasses which had slipped down on his nose.

"I don't know anything except that I was at the hotel to deliver the wedding gown. I must have been out of my mind to accept the job of cleaning it. I didn't even know who Olivia Torkelson was planning to marry until it was too late."

Nat took a sip of beer and pushed the glasses back up on his nose. "So you saw the bride just before she was killed?"

"Is this off-the-record?"

Nat cringed, but he finally nodded. He hated things that were off-the-record.

"Promise?"

"Okay, I promise."

"I actually helped her get into her wedding gown. She was alone when I left, but no one saw me go because I slipped out a stairway."

"No shit," Nat said.

"I would have been on my way back to the cleaners, but I forgot her veil and had to take it back upstairs. That's when I found Larry in the room bending over her body."

"I hear they took him down to the police station for questioning, but they let him go."

I wasn't about to tell him that I'd been there, too. "Do you know if they have any other suspects?"

"As a matter of fact, when I checked tonight, I found out they've arrested someone else and are questioning him."

It was probably Ryan, but I asked anyway, "Who was it?"

"Her brother."

At long last, I had confirmation.

"He supposedly had a fight with his old man who threatened to call the police on him. He claims he got as far as the bar when he saw cops and decided to get out of there, but he says he had no idea they were there because his sister had been killed."

"Do you think the police will buy that?"

"I don't know. The kid says he hid out in the basement for awhile, then climbed in an unlocked truck, and fell asleep under some stuff in the back until the driver came out and drove away. Can you believe that some dummy had left his truck unlocked?"

Every word, I thought, because that would explain why Ryan had stayed in the truck so long while he waited for the dummy to come back and haul him away from the crime scene.

My silence must have made Nat wonder. He eyed me suspiciously. "Great Jumping Jack Flash," he said. "Don't tell me it was your truck from the store?"

When I try to lie, I've discovered that it's better to answer a question with another question. "Why on earth would you think it was me?"

"Because you're beginning to itch." He pointed at my hands. "And you always itch when you lie."

I looked down where the fingers on my right hand, without my even knowing it, were scratching my left palm. "It must be an allergy."

"We know each other too well for that. You can't fib to me unless the lights are out and I can't see you." He was referring to another time when he'd kept an all-night vigil with me at the cleaners after the place was burglarized and trashed. That's the only time I'd ever pulled the wool over his eyes, so to speak, and gotten away with a fib.

"I'm just nervous about what I'm going to do with Mom," I said, figuring that might divert his attention.

It did. I could tell he was trying to suppress a smirk. "So what *are* you going to do with her?"

"Get her a hotel room someplace as far away from here as possible. At least she'll have a car this time so I won't have to chauffeur her around town."

"She was actually pretty nice to me on the phone," he said, taking another swig of beer. "She said she was sure I'd turned into a mature, responsible adult, but she reminded me about how mad she was that time we went to that all-night horror film retrospective. She thought we'd gone to a motel."

I snorted. "Yeah, right." Then I paused, bent my head to one side, and squinted at him. "You know, I think it's time you got a haircut so you'll look like a mature, responsible adult."

"Huh?" he asked, stunned at my suggestion.

I was actually thinking about Ryan and the fight he'd had with his father over a haircut and his drinking.

"Why don't you cut your hair?" I repeated.

I knew the answer. Nat thought he resembled John Lennon, so he kept his dark hair longer than the current fashion and still wore the granny glasses long after they'd gone out of style. He did look a little like the famous Beatle if the light was just right, but it was time for him to grow up.

I told him that.

Nat finally decided to go on offense. "You're just trying to change the subject to get me off your back. So come on, Mandy, were you the one in the van?"

"If I tell you, will you leave?"

He nodded.

"And it has to be off-the-record, too."

He nodded again, but this time it was as if the up-and-down movement of his head was giving him a migraine.

Once I'd extracted this sacred promise, I finally admitted that I'd been held up by Olivia's brother at Bic-point and forced to drive him to downtown Denver.

Nat started to laugh.

I stopped him and swore that if he ever wrote about it I would torture him with some fate worse than death. Perhaps make him smoke a cigar, which I remembered had made him violently ill when we were kids.

"What's Stan think about all this?" Nat asked suddenly. He tolerated my on-again-off-again romance with Stan, even though there was a reporter/cop antagonism between them. "Has he heard about it?"

"He's upset about my being involved," I said, but I didn't add anything about our non-dinner or the fight we'd had.

"You know," he said, "maybe we should go on a double date sometime." By now, he was at the door and starting to leave. "I've been dating this gorgeous blonde goddess. I think I'm in love, Mandy."

So what else was new? Nat never fell for anyone unless they were blonde and at least four inches taller than he was. No wonder he had trouble establishing long-term relationships, especially when most of the women were so young they didn't even remember John Lennon.

"She's a kick-boxer, and she's really good."

With that, I took a hint and drop-kicked him out the door.

I made a half-hearted attempt to clean up the apartment on Sunday. I collected the week's supply of newspapers and added them to a pile in a corner of the room. I saved the papers for Mack, who conscientiously recycled them, and I needed to tie them up for him. But he was out of town, and I was out of energy.

Besides, the clouds had disappeared, and the temperature was in the eighties. I turned on my window air conditioner and slouched around in my pajamas, hoping my mother would call. In my fantasy world, Mom would say she'd had a change of heart and gone back to Phoenix to await the return of her beloved husband from his used-car golf tournament.

But the phone didn't ring all day. Not that I planned to pick it up until I listened to the answering machine and knew who it was anyway. Instead, I slept, fed Spot a couple of times, and had a long discussion with him about his taste in men. "You really are a bad judge of character," I said, as the cat gave me an indifferent look and started eating his food.

I'd called Alabama first thing that morning, hoping to catch Mack before he went to the hospital to see his brother. I left a message, but I didn't expect to hear from him until that night.

Finally, at seven o'clock the phone rang. Mack should be back at the hotel by now, and I hovered over the receiver waiting to pick up if I heard him or Mom at the other end of the line.

"Hi, this is Stan." He waited a few seconds while I tried to decide whether I wanted to talk to him or not. "Well, I guess you aren't there so I'll call back later." He hung up.

At eight o'clock, the phone rang again while I was cleaning Spot's litter box. By the time I picked up, Mom had started to leave a message.

"Hello, Amanda. I'm in Albuquerque, and I just wanted—"

"Mom, it's me. You don't need to come. In fact, I insist that you turn around and go back home right now. Everything is under control here."

"Did they find the person who killed Larry's poor fiancée?" she asked.

"Well, no," I said. This was based on what I'd heard on the evening news which had been my only contact with the outside world all day.

"Then I'm coming, and I will *not* take no for an answer. You and Larry could be in big trouble, and I want to be there in case you need me."

"I don't need you, and I'm not in big trouble." I began to itch, and I guess it was about that "big trouble" part.

"But I'm concerned about what the police will think about you being at the hotel. Why in the world did you go there, dear?"

"Would it make you change your mind about coming up here if I told you?"

"No, absolutely not."

"Okay, we'll discuss it once you're here."

"All right, dear. I can understand why you'd rather not get into it on the phone. The line might be bugged."

Oh, yeah, right. Mom watched entirely too much TV.

"I should be in Denver by four o'clock tomorrow," she said. "I'll stop at the cleaners on the way into town."

We said goodbye, and I hung up the phone, but I had trouble putting the receiver in its cradle. I was shaking too much.

It wasn't until I talked to Mack that I finally calmed down, and I didn't do that at first. He told me his brother was doing well and that he was planning on coming home Tuesday.

"Oh, thank God," I said, and then I began to blubber out the whole terrible story.

I could hear the worry in Mack's voice. "Look, do you want me to come back earlier? Maybe I can get a flight out tonight or early tomorrow."

"No, no." I shook my head for emphasis even though he couldn't see me. "I'm just glad you'll be back on Tuesday."

"I should have stayed and delivered that wedding gown myself," Mack said. "I promised you I'd do it, and I should have kept my word."

"Oh, God, no," I said. "You had to be with your brother, and besides, if you'd have been here, then you'd have been the one under suspicion. You were always my staunchest ally when Larry left me, and the police might think you killed his fiancée."

"No, they wouldn't think that. The only person I ever had it in for was Larry."

I tried to laugh, but I couldn't. "Anyway, I feel better just talking to you, and I'll be glad when you're back." I shouldn't have mentioned that.

"Like I said, I can come home sooner."

"No, Mack. Besides, my mother's coming up from Phoenix tomorrow so I'll be tied up with her tomorrow night."

There was silence on the other end of the line, then Mack asked, as if he hadn't heard me right, "Did you say your mother?"

"Yes."

"That's what I thought you said. I've changed my mind. I won't be back until at least a month from now."

This time Mack laughed, and so did I. It was a good way to end the conversation.

I pulled out my sofa into a bed, climbed under the covers, and reached over to turn off the light on the end table. This was my cocoon within a cocoon, but I still couldn't resist turning on the TV with my remote control to catch the ten o'clock news. Big mistake.

Olivia's murder was still the top story of the day. The station had a shot of the outside of the hotel, which they always seem to do with the murder scene these days. In the foreground of the picture, sticking out the same way Ryan's tux had stuck out on East Colfax, was my Dyer's Cleaners van with its name emblazoned on the side with the fresh-as-a-daisy logo underneath. I put the pillow over my head, but I felt as if I were suffocating. I removed the pillow and kicked off my blanket, but I was still suffocating. I got up and went over to the window to catch a whiff of cool air from outside.

That's one thing about Denver. It always cools down at night, and with windows on three sides of the apartment, I get a good cross-breeze.

I finally calmed down, and by then, I'd resigned myself to the fact that it was only a matter of time before reporters connected me to the crime, especially once they managed to interview some of the witnesses who'd been at the scene.

Almost as if it were preordained, the phone rang right then. I hoped it would be Stan. He'd said he would call later, and by now, I'd decided to talk to him. But because of the timing, I waited for the caller to start speaking into my answering machine. You can never be too careful when members of the press might soon be hovering over you like vultures.

The voice on the other end of the line confirmed my fear. It was a woman's voice, one I didn't recognize, and she sounded as if she were on a mission.

"Miss Dyer," she said. "I was wondering if I could have a word with you."

No way, Jose, as Nat would say. I wasn't getting hooked up with any more reporters this weekend. Nat was enough. I walked away from the telephone and stumbled back to bed in the darkness. I could still hear the woman's voice, even when I pulled the sheet and blanket over my head.

"I was hoping it would be convenient for me to stop by your cleaners tomorrow at ten o'clock," the woman continued, "but since you're not home, I guess I'll have to check back with you tomorrow."

I twisted my bedding around me as I turned away from the answering machine and made a mental note to remind my front counter personnel that I wasn't taking any calls tomorrow.

"Oh, by the way, my name is Charlotte," the voice continued. "I met you when Mrs. Torkelson asked me to bring you the scissors—just before Olivia was killed."

It took me awhile to disentangle myself from the bed

sheets and get to the phone. By the time I did, Charlotte had hung up.

That was the young woman I'd dubbed the gofer girl because Mrs. Torkelson kept ordering her to go for this and go for that at the hotel the previous day. What could Charlotte want with me?

CHAPTER 8

By the time I left my apartment in my freshly pressed uniform at six o'clock Monday morning, I'd decided I needed to have a meeting with my employees. I just didn't know how much to tell them. Some of them knew I'd been married to Larry, and a few had probably recognized Olivia's name on the news because of the wedding gown we'd had in the cleaners for the last month. In particular, my two employees, Julia and Ann Marie, would know I'd been at the hotel. Although there was no production back in the plant on Saturday, the women had been working the counter when I set off on my disastrous delivery.

I stopped at one of those street corner news stands and grabbed the early editions of the Denver papers. I pulled over to the curb and scanned them. For once, Nat hadn't told the public everything he knew. He'd omitted all the stuff about me. He was a good friend after all, but I wasn't too sure how long that would last. Not when the other members of the media might soon pick up on the connection between the van in the photo of the hotel and the murder. I even took a glance around the parking lot behind the cleaners as I pulled in and parked the van next to my car which I'd left in the lot since Saturday morning. There didn't appear to be any media types lurking around the back of the cleaners to accost me. Yet.

Since Mack wasn't here today, I arrived at the plant at six-thirty to open the door and be there when the rest of the crew arrived. Kim, Mack's assistant, who is Korean, arrived shortly after I did. He was the best cleaner/spotter we'd ever had, aside from Mack, and would be a worthy successor when Mack retired. I couldn't bear to think about that right now.

The rest of the crew began coming in a few minutes later, and it was apparent that Betty, the irascible former bag lady I was in the process of rehabilitating, had spotted the van in the TV clip of the hotel the previous night.

"I can't believe you managed to get yourself smack dab in the middle of that murder on Saturday," she said as she came in the door.

Ever since her boyfriend, a doll doctor named Arthur Goldman, had given her a TV, she'd become a dedicated couch potato who never missed a thing on the tube. In fact, I'd decided the best hope of keeping her off the streets was her addiction to the programs she rushed home every night to watch.

"Me and Artie were watching the news last night when we saw the van. You were there, weren't you? You got this bad habit of always getting yourself knee-deep in a shit-load of trouble, don't you?"

Little did she know quite how much trouble.

I could see the startled look on Kim's face. I didn't know if it was from Betty's language or if he'd caught the significance of what she was saying. Anyway, I realized it was probably only a matter of minutes before the news spread around the plant like a virus.

"Please don't say anything about this to anyone else, will you?" I asked, looking from Betty to Kim. "We'll have a meeting about it later today."

First I had to figure out exactly what I wanted to say, but

for the time being, I went up front to wait for my counter crew. While I waited, I made a reservation for my mother at a downtown hotel.

Julia, a mother of three, arrived first, and her young co-worker, Ann Marie, was just a few minutes behind the older woman.

"Remember that wedding gown I came to pick up on Saturday?" I asked. "Well, the bride was killed right before the ceremony."

"Gross," Ann Marie said, shuddering as if she were doing some kind of weird new dance.

"I heard about it," Julia said. "That's terrible. I hope you weren't still there."

"Unfortunately, I was, so if any reporters phone about it, please tell them I'm not available."

Both women nodded.

"But if someone called Charlotte—I'm afraid I don't know her last name—should phone, please put her through or come back and get me. Okay?"

They nodded again.

"I hope you'll be able to get along without me here at the counter this morning," I said. "Since Mack isn't here, I'm going to have to help Kim with the cleaning until we get caught up on the orders that came in on Saturday."

With that I went back to the spotting board and set to work next to Kim. It was a good way to avoid holding the meeting for awhile; being out on the floor was also a way to keep the gossip from spreading to the point of becoming an epidemic.

By mid-morning, Kim and I had things under control in the cleaning department. When the pressers first arrived, they'd started work on the garments that had been cleaned late Friday, and now we had the assembly line running for things we'd cleaned today.

I glanced at my watch. It was quarter to eleven. I'd decided that Charlotte wasn't going to call after all, so after I finished putting another dark load in the cleaning machine,

I'd decided to go to my office and do some serious thinking about what to say to the crew. I almost had the machine filled when Julia appeared from the call office.

"It's that woman you wanted to talk to," she said.

I tossed a handful of pants in the machine. "Will you start this load for me, Kim? I have to grab the phone." I started to my office so I could take the call in private.

"No, she's at the counter," Julia said.

I changed directions and followed her to the front of the building. I recognized Charlotte right away, but this time I looked at her more carefully. She had nice, even features, which could have been enhanced with a little makeup, particularly the use of an eyebrow pencil. Her eyebrows were so pale they faded into the rest of her face, and her light brown hair looked as if she hadn't combed it. She looked worried.

"Thank goodness, you're here, Miss Dyer," she said. "I'm really sorry to bother you, but I've been so upset about what happened Saturday that I needed to talk to someone. Is there some place where we can be alone?"

"Sure," I said, motioning her around the counter and through the door into the plant. "Follow me, but first, I never caught your last name. What is it?" I hoped it wasn't another Torkelson like Ryan to further confuse the mix.

"It's Horton," she said. "Charlotte Horton."

I led the way to my office where my visitor's chair was filled with sample swatches of new fabrics that we needed to test-clean. I moved them to a sofa and asked her to sit down. I took a seat behind the desk.

Charlotte was wearing a tan skirt and a short-sleeved white blouse that went with her rather prim look better than the fancy blue street-length dress she'd had on Saturday for her task of handling the guest book.

"What did you want to discuss?" I asked.

"I was just wondering—" She licked her lips nervously. "—I was wondering if you told the police about my bringing the scissors to Olivia's room. I was afraid to tell the detective about it, and I've been scared ever since. I'm afraid my fingerprints will be all over the scissors and the police will think I killed her."

This was the woman who'd backed up Larry's story that he hadn't gone in Olivia's room. Why should I try to reassure her? I guess it was because I tended to agree with her. "Oh, I don't think they'll assume you stabbed her," I said, putting on my most comforting smile. "Besides—" And I really hated to think about it, but maybe it would make her feel better. "—my fingerprints probably covered yours on the scissors. Unless, of course, the person who killed Olivia wiped off both sets of prints."

"So you didn't tell the police about me bringing you the scissors?"

"Well, yes, I did," I said, "but that's no reason to worry as long as you don't have a motive." I'd been hoping Charlotte had something to share with me about what she'd seen that day, but all she was doing was reinforcing the fact that I was the only person who seemed to have a motive.

Charlotte shook her head. "Oh, no, I didn't have any reason to kill Olivia. I just work in her father's law office, and she asked me to handle the wedding invitations and the guest book."

"Well then I wouldn't worry, although I think you should call Detective Perrelli and admit to him that you brought the scissors into the room."

"You do?" she asked.

I nodded.

"Okay, thank you. I'm sorry if I interrupted your work, but I didn't know who else to talk to, other than Olivia's parents, and I didn't want to bother them right now. Her father has closed the law firm for a few days." Charlotte got up and started to leave. "I wish Olivia had never involved me in any of this. I hated sending out all those invitations, especially to some of the people she had on the list."

"Excuse me?" I leaned toward her across the desk. "Don't leave yet. What about the invitations?"

Charlotte came back with seeming reluctance and sat down in the chair again. Her voice was almost a whisper when she spoke. "Olivia wanted me to send invitations to her old boyfriend and to Larry's ex-wife up in Aspen."

I did a double-take. "So she knew about Larry's ex-wife in Aspen?"

Charlotte nodded. "Personally, I thought she was asking for trouble when she told me to send her one. I even suggested that maybe she shouldn't do it, but she insisted."

Hallelujah. Here were more suspects—the second ex-wife and an old boyfriend—to add to the meager list so I wouldn't look as if I were the only one with means, motive, and opportunity. Okay, so the other suspects might not have been in the room when the body was discovered, but they could easily have been in the hotel and snuck into the room while I was gone.

Just then I heard a noise at the door. I looked over to see Betty, her short-cropped gray hair sticking up in spikes as if she'd just used some kind of Fast-Gro hair gel on it.

"Psst," the former bag lady said, motioning for me to come to the door. "There's something I need to show you."

I frowned. "Not now, Betty."

She ran her hands through her hair in agitation, which must have accounted for the spikes. "It's important."

I glared at her. "I'm busy right now. Go back to work, and I'll talk to you in a few minutes." I should have closed the door. In fact, I thought of asking Betty to do it as she left, but that might have alerted her to the fact that something was going on in here that was worth listening to.

I glanced at Charlotte, then took another quick look at the door. I was relieved to see that Betty had retreated. I'd half expected her to persist until I had to go out and see what she wanted, but I didn't want to lose my train of thought.

"What was the ex-wife's name?" I asked when I was sure Betty wasn't going to bug us anymore.

"Patricia Robertson. Apparently, she's a lawyer in Aspen, and she still uses her maiden name."

I knew full-well the name of the woman Larry had dumped me for. I just wanted to check to make sure Charlotte wasn't feeding me a line, and she had the name right.

"And who was the boyfriend?" I continued.

"His name's Richard Willis," Charlotte said, brushing her blunt-cut hair away from her face. "He used to be a paralegal in the office, but he left when Olivia gave his ring back. After all, she'd stolen him away from his old girlfriend, who just happened to be her best friend. Then Olivia just cast him aside like an old shoe. He was really angry."

This was getting more and more interesting. "And who was the old girlfriend? Was she invited to the wedding, too?"

"No, not invited . . ." My hopes were dashed, but only temporarily. Then Charlotte leaned over toward me. "She was the maid-of-honor, Karen Westbrook."

The name sounded vaguely familiar, and I tried to remember where I'd heard it.

"They made up after Olivia dumped Richard," Charlotte continued.

"What did she look like?"

"She's tall and blonde."

So Karen was probably the first woman in the room after me, the one I'd thought I recognized.

"And who was the bridesmaid who accused Larry of going into Olivia's room?"

"Oh, her name's Victoria Burnett. I don't know much about her except that she didn't like Larry, but Olivia wanted her in the wedding anyway."

Wow. This was more than I had any right to expect. "Olivia seemed so sweet and gentle," I said, using Larry's words to describe his fiancée. "I can't imagine that she'd actually try to start trouble at her own wedding."

"You didn't know Olivia very well, did you?"

Well, no, I hadn't.

"She had that vulnerable quality about her," Charlotte said, "but she had a vindictive streak, too, and I think she wanted to rub it in to everyone about what a great catch she'd made."

I usually wasn't this bad a judge of character, and the picture Charlotte was painting didn't jibe with the shy, uncertain woman who'd been in my fitting room. "But she seemed so unsure of herself," I argued, "not even positive that she wanted to go through with the wedding."

"That's the way she wanted people to think she was, but she was always threatening us underlings. She made me readdress half the invitations because she didn't like my handwriting the first time."

"And you did it?"

Charlotte seemed embarrassed. "When I explained that it was cutting into my work time, Olivia let me know that I was climbing up the wrong tree if I thought I was going to get out of addressing the envelopes."

Climbing up the wrong tree? That didn't sound like something Olivia would have said if she'd wanted to threaten one of her father's employees, and for a minute, I almost wanted to giggle. It reminded me of a play I'd been in back in high school. I'd had the role of the nasty older sister, and at one point, I was supposed to say "You go to hell." Our prim, proper drama teacher just couldn't handle me saying that, yet she didn't want to lose the sister's line, so she had me say "You go jump in the lake," to which Sis said "You run your own errands." Somehow it just wasn't as funny or as much of a threat if the errand was to jump in a lake, not go to hell.

I'm easily sidetracked when I'm overwhelmed with information, and I realized Charlotte was still talking. I tried hard to get my concentration back as I juggled my picture of Olivia with the one Charlotte was painting.

"—and Olivia said her daddy had told her she could use me for anything she wanted me to do, and that she could get me fired just like that." Charlotte snapped her fingers for emphasis.

Double wow. Maybe I was as bad a judge of character as Spot. Only yesterday I'd criticized the cat for liking Larry. I needed to go home and apologize to my feline friend. And I made a mental note that even Charlotte could be a suspect. She was giving me such a different picture of Olivia than I'd had, and she seemed so bitter.

Charlotte must have read my mind. "If you don't believe me, then ask yourself one question: Why do you think she came to you to have the dress cleaned?"

I was half out of my chair. "Why?"

"Because she knew you were Larry's first wife. She got a big kick out of that."

"Damn." I sat back down. I couldn't really believe it. Why would anyone come to their fiancé's ex-wife voluntarily for help? For all she knew, I could have botched the wedding gown so badly she couldn't have worn it—or left pins in it so it would have poked her during the ceremony. Oh, yeah, Mandy, there's a real way to get even with someone, and if the cops only knew that about me, they would have me in jail right now. This momentarily diverted me again, and just when I'd thought of something else I wanted to ask Charlotte.

I was even further distracted by a male voice outside the door. "What you doing there, Betty? Juan wanted me to come find you."

"Shh." Betty's voice was a hiss. "I'm waiting to see the boss lady."

Jeez. She'd probably been eavesdropping all this time.

"Betty," I yelled. "I said to get back to work. I'll catch you in a minute."

She peeked in the door, gave me a dirty look, and then disappeared.

What was it I'd wanted to ask Charlotte? It had seemed important, and it would bug me all day if I didn't think of it. I doodled on a scratch pad, which I'd already filled with stars, arrows, the names Charlotte had mentioned, and their connection to Olivia. For good measure, I added Charlotte's, then finally remembered the elusive question.

"Did Olivia ever mention anything to you about receiving a threatening note that said she'd be really sorry if she married Larry?" I put the emphasis on the word *really*, the way Olivia had when she'd mentioned it to me.

Charlotte looked surprised. "No, I never heard of that, but I can see why she might get nasty letters after I mailed out all those invitations."

It was too bad Olivia hadn't told Charlotte about the note since she'd apparently mentioned so many other things to the gofer girl during the months before the wedding.

"Either that," Charlotte continued, "or she was just telling you a tale to make herself seem more helpless."

I didn't think so because I'd heard her talking to someone else about it on the phone. Either that or she'd been conning them too, but hopefully the police had found someone else to corroborate the story by now, even if Charlotte couldn't.

I thought of something else. "Do you still have the guest list Olivia gave you?"

Charlotte shook her head. "No, I don't know what happened to it. When I finally addressed the envelopes to her satisfaction, she had me seal and stamp them, and then I returned the whole thing to her."

I suppose it had been too much to hope that Charlotte would still have the list, but I decided to offer her my advice, based on crossing paths with the police department on a few other occasions. "You need to go to Detective Perrelli and tell him everything you've told me about the people on the list." When Charlotte looked dubious, I added, "It's the best way to keep him from being suspicious of you." And of me, too, but I didn't say that.

"I guess so," she said.

I asked her for her phone number and jotted it down, even though I thought I would remember it anyway—the same prefix as the cleaners, followed by 3456. Then I walked her into the plant and pointed her to the front door. "I need to find out what my employee wants," I said, "but I'm glad you came to see me. You need to let Perrelli know that a lot of people could have had a motive to kill Olivia."

She smiled weakly and left.

I knew one thing for sure. I was going to call the detective myself, give him Charlotte's phone number, and tell him what she said. The last time something like this had happened, I'd left it up to a friend to talk to Stan, and the friend had waited so long that it got us both in hot water for withholding information.

I turned around and headed for the laundry department, where I found Betty putting a load of blue jeans in the washer.

"All right, Betty, here I am. What was so important that it couldn't wait?"

"You're in shit way over your head, boss lady. I didn't know you'd been married to that guy whose fee-an-say was killed."

I couldn't hide my anger. "You had no business hiding outside my office and listening to our conversation."

Betty snorted. "That's not where I heard it." Then she shrugged. "Well, I heard it there, too, but it was on the TV when I was in the break room having lunch. I was trying to get you to come watch it."

Okay, so maybe I owed her an apology about where she'd obtained the information. And she was right about one thing—the shit had hit the fan, and I had to start doing some serious damage control.

CHAPTER 9

I'd been considering telling the crew a watered-down version of Saturday's events, but now that the news media knew I was the ex-wife of the groom, I decided it was time to let it all hang out. It was better if the employees heard the whole story from me rather than from one of the talking heads on TV.

My decision was confirmed when Ann Marie came back to the cleaning department to tell me that a reporter was on the phone and wanted to talk to me.

"Just tell him I'm not available right now," I said.

I went to the front counter a few minutes later and gave her and Julia "the rest of the story"—namely that the groom was my ex-husband, Larry, but I asked them not to talk to the press about it. I was confident Julia would honor my request, but I wasn't so sure about Ann Marie. She looked too excited, especially when she mentioned that the reporter who'd called was her absolutely favorite TV person, Jason Hendrix.

"He has a real dreamy smile," she said, "and I saw him once in person, and he's got a—like, you know—real cute butt."

I asked the women to cover for me at the counter and said I didn't want any calls or visitors, not even any salespeople from our distributors, while I assembled the rest of the crew in the break room. I had Juan from the laundry set up a few extra chairs around the tables where employees normally ate their lunches and took their coffee breaks.

Then I tried a technique I'd learned from one of my grade school teachers: give the class troublemaker a job so she won't run amok during the meeting. In other words, I asked Betty to sit by the back door and be room monitor. Hopefully, being guardian of the door would make her feel responsible so she wouldn't heckle me like a protester planted in the audience at a political rally. Naive me.

"Some of you may have seen the news on TV here in the lunch room during your break," I said, trying not to glance back at Betty who had a strange, thoughtful look on her face. It was always dangerous for her to think too much because she was likely to come up with some off-the-wall remark. "The report mentioned that I delivered the wedding gown to the hotel that was to be the site of a wedding between Olivia Torkelson and Larry Landry."

I could tell by the almost hushed reaction of my employees that I had their full attention. Why couldn't they be that way when we had our periodic meetings to review OSHA's safety requirements, or the definition of what constituted sexual harassment?

It was also apparent that most of the crew had seen the news broadcast, or if they hadn't, the information had been transmitted to them by their friends. All except for Lucille, who marked in clothes at a counter on the opposite wall from the call office. She was so grouchy that most of her coworkers stayed away from her; therefore, she was usually out of the loop for the rumor mill. That isn't to say that she didn't like raunchy gossip as well as the next person. At any rate, she was the only one who let out a noticeable gasp when I mentioned Larry.

"And as some of you know," I continued, unable to keep from looking at her, "Larry Landry is my ex-husband."

I was sure the old-timers remembered when Larry had dumped me. I'd been working part-time at the cleaners, and Larry used to drop me off and pick me up in our old clunker of a car on his way to law school. Then he announced he wanted a divorce, which was shortly before Uncle Chet died and left me the cleaners. It had been a double-whammy, which I got through only because of Mack's advice and support.

Most of the employees from before I inherited the cleaners were polite enough not to gasp the way Lucille had at the mention of Larry's name. I was sure she'd have a few well-chosen words to say to me later about how none of this would have happened if my uncle were still alive.

"What I feel you should know—" My mouth seemed to have dried up, and I tried again. "What I want—" Actually what I wanted was to sneak off to my office and lock the door.

"Betty, would you please get me a glass of water?" I asked her because she was the closest to the water fountain, but I'd no sooner made the request than there was a commotion at the door.

At first, all I saw was a flash of colors that looked like a huge bouquet of flowers being delivered for my curtain call. Unfortunately, as my vision cleared, I realized it was my mother in one of her ruffled print dresses. Oh, God, she wasn't supposed to be here until four o'clock.

The scent of Chanel No. 5, her favorite perfume, wafted around her as she clattered into the room in three-inch heels looking as if she had just burst into bloom or, at the very least, was on her way to an afternoon tea. Most mothers would have worn a pants suit, if not jeans, for the 450 mile car trip from Albuquerque. Who ever heard of anyone wearing heels and flowered chiffon for such a drive?

"I hope I'm not interrupting," she said, fluffing her blonde hair, delighted to be the centerpiece on an otherwise dull table.

Julia followed her inside. "I tried to make her wait out front until the meeting was over."

"Hey, you can't come in here, lady," Betty said, jumping to attention, and turning from benign protector of the door to barroom bouncer.

Mom pushed her aside, which I knew at once was a big mistake.

Before Betty decided to push her back, I yelled, "That's all right, Betty. You can let her in." I glanced around the room at the rapt audience. "For those of you who don't already know her, this is my mother, Cecilia Smedley. Why don't you have a seat back there, Mom, until we're finished?"

Juan, who'd been sitting on the other side of the door from Betty, moved over one chair to let Mom sit by him, but that wouldn't do for my mother. She click-clacked on up to where I was standing and seated herself in a chair directly in front of me.

The recovering bag lady gave her an angry look, which turned to disgust as Mom carefully arranged her skirt as if she were a Southern Belle at the spring cotillion.

I felt as parched as a prospector lost in Death Valley for a month, and I needed water more than ever. I decided to try a different tack, however.

"Juan, would you bring me a glass of water?"

Betty was having none of that. She pushed him aside, ran water in a paper cup, and raced toward me as if this were some sort of popularity contest. Mom looked her up and down as she approached, and I could tell Mom didn't think much of Betty's bilious green polyester pants suit, which was one of the few things Mom and I would probably agree on during her whole ill-advised visit to Denver.

Just before she reached me, Betty seemed to trip, spilling most of the water on Mom's skirt before she regained her footing.

"Whoops." Betty grinned wickedly. "Sorry about that."

"Of all the clumsy—" Mom's voice trailed off as she grabbed a lace-trimmed handkerchief from her purse to swipe at the water on her dress.

"Want me to get you some more water, Mandy?" Betty asked.

Since there was no way I was going to believe that clumsiness had anything to do with it, I declined the offer and grabbed the cup from her hand. "No, this will be fine, Betty. Just go back to your seat."

For a minute I thought she was going to ignore my request and grab the seat next to Mom, but she turned around and went back to her station at the door. Juan, whom I should have put in charge of the door, rushed forward with some paper towels for Mom to sop up the water while I drank the thimble-full still remaining in the cup.

"As I was saying—" What had I been saying? I tried in vain to think what it was. "At any rate, I was not aware of the name of Miss Torkelson's fiancé when I agreed to alter and clean her wedding gown." I wished now that I'd thought out what I was going to say before the meeting, but I tried to edit as I went along.

"Anyway—" Why did I keep using such superfluous expressions all the time? It was as bad as Ann Marie with her "like, you knows." I finally forced myself to continue. "So by the time I realized who her fiancé was, it was too late to do anything about it."

At the other end of the room, I saw Betty wiggle in her chair. She actually had her hand in the air as if she wanted to be excused to go to the bathroom. I guess in some way I could take satisfaction in the fact that she was at least beginning to follow some rules, instead of just blurting out whatever was on her mind, but it was very distracting.

"Not now, Betty. Wait until I'm finished."

I was so rattled that I'd completely lost my train of thought again. "At any rate—" Damn, there I went again, but at least the phrase gave me time to pick up the frayed threads of my thoughts. "—it was my plan to have someone else deliver the wedding gown to the hotel Saturday. Unfortunately, no one was available, and I had to do it myself. I made the delivery to the hotel and returned to the van for the veil." I was just about to mention the scissors when I realized I was probably telling more than I should. I needed to wrap it up quickly and get out of there. "When I returned to the room," I continued, "Larry had just found his fiancée—" A lump replaced the dryness in my throat. "—his fiancée's body." I gulped for breath.

"My poor Mandy," Mom said as she put the sodden handkerchief to her mouth.

"Can I say somethin' now?" Betty asked.

"I'm not finished." I glared from Mom to Betty. If looks could kill, they would both be dead by now, and I knew the moment I zapped them with the scalding glance it hadn't been a wise thing to do. My crew might actually think I was capable of killing someone.

"Anyway, that's all I know about the murder. I've told the police what I've told you." I didn't mention how many times or in what detail I'd repeated the story to the cops, but it didn't seem prudent to do so. "Unfortunately, this may bring some unwanted attention to Dyer's Cleaners, but I'm sure we can weather this period just the way we did that other terrible incident when the man was killed here in the plant."

I probably shouldn't have reminded my crew about that other time, but everyone knew about it anyway. It was just that pretty soon people were going to think the place was jinxed because of all the bad things that happened to its owner and be superstitious about working for me.

"If any reporters approach you to talk about the case," I continued in a panic to wind up, "I would prefer that you say no comment, but if you feel obliged to speak, I hope you'll tell them that this is *not* disrupting work here at the plant. And I want to emphasize that at no time should we let this crime distract us from the careful attention to detail we always give our customers' clothes."

My speech was disintegrating into the kind of gobbledygook I hated in other bosses, but I didn't know what else to say. I wished Mack had been here to help me with the speech.

"You can all go back to work now," I concluded. It was the best I could do.

I saw Betty's hand in the air again.

"Can we wait until the meeting is over, Betty?"

"But I wanted to say somethin'."

"Very well, go ahead." I prayed it would be something innocuous. Maybe something about how everyone ought to rally around "the boss lady" by turning out the best damned product they could.

Betty rose as Mom turned around and gave her a disapproving look.

"I heard that your ex's *other* ex-wife was invited to the wed—"

She was about to bring up what she'd overheard from Charlotte outside my office door, and I think I actually stomped my foot to shut her up. "We don't need to discuss that here. The meeting is over. We'll talk about this in my office, Betty." I gave her another laser-beam glare. "*Now.*" I started to leave, but Mom stopped me by tugging on my hand.

"I'm so sorry about this, Amanda." She rose and gave me a hug. "I got here as soon as I could." There were tears in her eyes as she pulled away from me. I didn't doubt her sincerity, but I hoped her mascara wouldn't start to run, not to mention the fact that one of her contact lenses might fall out. I don't know why I thought about that, but I suppose it was because it was too painful for me to think of anything else.

I glanced around the room and noticed that the rest of the crew seemed unwilling to tear themselves away from this little drama, unlike the OSHA meetings they always fled as if someone had set off the fire alarm. I headed for the door, and they followed reluctantly.

When I reached my office, I turned, expecting to find Betty right behind me. Instead, Mom almost ran into me. I guess I'd been too upset to hear the clicking of her heels following me across the epoxied floor of the plant.

Before I could stop her, Mom sat down in the chair I'd cleared earlier for Charlotte. Betty trailed after her. She gave Mom a dirty look for taking the only chair, then plopped down on the sofa, unconcerned by the fact that it was covered with fabric swatches.

Mom glowered back while I tried to make up my mind which one of them to banish from the room. Finally, I decided, why bother? I'd go ahead and say my piece to Betty even if it was against my normal policy to do so in front of other people.

"I do not want you to repeat anything you heard when you were snooping outside my door a little while ago. Do you understand, Betty?"

She shrugged. "I just thought if this Larry-fella's other ex-wife and the bride's old boyfriend were invited to the wedding—"

She had Mom's attention now, if not her approval.

I put my hands on my hips to show how really ticked off I was. "Betty, I said not to repeat any of that."

"But I was thinkin' maybe me and the rest of the crew oughta go out and track them down to see if they had alibis."

"No."

"But what I found out about the dead guy in the alley helped you solve that other case."

"What other case?" Mom said, turning to me.

I shook my head as if I didn't know what Betty was talking about. The gesture had all the effect of trying to stop a moth from flapping its wings against a porchlight.

"What case?" Mom repeated, her own hands fluttering to the ruffles at her throat as if she were that Southern Belle again and might fall into a sudden swoon.

Betty stood up proudly. "Mandy and me figured out who killed the guy when nobody else could."

Before she had a chance to sit down again, I grabbed the retired bag lady by the arm and escorted her out of the room. For what it's worth, I was almost tempted to keep right on going and toss her back out on the street where she came from.

"I don't want you to say one more word about trying to find out if Larry's second wife or anyone else has an alibi. Never. Not to anyone. Am I understood?"

Betty nodded, then gave me an evil grin. "I'da never figured you to have a mother like that, boss lady. She looks like a garden where they've spread too much fertilizer."

I felt a hysterical urge to laugh, but I pulled myself together. "We'll discuss the eavesdropping incident again later, Betty."

With that I spun around and returned to my office, where Mom had a disapproving look on her face. "Who was that dreadful woman, anyway?"

"Her name is Florence Lorenzo," I said, which was the name on her Social Security card. "But everyone calls her Betty." I didn't add that people used to call her Betty the Bag Lady. I was sure that wouldn't make my mother think any more highly of her, although it probably wouldn't have made her think any worse.

"Well, somebody needs to spill something a whole lot worse than water on that horrible green outfit of hers," Mom sniffed. "I didn't know anyone wore polyester like that anymore." She said polyester as if it were some sort of social disease, then abruptly shifted directions. "And what was that she said about a dead man in an alley?"

"I'll tell you about it later. Right now I have a lot of work to do before I leave." I went over and reached in my purse for a hotel confirmation number. "I reserved a room for you at that same hotel where you stayed the last time you were here. I'll try to get away by seven so we can go out to dinner."

Mom started shaking her head before I finished talking. "No," she said, "I came here to be with my little girl, and I intend to stay with her." I guess she chose to refer to me in the third person and as her "little girl" to perpetuate her personal myth that I was still a teenager and she couldn't be any more than thirty-five herself. "I've been taking some new allergy medicine, and I think I'll be able to tolerate your cat better this time."

The problem was, could Spot and I tolerate Mom? I knew the answer, and I finally wound up saying I'd stay at the hotel with her, at least for tonight. Okay, I know that was against my earlier ironclad resolve, but once I had her safely ensconced with room service, I could probably break away and return to my apartment alone. I hoped.

Once she'd extracted the promise from me to stay with her at the hotel that night, she finally got up from the chair and headed for the door. I suppose it was premature of me to think she would leave without a final few words for me to mull over in her absence.

"But you know," she said, turning to me with a thoughtful look on her face, not unlike Betty's, "distasteful as that woman is, what she said makes a lot of sense. Maybe I could talk to Patricia and see what she was doing Saturday."

I actually moved my head back as if Mom had landed a blow squarely in the middle of my jaw. "Patricia? You are talking about the woman Larry dumped me for, aren't you?"

"Well, yes, his second wife."

"That's the worst idea you've ever had." Of course, it was really Betty's idea, but I guess middle-aged meddlers come in all kinds. "Forget it, Mom. Erase it from your mind right now."

I grabbed her by the arm the way I had Betty, planning to

escort her to her car before she got another hair-brained idea to go with her bouffant hairdo.

"But I met her once, you know," Mom said as we walked in step to the front door.

I came to an abrupt halt, forcing her to stop, too. "You never told me that."

"I didn't want to upset you, dear, when you were still carrying a torch for Larry."

She winced as my hand tightened on her arm, and it was with great effort that I finally released my grip on her elbow. "I wasn't carrying a torch for Larry."

"Very well, Amanda, if that's what you say."

This is what I hated about conversations with my mother. They always made me feel like a pouty, put-upon teenager.

"I was furious at him," I said. "I wanted to pull his gelled hair out by its roots, but I was not carrying a torch for him. In fact, I don't think people even say 'carrying a torch' anymore. It's something from a few generations ago."

Now it was Mom's turn to pout. She was sensitive about her age, fifty-four, and she didn't like to be reminded of it.

I saw her lower lip begin to quiver, and Harry on the press line gave me a shocked look, as if I were guilty of some form of parental abuse.

"I'm sorry," I said. "And even though you may have met Patricia, I do not want you to call her. Do you understand?"

"Oh, all right, Amanda."

"The police are aware of her, and they'll be talking to her," I added for emphasis.

With that we continued our trek to Mom's car. I was sure she'd have more to say about Patricia tonight, and as a matter of fact, I planned to ask a few questions myself as to where and under what circumstances she'd met Larry's second wife.

CHAPTER 10

Sometimes I'm thankful when I have a lot of work to do, and this was one of those occasions. Otherwise, I would have fixated all afternoon about my mother's revelation that she'd met the second Mrs. Landry, not to mention what devious plan she might come up with to continue the relationship.

But once I had Mom safely tucked in her Lexus, I turned my attention to the task of calling Detective Perrelli. I reached his voice mail and relayed the information about Charlotte Horton, along with her phone number. Then I briefly outlined the names she'd given me so he would know there was a whole bunch of other suspects out there besides me and the gofer girl.

That done, I put the scratch pad in a desk drawer away from the prying eyes of Betty or any other employee who might wander into my office. I went out and helped Kim at the spotting board in the cleaning department, and did a long-overdue check of our inspection and bagging system to see that the clothes were cleaned and finished properly before being returned to the customers.

There was an ulterior motive to that latter task. It freed Patty, whose main job was to inspect, assemble, and bag the clothes, to help out at the counter. Working the counter is a job I normally do in the late afternoon, but since any customer I didn't know could be a reporter in disguise, I deviated from the usual routine.

The inspection station is at the front of a conveyor loop that goes around the plant and is adjacent to Lucille's mark-in table. I'd no sooner begun to do my inspection when Lucille came over to me and began to criticize. Surprise, surprise.

"You should check out your customers before you take on their work," she said. "Remember how your uncle used to check all the references of his charge customers in the old days?"

Good old days was what she meant, and sometimes I wondered if Lucille, who'd just recently quit dyeing her tightly permed gray hair, had harbored a secret crush on Uncle Chet, the way she always spoke of him with such awe. Maybe she'd even hoped that something would work out between them after his wife died when I was a teenager.

"We don't have to do that anymore," I said. "As long as their credit's good, that's all that matters." What I really wanted to say was that we weren't the CIA, for God's sake, and didn't need to check on whether our customers had ever been engaged in subversive activities. Of course that wouldn't have deterred Lucille, even if I'd mentioned it.

"Chet would never have accepted the work from Olivia Torkelson under the circumstances," she said. "He would have checked her out and refused the work when he found out she was marrying *your* ex-husband."

I sighed. "Yes, I suppose he would have, but I'm not my uncle, and it's water under the bridge now, isn't it?" The thought flitted through my mind that I might not have inherited any of Uncle Chet's wisdom, but I must have picked up my conversational skills from my cliché-ridden friend Nat. Who says that heredity is more important than environment? I even considered adding something about "There's no sense closing the barn door after the horse is stolen," but I let it go.

"It's going to be bad for business," Lucille said. "You mark my word."

I glanced up at our clock. It was four-thirty. "You should have been off work half an hour ago."

She pursed her lips. "I suppose, but the next thing I know, you'll be cutting my hours because we'll have lost most of our customers." With that, she cleaned off her work area, retrieved her purse from under the counter, and left.

I finished the inspection, checked to see if Patty had put tissue paper in the sleeves of all the clothes, and gave an A-plus to her work. Then I went out front, praying I wouldn't walk into a TV news crew with a video camera waiting to interview the "most likely" suspect in Olivia's murder.

Happily, there was only the usual array of customers who made no indication that they'd heard Lucille's dire predictions for the business. That's d-i-r-e, not Dyer as in my name or the name of the cleaners.

I complimented Patty on the inspections, told her she was free to go home now, and stopped to chat a minute with Arlene Whitney. She's a bank vice president who was one of our best customers and had given me a piece of information that helped unravel one of the puzzles in that murder of the "man in the alley" that Betty had referred to earlier.

Theresa, my afternoon counter manager, returned from the conveyor with a big order for Arlene. Once she took Arlene's money and cleared the computer, I had a brief conversation with her about the murder on Saturday. Julia from the morning crew had already filled her in, and Theresa said she'd deflected a few more calls from the media that afternoon while we were in the meeting. I thanked her, went to the computer, and typed in the name *Karen Westbrook*.

Customer accounts can be activated by either the person's

name or phone number, and this time the name came up on the screen. It was my lucky day.

Karen Westbrook, Olivia's maid-of-honor, was one of our customers. That explained why the name had rung a bell when Charlotte mentioned it. It probably also explained why I'd thought one of the women in blue satin looked vaguely familiar in the hotel room that day. I bet Karen was the one who'd screamed when she saw Olivia's body and Larry bending over it.

The computer told me that Karen lived just a few blocks north of the cleaners. It also told me that she had an order on our conveyor. I couldn't believe my good fortune. According to the computer, Karen had dropped off the order on Friday and wanted to pick it up Tuesday. That was tomorrow.

I flagged the computer with a notation which told whoever waited on her to come and get me when Karen came in. Maybe I could find out if she'd recommended Dyer's Cleaners to her friend Olivia, or if Charlotte's story was true, and Olivia had maliciously sought me out because I was one of Larry's ex-wives.

I was out of breath by the time I reached my mother's hotel room. I'd taken the time to change out of my uniform into brown slacks and a cream-colored silk blouse before I left the cleaners. It was seven forty-five, and Mom would probably be irritated that I was late.

When she answered my knock, she didn't even mention my tardiness. I should have been suspicious right then.

"Where do you want to go for dinner?" I asked. I'd been thinking of taking her to the Brown Palace Hotel, one of her favorite places to dine. I'd even thought we could walk there, because it was such a pleasant evening, but I discarded that idea when I saw her high-heeled sandals that looked as if she could hardly stand on them, much less walk.

Mom had changed from her flower-garden dress to an attractive linen suit. The only trouble was that it was in blushing pink and made her look like a flamingo.

"I thought maybe we could try one of those microbrewery places in LoDo." She mentioned Home Run Henderson's, one of the hot new restaurants that had sprung up in Lower Downtown once the Rockies built their new baseball stadium nearby. I nodded my head, but what I should have done was wonder how she'd even heard about it. However, she had a lot of friends from Denver who wintered in Phoenix and then returned to Colorado for the summer. I foolishly decided one of them had recommended it to her.

"Okay," I said. I waited while she grabbed her matching pink purse and shut the door to her room, then led the way down the corridor to the elevators. I was silent until we were in my Hyundai. I'd insisted on driving it because it might be easier to park than Mom's Lexus if we were lucky enough to find on-street parking in LoDo.

"So," I said when we were seatbelted inside the car. "Just where did you meet Larry's second wife, Patricia."

"Oh, you're not going to start that again, are you?"

I was the picture of calm. I could even drive and make logical arguments at the same time. "I didn't bring it up, Mom. You were the one who mentioned it this afternoon."

"Very well, Amanda. If you must know, Larry and Patricia were in Phoenix one time and took Herb and me out for dinner. Are you satisfied?"

Well, satisfied probably wasn't the right word, but at least I'd found out what I wanted to know. She hadn't instigated the meeting; it was lecherous Larry's idea. "Okay, Mom, we'll drop it, but I don't want you to even think about calling her and trying to grill her about her whereabouts on Saturday. It would look bad for me if my mother started snooping around."

I let Mom off at the entrance to Home Run Henderson's and told her to go inside and make a reservation while I parked the car. Mom was waiting for me with a hostess when I got to the lobby.

"Will the rest of your party be joining you later?" the hostess asked when I joined Mom in the restaurant.

"We'll be seated now," Mom said, and before I could ask what the hostess meant about "the rest of our party," the woman whisked us off to our table, which had four chairs at it. That was a relief. For a moment, I'd been afraid she was planning a party with a bunch of her old Denver friends.

The table was in front of a ceiling-high window that gave us a ringside view into the microbrewery where the restaurant made its private-label beer. The huge vat with its copper tubing looked like a moonshiners' still for a clan of backwoods giants.

"Your cocktail waitress will be here soon to take your drink order," the hostess said.

Mom nodded.

"What did the woman mean about *the rest of our party*?" I asked as soon as the hostess departed.

Mom acted as if the din of other diners made it difficult for her to hear, but this was Monday night and the Colorado Rockies were on the road so there wasn't the usual raucous crowd of after-game revelers. I knew damned well she could hear me, but she was looking around the darkened room with an interest she usually reserved for more glamorous places.

"I do wish the waitress would get here to take our drink order," she said and raised her hand to a server at the next table, who continued to ignore her.

Then her eyes settled on something near the door, and just as I was about to inquire again about "the rest of the party," I glanced over my shoulder at what had caught her attention. No need to ask the question now.

Larry was coming toward us, and he smiled when he spotted Mom. That was before he noticed me, and to his credit, he seemed as unhappy to see me as I was to see him. But this explained where she'd heard of Home Run Henderson's. My ex-husband always did like the "in" places.

I couldn't believe the audacity and poor judgment of my mother to invite him here. Surely, she didn't harbor dreams of getting us back together, especially under the circumstances, but you could never tell about Mom. She'd tried her damndest to arrange something the last time she came to Denver.

"Mom," I said in a voice as frosty as one of Home Run Henderson's beer mugs. "This was a really bad idea, and I'm leaving right now."

She grabbed my hand. "At least say hello."

Images flashed through my mind of the *Trib*'s gossip columnist, Sparky Malone, whom I'd met through Nat. This was one of his favorite haunts, and he would relish spotting this little tête-a-tête. I could just see his lead paragraph in a column later on this week:

> *Seen with their heads together at Home Run Henderson's Monday night were Mandy Dyer, dry cleaning entrepreneur, and her ex-husband, the legal eagle Larry Landry. Strange indeed since they are both possible suspects in the murder of Larry's fiancée last Saturday. And who was the mystery woman in shocking pink that they were seen having dinner with?*

Larry was wearing a white tennis shirt, the better to set off his deep tan, and a pair of tan pants. He seemed reluctant to join us; however, he didn't change directions.

I saved him the trouble. "Hello, Larry. I was just leaving. I trust you'll be able to return Mother to her hotel."

He nodded, but at the moment I didn't care if she got a ride or had to walk the whole way in her pointy-heeled pink shoes.

"Goodbye." I started for the door, but like a female version of Columbo, I returned and slipped back into a chair so as not to draw undue attention to our table.

This might be my only opportunity to ask Larry an important question I'd forgotten about Saturday night in the panic of hearing he'd contacted Mom. "Did you ever tell Olivia that I was your first wife?"

Larry looked appalled that I would ask such a thing. "She knew I'd been married before, if that's what you're asking."

The cocktail waitress who'd ignored Mom a moment before was at our table faster than a runner trying to steal second base once she spotted Larry. She was wearing an abbreviated version of a Rockies shirt and an incredibly short skirt.

"Hello, Larry," she said flirtatiously. "I haven't seen you for awhile. What can I get for you?"

Oh, yeah, he'd been here before, but maybe the waitress didn't know his last name. She gave no indication that she'd heard about the murder.

"I'll take something with an umbrella in it," Mom said as if she were in a Polynesian restaurant.

"All we have is beer and wine," the waitress said, never taking her eyes off Larry.

"The usual," Larry said.

"Wonderful," the waitress trilled.

I could tell Mom wasn't happy at being ignored. "Oh, very well," she said, "give me a Chardonnay with a twist of lemon and please hurry, dear."

For a minute, I thought the waitress was going to say something nasty that would make us the center of attention.

I slipped down in my chair and tried to look inconspicuous. "Nothing for me, thanks."

The cocktail waitress glowered at Mom and left, but I was afraid she might try Betty's trick from earlier in the day and dump the wine in Mom's lap when she returned. I needed to get out of there—fast.

"As I was asking before, did Olivia know that you'd been married to me—Mandy Dyer, a dry cleaner? Just yes or no."

I guess Larry the lawyer didn't like being treated like one of the witnesses he cross-examined in a courtroom. "Well, no," he said nervously.

"And you never mentioned it, even in passing?"

"I think I did say once that your name was Amanda and you were an artist."

Yep, that sounded like Larry, all right. Never let it be known that he'd once been married to a woman in a service industry. It also eliminated one way that Olivia could have found out I was Larry's ex.

"Okay, I'll see you later." With that, I made my escape, despite Mom's final plea for me to join them for dinner.

It wasn't until later as I was driving aimlessly around Denver that I thought of something else I should have asked Larry. I wondered if he'd been the one Olivia had been calling about the threatening note that day in the fitting room.

I drove some more, giving serious consideration to fleeing the state or, God forbid, stealing Mom's idea—well, Betty's actually—and driving up to Aspen to talk to Patricia, a woman I'd never met and didn't particularly want to know.

"Forget that," I muttered to myself as I finally came to my senses and turned off a freeway exit just before I started up Mount Vernon Canyon into the mountains.

What I needed was to stop some place for dinner. I hadn't had anything to eat since a quick bowl of cereal before I went to work that morning. What I *really* needed was to talk to Mack, and in lieu of that, I even considered going back to the German restaurant on Capitol Hill and unburdening myself to the kindly waitress from the previous night. The only problem was that I didn't want Greta, as I'd come to think of her, to bear the pain once again of commiserating with "the woman who dined alone." I settled for stopping at a Denny's that I spotted just off the interstate.

Once fortified with a meal, I went home to feed Spot. I

had trouble finding a parking spot near the old Victorian house where I lived in the top-floor apartment.

I finally had to park several blocks away and walk to my apartment. It was a warm night, but so late—nearly midnight—that there weren't any people out and about. Earlier in the evening, I was sure there'd been a lot of foot traffic from joggers and people walking their dogs. Now there was only me. My footsteps echoed on the sidewalk to the accompaniment of music from an open window somewhere in the neighborhood. In the distance, I could hear the hum of traffic on Colfax, and closer at hand, a chorus of crickets that sounded like a hundred squeaky bedsprings.

All I wanted to do was get upstairs and go to sleep. I'd be darned if I were going to join my mother at her hotel, promise or no promise. I would call her and tell her that I couldn't make it tonight. Maybe I'd say that Spot needed me, which she'd know wasn't true. But who cared, after the dirty trick she'd played on me?

Even though I'd relaxed somewhat from my earlier agitation, I still scanned the street for signs of anyone in the shadows, and I held my shoulder bag close to my body, my hand firmly attached to the metal ring that connected the purse to its strap.

Everything was peaceful. I was almost home, only one house away from my building when it happened. Suddenly, someone burst out of a parked car and jumped in front of me, blocking the path to my apartment and safety.

CHAPTER 11

I took a step backward, then froze, unable to either advance or retreat. I was afraid the person would rush me if I tried to move.

I strained to see who it was. Unfortunately, the street light at the next corner probably lit up my face, but it only silhouetted whoever was in front of me. All I could see was that my assailant looked like a man. He was wearing a baseball cap, which further shielded his face from view. I was ready to scream if he came any closer, but he didn't.

"Mandy," he said. "That's your name, isn't it?"

There was a moment of silence in which the only sounds were the crickets and my hand sliding into my shoulder bag for a can of pepper spray.

"Who are you?" I finally managed to get out as I fumbled for the spray. Damn, all I could find was a package of Life Savers. Fine lot of good it would do me.

"Look, I just need to talk to you," the man said.

I took my hand out of my purse, clutching the Life Savers and ready to swing the bag at him if he made any sudden moves. "Who are you?" I asked again.

"I'm Ryan Torkel—"

Oh, God. It was Olivia's brother, the guy who'd put his

Bic to my back in the van, and I didn't let him finish. "Get away from me or I'll use my pepper spray."

I shoved the Life Savers toward him, my finger on top of the roll of peppermint-flavored candies.

Ryan stepped back and shielded his eyes with his hands, which was probably a good thing since he might have recognized the familiar blue packaging of the Life Savers. When no whoosh of spray came, he lowered his hands and put them out palms up in front of him, perhaps to show me that he wasn't armed with his lighter.

I pulled back the pretend pepper spray before he could get a good look at it. "What do you want?"

"I just want to talk to you."

The police had obviously released him, and if he'd found out that I was the ex-wife of his sister's fiancé, I wasn't so sure that his motives would be strictly conversational. But why had they released him? Maybe they couldn't make the murder charge stick, but what about the one for forcing me at Bic-point to drive him away from the hotel? That ought to be a serious enough charge to keep him locked up for awhile.

"All right, talk, but if you don't do it soon, I'll use this. I swear." Tough talk for a person with no ammunition, but I shook the Life Savers in my hand, just so he'd know it was going to put out a potent spray.

"I'm looking for my wallet. I think I lost it in your van."

"You what?" Maybe he didn't actually know my connection to Larry after all.

"I lost my wallet. I got no driver's license or anything. That's why my buddy drove me over here to wait for you."

My eyes did a quick sweep toward the car as my hand squeezed the Life Savers so hard I was sure I'd crush them. There was someone in the car, and I wasn't sure the old-pepper-spray-in-a-blue-wrapper trick would work on him.

"Look, I'm sorry for what I did Saturday," Ryan said. "I wasn't thinking straight and I panicked because I've been in some other scrapes with the law, and this would have been about the last straw. I heard someone had been killed in the hotel, and I just wanted to get out of there. I didn't know it was my sis—sister." The guy lost it at that point and sounded as if he were about to cry.

"I'm sorry," I said even though this was the guy who'd almost scared me to death *twice*. "But how'd you know where to find me?"

His voice sounded shaky as he spoke. "I heard it when that cop arrested me, and your name and address is in the phone book."

I'd sworn the last time someone had tracked me down that way that I was going to have my address deleted from the White Pages. So much for good intentions.

"Well, I don't have your wallet."

"I thought maybe it fell out inside that delivery truck of yours."

"If it did, then the police have it. They searched the truck, and they'd have found it if it were there."

The silhouette shrugged or trembled, I wasn't sure which. "I- guess I could have lost it later on. I don't dare drive without it."

The fear about driving without a license seemed ridiculous from a guy who'd made me chauffeur him downtown under threat of bodily harm, but I didn't say so.

"I'm in enough trouble already about what happened in your van. I'd never have done it if I hadn't been drinking and already in trouble with the cops."

There was so much pain in his voice that I loosened my hold on the Life Savers. "So why aren't you in jail right now?"

"I made bail, and they let me out a little while ago."

I wondered if he'd reconciled with his father who'd posted bond, but I didn't plan to ask. I wanted to go up to my apartment and try to pull myself together. I felt as if I were on a serious downhill slide after the adrenaline rush and bit of bravado with the Life Savers.

I thought about warning him that his bond might not be worth much when I told the police that he'd accosted me again, but I decided that might not be a wise idea, either.

"Look, I can't help you," I said instead, "and I have to go now. I have someone waiting for me in my apartment, and they'll be coming down here to look for me if I don't get inside." Another bit of bravado, but I was crashing fast. I needed to get away from Ryan before I had a total meltdown.

Apparently, he didn't notice, or even if he did, he was through with me. "Sure," he said and moved aside.

I very carefully edged around him, holding the Life Savers out menacingly and facing him all the way up the steps leading to the front door of my building.

And then something occurred to me, and even though my legs were quivering as if I were standing on a fault line in an earthquake, I knew this might be the only chance I'd have to ask. I turned, reasonably sure that Ryan hadn't found out who I was (other than the woman who'd provided him with an escape from the hotel) and that he wasn't going to hurt me.

"I was wondering about something, Ryan," I said, choosing my words carefully. "I heard a rumor that your sister had received a threatening note that said she'd be sorry if she married Larry Landry. Do you know anything about that?"

He'd opened the car door, but he came over toward the stairs. I moved a few steps closer to my own door, but he stopped on the sidewalk down below the steps.

"Yeah, come to think of it," he said, "I do remember that."

I was relieved that someone could back up my story. "You ought to tell the police about it."

Ryan shrugged. "It was just a dumb note from some quack, and I told her to forget about it and throw it away."

"And did she throw it away?"

"I think so."

Too bad if she'd followed the advice of a brother who didn't have a good track record for making wise decisions. "Do you remember exactly what it said?"

He shook his head. "No, all I know is that it was on blue paper, and the person who sent it had cut words out of the newspaper for the message."

A little shudder ran through me, either because of how badly Ryan had scared me, or at the thought of someone taking the time to cut out all the letters to make up such a threat. That sounded more ominous than a handwritten note, tossed off in a fit of anger, or something whipped up on the computer.

"Well, tell the police about it." I turned and made a dash for the building.

Once inside, I watched through the pane of glass on our less-than-secure front door as Ryan got in the car with his unknown friend and drove away.

That's when I finally fell apart. I got shakier with each step I took until I reached my third-floor apartment. I sat down on the top step outside my door to catch my breath and try to recover some of my composure.

The only thing that finally let me get a grip was the satisfaction that Ryan might have held me up with a Bic but I'd held him off with a package of Life Savers. Fair is fair. I chuckled at the thought, rose to my feet, turned the keys to both the lock and the dead bolt on my door, and entered my apartment.

The control I'd tried so hard to regain collapsed the moment I got inside. It was replaced by another bout of fear, and whether it was real or imaginary I didn't know.

CHAPTER 12

As soon as I turned on the light, Spot jumped to the back of the sofa and hissed at me, arching his back so that the fur stood up as if he were one of those cut-outs of a black cat on Halloween. Only trouble was, Spot was the color of a pumpkin, and this was decidedly strange behavior.

Spot generally greeted me with calm disdain, even when he was hungry. Indifference was his middle name.

I went over to him. "What's the matter, Spot?"

He hissed, bounded off the sofa, and streaked toward my walk-in closet, which was his hiding place when he was annoyed with me or wanted to be alone. But this wasn't right. He should be hungry after being left alone until midnight. Usually after this length of time, his indifference was tempered with a begrudging desire for food and the realization that I was the person who fed him.

I glanced at his food bowl. It was empty, both the side for the food and the one for water. He seldom drank all the water, and when I went over to the bowl, I saw that there was water pooled on the floor as if someone had accidentally kicked it and the water had sloshed out.

The hairs on my arms stood up, the human version of Spot arching his back. Something was wrong here, but I didn't know what. My eyes swept around the apartment. I didn't see anything else wrong, but I couldn't get over the idea that something was strange. I went over to the huge walk-in closet and turned on the light. Nothing stirred except Spot. He raced out the moment I approached and ran behind the sofa.

I ran over and looked behind the counter that separated the kitchen from the living area of my studio apartment just in case someone was crouching there, but no one was. I went on down the short hallway to the bathroom and peeked inside. The shower curtain across the tub was closed, not open the way I always left it, and I couldn't take my eyes off it. It reminded me of *Psycho*. Someone could be hiding on the other side. I lunged for it and shoved it open. Nothing. I didn't realize how scared I'd been until I fell to my knees and started to put my arms on the side of the tub. That's when I noticed it. The seat on the toilet was up as if a man had used it. I pushed myself as far away from the toilet as I could get and looked at it with horror. Someone had been here. I'd been home alone all day yesterday, and I knew I hadn't left it that way.

Once I managed to haul myself to my feet, I lurched out of the bathroom and ran through the hallway to the window that led out to a fire escape where Betty and Spot had once hidden when I'd had another break-in. The latch on the window was locked. I went back to the front door to make sure I'd locked it as I came in. I pulled the chain across it as triple protection.

I felt as if I were going nuts. On the occasion of the other break-in a year ago, I'd known I'd been burglarized. The place had been trashed as the thieves looked for a valuable dress that they thought I had. This time there was no hint as to what the burglars might have wanted. Only a closed shower curtain and a toilet with the seat up. Could I have left them like that? No way. And even if Nat or Larry had used the toilet Saturday night—which they hadn't—I'd been here alone all day yesterday.

So the only conclusion was that an intruder had been in my apartment at some point since I'd left home this morning. Someone so crazy that the person wanted to let me know he'd been here by leaving me clues and a decidedly spooked cat. In a way, it was more scary than the other break-in because there was no evidence or explanation of what the person wanted. It seemed as if he'd simply wanted to invade my space and make me feel that I was no longer safe even within my own private sanctuary.

And how could the person have gotten in? On the other occasion, someone had taken a crowbar and forced the door. This time, there was nothing. Then I thought of the two keys I kept above the sill outside the door in case I ever locked myself out. Dumb of me, but I locked myself out once years ago when I'd been married to Larry, and it had been a major inconvenience to get a locksmith over here to let me inside. But easier than it would have been to find Larry, who'd probably been at a singles' bar with his friend Brad the Cad.

I'd had a duplicate set of keys made and put them above the door, but I'd never needed them since that one time. The question was, who knew about the keys above the doorway. Larry was the only person I could think of. Had he ever mentioned it to Ryan or someone else? Could Ryan have come in before I got home, looking for his wallet or God knows what, and then waited for me outside?

I took off the chain, unlocked the dead bolt, and peered out on the landing and then down the stairs. There was no one either in front of or below me. I needed to get the keys. I dashed out on the landing, stretched up for the keys, and felt along the sill. For a moment, I didn't think they were there, but then I found them. I'd thought I'd put them above the center of the door, but they were at the side.

My fingers were dirty from the dust along the sill. I looked at the keys. They appeared to be clean, not dusty the way they should have been if they'd been on the sill all these years. And just because they were still here didn't mean the intruder couldn't have taken them and had a second set made while I was wandering all over the city tonight. My hands as well as my legs were shaking now, and I went back inside, locked the dead bolt, and pulled the chain across the door. But I wasn't done yet. I ran over to my dinette set and got one of the chairs to prop under the doorknob. Just as I lifted it, the phone rang. It scared me so much I dropped the chair at the same time my heart dropped out of my rib cage.

I grabbed the receiver.

"Amanda, where are you? I thought you'd be here when Larry brought me home. You said you were going to spend the night."

I didn't want Mom to come running over here so I didn't dare tell her that I thought *maybe* I'd been burglarized or at the very least, victimized. "Sorry, Mom. I can't make it tonight after all."

"It's because of Larry joining us for dinner, isn't it?"

"Did he know I was going to be there, or did you plan it as a surprise for him, too?"

"Well, no, he didn't know, but I thought it might be a good idea if we got together and discussed what each of us knew." I couldn't tell if she was lying or not; she was better at it than I was. "You're mad at me, aren't you?" she continued.

Mad, yes, and wondering if Larry could have popped over here after dinner and let himself in to wait for me so that we could discuss how irritated he was as well. I thought it unlikely because he'd been waiting outside on the landing when he stopped by the other night. But could he have let himself in for some other reason, or perhaps had one of his friends—his buddy Brad the Cad, for instance—search the place for something to show that I was involved in the murder of his fiancée? He couldn't have been looking for anything of his. All remnants of my former husband had long since been purged from my apartment.

It was all too weird even to contemplate, although Larry was the one person involved with the case who might have known that I wouldn't be home tonight.

"You're mad, aren't you?" Mom repeated, and I realized that I'd been off somewhere else, weaving my own eerie scenario for what might have happened here.

"Okay, I'm mad, but—"

Mom began to sniff, a prelude to tears. "I'm sorry."

"But," I said firmly, "that isn't the reason I can't stay at the hotel tonight. Something is wrong with Spot, and I need to stay here to make sure he's okay."

Wasn't that what I'd been thinking about saying to her earlier in the evening anyway—my cat needs me?

"I'm really sorry," she said.

"Okay, but answer me one thing—how long has it been since Larry dropped you off?"

"A couple of hours—maybe ten o'clock. I've been calling you ever since."

I glanced at the answering machine. Eight calls.

"Can we have dinner tomorrow night?" Mom continued. "I promise I won't invite anyone else along."

"Fine," I said, "but I have to go now."

Why did I always have to be the one to make it seem as if everything was all right.

I hung up and began a more thorough search of the apartment to see if I could find anything that had been stolen. I didn't find a single thing.

Could all this be a figment of my imagination? Conceivably, I could have pulled the curtain across the bathtub after my shower this morning, but I hadn't put up the toilet seat. I couldn't be that far gone. I picked up the chair I'd dropped a few minutes earlier, took it over to the door, and jammed it under the knob. And after some serious brooding, I called the police to make a report about Ryan accosting me outside and the subsequent feeling I had that someone had broken into my apartment.

I checked my answering machine while I waited for the police. Mom was right. She'd called me seven times. The other call was from Mack in Alabama. He said he'd be home on schedule the next afternoon and would pick up his truck at the airport and stop by the cleaners on his way home.

But there was no call from Stan. I was thinking about him when two cops arrived. They announced their presence by yelling through the door.

I removed the barricade from the door and let them in. They introduced themselves as Officers Martino and Wheeler. Martino wrote down the information about Ryan and my account of the scared cat, the spilled water in his dish, and the closed shower curtain. Then I told them about the toilet seat.

The men looked at me as if I'd flipped my lid. I was so overwrought that I had to fight the urge to laugh hysterically at such an apt description of my current condition. It was an effort to pull myself back together.

"Was there any evidence of a forced entry?" Martino asked, still taking notes.

"No." I mentioned the keys above the door, but I had to admit that they were still there when I went to retrieve them.

"Is anything missing?"

"Not that I can find."

"Does any man have a key to your apartment? Maybe he let himself in and used your bathroom."

"Only one person has a key, and he's in Alabama."

"What about the landlord?" Wheeler asked.

"No, he never comes over unless something needs to be fixed."

I could almost hear them thinking that I probably had keys out all over the city.

Martino shook his head at my non-burglary and didn't offer to fingerprint the toilet seat. "Well, if you find anything missing later, be sure to file a report," he said.

It was only after the two officers left that it occurred to me that my intruder might have been a woman. What better way to send me off on a tangent than raise the toilet seat so that I'd think my intruder was a man.

It didn't matter. I changed into a pair of jeans and a T-shirt, slipped on a pair of rubber gloves, and went into the bathroom. I cleaned out the bathtub, and then I scrubbed the toilet inside and out. That done, I tossed the gloves in a waste basket and scrubbed my hands until they hurt.

The only thing I could take comfort from was that the police had a record in case the incident ever came back to haunt me.

Unfortunately, the haunting started immediately. I turned off the air conditioner in the window, but I didn't open any of the windows that night the way I normally do to let in the cool night air, and I even closed the one that I always kept open a crack so Spot could get fresh air. I didn't know if I could stand it in the stuffy room, but I wanted to be able to hear any unusual noises.

One thing I knew for sure. I couldn't bear to take a shower tonight. I slipped out of my grungies, put on a clean T-shirt, and pulled out my sofabed. When I did, Spot went streaking back into the closet. I kept the light on by the bed as I flopped down on it and listened for footsteps on the stairs. All I heard were the creaking sounds that old houses make in the night.

I finally fell asleep, and when I awakened a few hours later, Spot was lying at the foot of the bed. It was very strange. He never does that. It was as if he too were still frightened of the phantom intruder.

CHAPTER 13

I bolted upright in bed. I couldn't think what was wrong, but I knew something was. I finally remembered my scary encounter with Ryan and the even more unnerving conviction that someone had gotten into my apartment while I was gone the night before.

Not only that, but I'd overslept. It was ten minutes to six, and I had to be at work at six-thirty. I must have forgotten to set my alarm, and I was going to have to forego all my morning amenities—even my wake-up shot of caffeine—if I was to get to work to open up for the crew.

I headed for the bathroom, then stopped when I got there. It was all I could do to peel off my T-shirt and get in the tub. I locked the door before I did, but I couldn't bring myself to close the shower curtain. The idea of closing the curtain brought back images from last night of *Psycho*. I wondered if I'd ever be able to close the curtain while I showered without feeling that someone might be on the other side waiting to stab me.

The water spilled out on the tile, but I didn't care. It had a tranquilizing effect on me, and I felt better when I climbed out, toweled myself off, and mopped up the water from the floor. The sense of well-being lasted while I dried my hair and put on my beige and yellow uniform. It was when I grabbed for my toothpaste on the counter by the washbasin that I lost it again. Everything in the room seemed tainted. I would have to buy a whole new supply of toiletries, but for the time being, I washed out my mouth with some Listerine from the medicine cabinet, put on lipstick from a tube I had in my purse, and popped a Life Saver in my mouth from the package that had so recently been substituted for pepper spray. That would have to suffice as "breakfast" until I got to work and sent someone out for doughnuts. So much for making breakfast the most important meal of the day. And while I was shopping, I would have to buy another package of Life Savers, too. You could never tell when a person might need a weapon.

By the time I was fortified with several cups of coffee and a couple of chocolate-covered doughnuts, thanks to an emergency run to the doughnut shop by Juan, the fears from the previous night began to fade. In fact, the only reference any of the crew made to the day before was when Betty hailed me with a gleeful question about my mother, referring to her as "the lady who looked like an overgrown garden."

I helped Kim load the cleaning machines and spot the garments that had been dropped off the previous afternoon. Thank God Mack would be home today.

He'd promised to stop by the cleaners as soon as he got back to town. Hopefully we could have a drink at Tico Taco's before I had to meet Mom for dinner. I knew Mack would decline to join us because he said she made him crazy. Welcome to the club.

At nine o'clock, I checked with my landlord to tell him I was changing my locks at the apartment. I asked him if, by any chance, he'd gone into the apartment the day before, but he hadn't. Then I called the locksmith. I'd used the same man to put in new locks at the plant. Only trouble was he said he couldn't get to the job until the next day. I agreed reluctantly, and said I would meet him at the apartment at eight o'clock.

Before I could get back to work, I got a call from Stan. He was upset. "I just heard about what happened last night. Why didn't you call me? I would have come over."

I felt like saying that, for one thing, he'd never called me back the way he'd said he would and I was still irritated with him. "It was no big deal," I finally said instead. He'd have known I was lying if he could have seen me begin to itch. "But what's going to happen to Ryan now, and why wouldn't you tell me his name Saturday night?"

"The judge will probably revoke his bail, and I didn't tell you because we were checking it out. He didn't have any ID on him when he was arrested." I didn't say anything, and he continued, "Look, I'd like to make it up to you for the other night. How about dinner tonight?"

"Sorry, I have plans with Mom."

"What about tomorrow night?"

"Okay." I still wasn't ready to forgive him completely, but we agreed on a time and place to meet before we hung up.

I returned to the spotting board and began working on a blouse with a salsa stain on it. I knew what it was because the customer had identified the stain when she brought it in and one of our counter people had flagged it with a piece of red tape so the person doing the spotting wouldn't miss it.

"Hey, Mandy," Ann Marie yelled from halfway across the plant. "That customer you wanted to see—Karen Westbrook—is at the front counter to pick up her clothes. She thinks I'm getting her order, so you'd better hurry if you want to talk to her."

I put down my bottle of spotting solution and headed toward the front of the building. Ann Marie started to detour to the conveyor to get Karen's order.

"I'll take care of it," I said and grabbed the ticket, running a scanning gun over the bar code so the conveyor would stop at the correct spot for me to retrieve the order. It was so much easier than back in the days when we had to go through every bag filed under the first letter of the customer's last name to find his order.

"Oh, yeah, and I forgot," Ann Marie said as she waited for me. "Detective Foster called yesterday, but you were in that meeting and I told him you weren't taking any calls."

"Thanks, Ann Marie." I hoped I didn't sound as irritated as I felt. No wonder Stan hadn't left a message for me at home last night. I guess Ann Marie figured if I wouldn't let her talk to the TV reporter with "the cute butt," she wouldn't pass along Stan's message to me in an expeditious fashion.

I grabbed the order, a navy blue blazer and a pair of white slacks, and followed Ann Marie to the call office.

"Karen Westbrook?" I asked, but I'd already recognized her, even though she was now wearing a crisp white tennis outfit instead of a floor-length blue maid-of-honor gown.

She had long blonde hair, worn the same way that Olivia had worn hers the day she'd come to the cleaners, but there was a sharp edge to her features that Olivia hadn't had. Besides, she was much taller and more athletic looking than Olivia and had a deep tan instead of Olivia's pale waiflike look.

For the wedding, both women had worn their hair up in elaborate styles, and I'd been right about which one she was. Karen was definitely the person who'd let out the bloodcurdling scream at the sight of Olivia's body on the floor. A few seconds later, the dark-haired bridesmaid had pointed an accusing finger at Larry as the killer of his bride-to-be.

Karen nodded, and I could tell that she remembered me, too. She gave me such a wary look that I was sure she'd heard I was one of Larry's ex-wives.

"Are you dropping something else off to be cleaned?" I asked. I'd noticed that she was carrying a big plastic bag from Fabergé, a high-fashion dress salon in the neighborhood.

"Uh—yes," she said, but she looked as if she were having second thoughts about giving it to me.

I hooked the hangers for her pick-up order over a slick rail at the counter and reached for the bag. She held on to it, then finally made up her mind and thrust it at me. When I opened the bag, I realized her reluctance to let me have it. It was the taffeta gown from the wedding.

"I can't even stand to look at it," she said, speaking rapidly. "I keep remembering . . ." She puckered up her face as if she might start to cry. "Anyway, all I want is to get it cleaned so I can get rid of it. Maybe I'll put it in one of those consignment stores."

Here was my opportunity to inspect the gown of one of the participants in the wedding. It was more than I had any right to expect. I wondered if there was blood on the gown or something else that might indicate an earlier trip to Olivia's room, but I wasn't going to look for it right then. I printed out the ticket, handed a copy to Karen, and put the original in a bag with the gown. Then I put the bag on the floor, not in the laundry cart for Lucille to mark in. This one was for me.

I made change for the order Karen was picking up. "I was wondering if I could ask you something."

Karen glanced at a couple of other customers who'd just entered the call office. "Right here?"

Apparently she was reluctant to answer questions with other people looking on. I wasn't too eager to talk in front of them myself, especially since one of the people was a man I'd never seen before. He could be a reporter masquerading as a customer.

"Why don't we go over there?" I motioned to our fitting room in a corner of the call office.

She still looked dubious so I didn't wait for her to respond. I grabbed her order and led her to the fitting room where I'd earlier pinned up Olivia's grandmother's wedding gown in preparation for the alterations. Ordinarily I don't conduct business in the fitting room, but it was designed to accommodate several people in case someone such as the mother of the bride came along.

I hung Karen's order over a hook and glanced up at her. She was about four inches taller than my five-five, and I couldn't help thinking that she was exactly the type of tall, blonde woman that Nat always seemed to fall for.

I invited her to sit down so we'd be at the same level, but I decided not to close the door. I didn't want her to feel uncomfortable about being in a closed room with Larry's ex-wife. For all I knew, she could have been thinking I was the murderer. After all, I was wondering the same thing about her.

"You're Mandy Dyer, aren't you?" she asked finally.

"Yes, and I know you and your family have been customers of Dyer's Cleaners for some time," I said, quoting from information I'd gleaned off our computer. "What I wanted to know was if you might have recommended Dyer's Cleaners to Olivia as a place to get her gown altered and cleaned."

I was hoping her answer would be yes. I didn't really want to believe that Charlotte Horton was right and it had been pure spitefulness on Olivia's part to come here.

Unfortunately, I could see Karen shaking her head even before she spoke. "No, it wasn't me," she said, her words running together, "and I don't think my mother ever talked to her about it, although I can ask."

"I'd appreciate it."

She looked relieved that this was all I'd had on my mind. "I guess you want to know why she brought the gown to you, huh, seeing that you're Larry's ex-wife?" Her words continued to tumble out so quickly that I assumed it was just her normal speech pattern.

I decided I might as well be truthful. "I was wondering if she knew who I was when she came here, or if she was referred by someone and it was just a coincidence. Is there anyone else you can think of who might have recommended us to her?"

"Well, I recommended your cleaners to someone once, but—" She paused and shook her head. "No, it wouldn't have been him?"

"Who?"

"Oh, a guy named Richard Willis who used to come here, but I'm sure he wouldn't have said anything to her."

Richard Willis. Wasn't that the boyfriend that Olivia had stolen away from Karen?

"Any other ideas?"

"The only person I can think of is Vicky Burnett. She was one of the bridesmaids, and I know she's been working at her brother's shoe store here in Cherry Creek this summer. She had to get off work Saturday for the wedding."

Ah, yes, the bridesmaid who had made the accusation against Larry, and according to Charlotte, had disliked him. I thanked Karen for her help and started to leave.

Karen seemed to have something else on her mind now that she knew the innocuousness of what I'd wanted.

"Do you think Larry could have killed Olivia?" she asked. "I know the police questioned him."

"The police questioned all of us."

"But they took him down to police headquarters."

"And they let him go," I pointed out.

She nodded, and now she was speaking in such a rush that I thought she must surely belong to the Fast Talkers Society of America. "I know, and I couldn't believe they'd even question him. He seemed so broken up about the whole thing when I saw him last night, but Vic—" She stopped mid-sentence. "Someone said she heard he'd been abusive when the two of you were married. It isn't true, is it?" She gulped for air as if she'd finally gotten something off her chest that had been troubling her.

I took that opportunity to double-check, "Vic? Vic who?"

Karen seemed embarrassed. "Oh, you know, the bridesmaid I just mentioned. She's not right, is she? She even told me Larry tried to hit on her after he was engaged to Olivia."

"No, Karen," I said about the abusiveness. Personally, I thought that hanging out in singles' bars when we were married and letting me put him through law school, then dumping me, was pretty damned abusive in a non-physical, non-verbal way, but I wasn't about to tell her that. As for him "hitting on" Vicky, I wouldn't put it past him.

"He's such a sweet guy, and he seems so devastated by everything," Karen said.

The remark made me wonder if she had designs on him herself. Could she have killed her friend so she could steal Olivia's man? After all, Olivia had once stolen Karen's boyfriend, and it had seemed weird to me when Charlotte had said that Karen and Olivia became best buddies again after the mutual beau was out of the picture. That was a little more forgiveness than I thought I could muster in a similar situation. In fact, it was so strange that I suddenly wanted to get out of the fitting room and go looking for other clues on that blue taffeta gown of hers.

Karen started to get up, but this would probably be my only chance to find out what else she and her friends were gossiping about. "Did you ever hear about a threatening note Olivia received before the wedding?"

Karen's eyes widened. "No, what did it say?"

I shook my head. "All I heard was that it was on blue paper and used words that had been clipped out of a newspaper."

"I sure never heard of that." She gave a little shudder, and this time she did get up.

I rose, grabbed her cleaning order, and handed it to her. I might have offered to carry it to her car, but she seemed able-bodied enough to do it herself. In fact, as I took a better look at her in the tennis outfit, she looked as if she worked out regularly and might be quite capable of jamming a pair of scissors into someone's heart.

"You can pick up the dress Thursday," I said. We could actually have had it ready the next day, but I figured Karen was in no hurry. Besides, I wanted to inspect the garment with a microscope if necessary, and see what I could find.

As we came out of the fitting room, I saw Charlotte Horton, who'd given me the interesting information about Karen the day before. She was sitting on one of the yellow velvet chairs in our call office, apparently waiting for me. She looked painfully plain next to the blonde maid-of-honor. She was wearing a gray suit with a long-sleeved white blouse that stuck out from under the jacket sleeves. The outfit seemed too warm for summer.

The two women exchanged polite greetings as Karen left, but it was obvious they weren't close friends.

I went over to Charlotte, but before I could ask what she wanted, she stood up, brushing her straight brown hair back from her face. "What was Karen doing here?"

"She and her family are customers of ours, but I didn't realize that when you told me about her," I said. "I thought she might have been the one who recommended that Olivia bring her gown here, but she wasn't."

Charlotte looked outside as Karen got in her car. "Oh, I thought she might have been grilling you about Larry. I wouldn't be surprised if she tries to set her cap for him now."

"Do you really think so?" That was exactly what I'd been thinking, although "setting her cap" isn't exactly the term I would have used.

Charlotte shrugged. "The reason I came by was to let you know I talked to the detective and to thank you for encouraging me to do it. It's a big relief to have it off my conscience."

"Sure, any time." Maybe I should start billing myself as the dry-cleaning psychiatrist.

She leaned over toward me. "I also found out something else that I told the detective about. One of the other secretaries said that she saw Karen and Olivia's old boyfriend, Richard Willis, in the hotel the day of the wedding."

Aha. The plot thickened, and I wanted to talk to her some more about it. "Why don't you come back to my office, and we'll have a cup of coffee?"

"I'm sorry, but I have to go." She started to the door as Karen's car pulled out of our parking lot.

"Are they reopening the office today?" I asked.

She stopped. "No, why?"

I pointed to her suit. "I thought you were dressed to go to work."

She gave a nervous little laugh. "No, but I better hurry. I have to make a condolence call on the Torkelsons, and I'm really dreading it."

I didn't blame her for that.

I didn't find any suspicious stains or other clues on Karen's gown in the next twenty minutes. In fact, the only thing I saw that was out of the ordinary was a safety pin where she'd pinned up part of the hem, and even that wasn't really unusual. You'd be surprised how many seams and hems we find, even from our most wealthy customers, that have been stuck back together with safety pins and even masking tape.

So the only thing I really achieved was to make my grouchy employee, Lucille, mad at me for usurping her space at the mark-in table. Normally, I waited until she went home to do any serious detective work on the clothes, and when it came right down to it, I'd only done it once with a bloody suitcase when I'd had the opportunity to examine the clothes of a murder victim. This time I sent Lucille on a coffee break.

She returned as I was stuffing Karen's gown back in the laundry bag because I wasn't yet ready for it to be cleaned. "It's about time." She watched as I pulled the drawstring on the bag and started to take it away. "Aren't you going to put that dress in the cart with the other clothes?"

"Nope, not yet." I took the gown and headed to my office with it. I came to an abrupt halt when I was halfway there.

Wait a minute. In Karen's rush of words a few minutes

earlier, she'd said that Larry had seemed so broken up when she talked to him *last night*. But Larry was with my mother last night. Mom said he'd dropped her off at the hotel at ten o'clock. When had Karen seen him? Had they run into each other accidentally at Home Run Henderson's, or had he gone over to Karen's house later for a little consolation, the way he'd done with me Saturday night? The unmitigated lout.

Too bad I hadn't found any clues on her clothes, and I wondered if the police had found anything, especially blood on any of the clothes of other members of the wedding party. I knew Stan wasn't about to tell me. But maybe I could find out from Nat, crime reporter par excellence.

And damn it, there should have been blood on somebody. When a killer stabs someone, whether it's with a knife or a pair of scissors, there should be blood.

If there was no blood, did that eliminate the people in the wedding party and mean that it was someone else? Olivia and Karen's ex-beau or Larry's second ex-wife, for instance? If it were someone outside the wedding party—maybe with blood on his clothes—wouldn't that person have fled down the stairs? And if he had, then shouldn't I have run into him on the way up those same stairs with the wedding veil? Unfortunately, I hadn't.

I picked up the phone again and called Nat. I was lucky to catch him at his desk at the *Trib*.

"Anything new on Olivia's death?" I asked.

"What'ya wanta know?" Nat said in his usual slangy way.

"I wondered if anything has come back from the lab about fingerprints on the scissors or anything?"

"They were smudged. That's all I've heard."

Damn. I wondered if that meant they'd find my prints on the scissors and arrest me. "What about blood on anyone's clothes?" I asked, hoping for some better news. "Surely the person who stabbed Olivia must have gotten blood on himself."

"Yeah, you'd think, but I haven't heard of any."

"So do the police think it was someone outside the wedding party who killed her?"

"I hate to tell you this, Man," Nat said.

I hated it when he called me Man.

"But," he continued, "the cops are leaning toward the theory that the killer used a plastic bag to hide the scissors from Olivia's view when he approached her."

My heart began to beat so hard it sounded like a call for help on a jungle drum. I was sure Nat was talking about the polyurethane garment bag that was over the wedding gown when I transported it to the hotel. I remembered that I'd seen the bag crumpled on the floor, not over the padded silk hanger where I'd left it, when I returned to the room and found Larry bent over Olivia's body.

"It had a lot of blood on it," Nat said, "so the cops figure it protected the killer from getting any blood on his clothes."

Why did it have to be the Dyer's Cleaners garment bag?

CHAPTER 14

I pitched in to help Kim, Mack's assistant, at the spotting boards until Mack arrived at three o'clock. If we weren't caught up in the cleaning department, he would want to roll up his sleeves and get to work.

When he arrived, the rest of the crew was so happy to see him and hear that his brother was going to be okay that they wanted to break for a party. No way. I was the boss, and I wanted him to myself. After all, he was my surrogate father.

"Are you okay?" he said as he gave me a hug.

"I will be now."

What I'd needed ever since Saturday was to talk to him. We went across the parking lot to Tico Taco's, the Mexican restaurant in the strip shopping center behind our stand-alone plant.

As we crossed the pavement between the two businesses, I saw that Mack was walking stiffly. It worried me. I always looked with fear for signs that Mack might want to retire soon. He was tall and reminded me of James Earl Jones with his gray hair, ebony skin, and deep voice, but now he seemed stooped.

"What's the matter?" I asked. "You're all bent over."

"It's just that I get cramped from sitting on those planes. They never give a person enough room for his legs, and I was glad when we got home to Denver."

I gave a sigh of relief. I decided he wasn't going to tell me he was planning to turn in his resignation so he could move back to Alabama to be with his brother. At least, not yet.

Manuel, the owner of Tico Taco's, seated us and brought Mack a welcome-home beer. I declined a beer myself so Manuel said my coffee was free. The way he hovered over us made me think he was worried about press reports connecting me to Olivia's murder.

I assured him that the police weren't looking at me as a suspect. Didn't I wish?

"That airplane food is for the birds," Mack told him. "I need some of your chimichangas—and hurry. I'm starving."

His urgent request sent Manuel to the kitchen, and Mack winked at me. "Thought he would never leave."

I began telling Mack what had happened since Saturday with only a few interruptions from Manuel to bring salsa and chips, refill my coffee, and finally return with the chimichangas. Luckily, two other groups of diners came into the restaurant or Manuel might have wanted to join us in the conversation.

"But I haven't told you about last night." I launched into how Ryan, the carnapper from Saturday, had accosted me in front of my apartment and then about the discovery of the intruder who had unnerved me so much because I couldn't really prove he'd been inside my apartment.

"Lordy, Mandy," he said. "You shouldn't leave your keys up on the door frame like that."

I wondered where the "Lordy" came from. It didn't sound like Mack. It must have been something he picked up from being back in Alabama.

"Did you get new locks put on today?" he asked.

"Yes," I lied and began to itch. Actually, I didn't want to

tell him that the locksmith had said he couldn't get there until the next day. If I did, Mack would want to run right out, buy new locks, and install them himself tonight. I wanted him to go home and get a good night's rest. He looked as if he needed it.

"Has the locksmith brought the new keys to you yet?"

"Yep, everything's taken care of." I suppressed the urge to scratch my nose and changed the subject to my mother.

"Oh, yeah, your mom," Mack said. "How is Cecilia, anyway?"

Actually, I hadn't gotten around to mentioning the embarrassing meeting with the crew and Mom's encounter with Betty, so I told him that, too. "It was kind of like *Barbie meets the Cabbage Patch Doll*, only worse."

Mack laughed when I told him how the two women had described each other, and it made me feel better to realize there was a humorous side to the whole experience.

It wasn't until Mack had finished his meal and I was on my third cup of coffee that I finally told him about Karen, the maid-of-honor, and the gown she'd just brought in to be cleaned. "I'd been hoping to find something like a blood splatter on it, but I didn't."

"Want me to take a look at it right now?" Mack asked.

"It can wait until tomorrow."

He nodded his head. "Good, I am pretty wiped out."

His comment made me glad I hadn't told him about the locks.

I hated to even talk about the smudged prints on the scissors and the fact that there was blood on our Dyer's Cleaners bag, which may have protected the killer from getting blood on his clothes, but I finally did.

"So maybe that's why the fingerprints were smudged," Mack said. "The killer could have held the scissors with the plastic and didn't bring them out until the last minute to stab her."

I loved being able to bounce ideas back and forth with Mack. "I was thinking maybe it was because the bridesmaids were wearing gloves, but I'm assuming the police checked them out."

And now that we were on a roll, I had another idea. I leaned over the table. "I know this is a long shot, but what about the tuxedos all the groomsmen wore? Maybe they were rented from one of the tuxedo shops we do wholesale work for. They might not have blood on them, but we might find something else."

Mack's eyes lit up. "Good idea. We clean the tuxes for a lot of the rental places on this end of town, and if both Larry's fiancée and her maid-of-honor came here, chances are the men arranged to rent their tuxes in the area."

I could always call Larry and find out, but I'd already had enough contact with him in the last few days to last forever. Better to try the tuxedo shops.

"I'll go call all the tux places on our route." I grabbed the bill and slid out of the booth.

"Give that to me," Mack said, snatching for the piece of paper.

"No," I said. "It's your homecoming present."

"It's on the house," Manuel said when we got to the cash register.

Manuel won. I would buy next time.

At his truck, Mack stopped me. "I'm sorry I wasn't here to make the delivery Saturday."

"Don't worry about it. I'm just glad your brother's doing well and that you're home at last."

"Me, too," he said. "See you tomorrow."

I stopped by at a convenience store in the neighborhood to buy a new toothbrush and some toothpaste. Call me weird, but somehow it made me feel less violated by the intruder. When I returned to the cleaners, the production crew had finished for the day. I called and made a reservation for

Mom and me for dinner and still had time to make some calls to tux shops before I headed up front to help Theresa and Elaine at the counter with the after-work rush.

I'd bailed out on my employees yesterday, but I couldn't keep hiding in the back room forever on the odd chance that some TV reporter would show up and want to interview me.

I grabbed my list of our wholesale accounts and started dialing rental places. I hit paydirt on the third call.

"Look, I heard you were at the hotel, Mandy, and I'm sorry, but I don't want anyone to know we were connected in any way to that murder case," Tony Marcano, the owner of Tony's Tuxes, said. "It might be bad for business."

"I just need to take a look at them," I said.

"Why?"

"Because it's going to be a whole lot worse for my business than it is for yours if the killer isn't found soon," I said. "I thought there might be some clue on the tuxes, even some blood splatters. Besides, we'll take special care to remove the stains if we find any."

I felt only a slight tingle of guilt for not adding that I'd have to turn anything like that over to the police before I returned it to him.

"And—and we'll clean them for free," I said. "How's that?"

Tony finally agreed. I figured it was the promise of getting the work comped that did it.

"Have the tuxes come back yet?" I continued before he had a chance to change his mind.

"Yep, the guys had to have them back by today."

"So our driver will be picking them up tomorrow?"

"Yeah, he generally gets here about ten o'clock."

I gave a sigh of relief. "So could you do me a big favor?"

"Sure. What is it?"

Who knew how many black tuxes Tony had rented out that week? "Do you suppose you could separate them out in different bags from the other tuxes that you rented over the weekend and mark them so I'll know which ones they are?"

"Okay, will do."

As soon as I got to the front counter, I checked the computer for Richard Willis, former boyfriend of both Olivia and Karen. Maybe Larry had told him about me at some point. After all, according to Charlotte, Richard had once worked at the law firm, and he could have talked a friend into recommending Dyer's Cleaners to Olivia out of pure spitefulness.

I copied down his phone numbers, both at work and at home. I could always use the pretext of offering him a fifty-percent-off coupon to regain his business. We did that sometimes to lure customers back to our cleaners, but this time I could slip in a question about the possibility of him having given Olivia a referral.

While I was on the computer, I checked for Victoria Burnett's name. It wasn't in our system, and the call to Richard Willis would have to wait.

By five-thirty, customers were stacked up at the counter. That's when I looked up and saw a familiar face, but not a friend's face nor even a friendly face. Unfortunately, it was the face I recognized only from TV—Jason Hendrix, the reporter with the "cute butt" that Ann Marie had admired. Just when I'd let my guard down and decided the press had given up on me.

He was like an airplane on final approach to a runway at DIA as he headed toward me, and he didn't mince words. "Miss Dyer," he said, "I wondered if you'd care to comment on the murder of your ex-husband's fiancée on Saturday."

Behind him, I could see a woman with a video camera. Its light was blinding, but I'd be damned if I would cover my face and flee to the backroom the way I saw people do on *Sixty Minutes* sometimes.

"I'm sorry, but the police have asked me not to comment," I said.

He ignored my answer as if I hadn't even spoken. "How did you happen to agree to clean the wedding gown for Larry Landry's bride-to-be?"

"Sorry. No comment."

"What happened when you got to the hotel?"

"Look, I'm busy, and unless you have some cleaning to pick up or drop off, I'd appreciate it if you'd move aside so I can wait on a legitimate customer."

He glared at me, and there was no hint of the dreamy smile Ann Marie had also admired.

When one of our regulars, a woman who worked in the cosmetic section of a department store at the nearby Cherry Creek Mall, handed me her ticket, I went through the door into the plant. It was all I could do to come back out to the call office when I'd collected her clothes.

Another customer was waiting behind her in line and Jason and his camera operator had dropped back to a position by the door. Finally he said, "Lady, this was your big opportunity to give your side of the story, but you blew it."

"I'm sorry, but I have no comment," I said and kept my smile in place, but it took a lot of effort.

He sneered at me, but at least he left. And I had to admit, Ann Marie was right. He did have a "cute butt."

I wondered if I'd be part of the "news at eleven"—only in Denver it came on at ten. I removed the pasted-on smile from my face.

"You did good," Theresa said in a whisper from next to me.

I realized I'd broken out in a cold sweat, but I kept working until there was a lull in traffic.

"Excuse me, Theresa, but I have to go in back and recover." Then I fled to the rear door of the plant.

I went outside and stood in the shade of the building while I tried to get a grip. These were the times when I wished I still smoked. I really wanted a cigarette. I was still standing by the door when Phil, our route driver, returned with the cleaning orders he'd picked up that day.

"You're late," I said. "It's almost six o'clock."

"I got hung up in traffic. The wife is going to be mad."

"So why don't I give you a hand unloading the truck?"

He looked surprised and happy at this unexpected offer of assistance. Together we unloaded the truck in record time.

We didn't have to carry the laundry bags very far because we mark in the route orders near the back door, and Juan from laundry usually does it.

"I was wondering if you'd do me a favor tomorrow," I said before he got away. "When you make the pick-up at Tony's Tuxes in the morning, could you bring the orders back right away?"

He looked as if he wanted to refuse, but after all, I'd just helped him unload the truck, so he agreed. I could hardly wait, and with something to look forward to, I went back out to the counter to meet the public. Fortunately, it didn't include any more TV personalities.

At six-thirty, I went to my office and changed into a cream-colored linen suit. Theresa said she could close up without me, so this time, I made it to Mom's hotel on time.

She was waiting for me with a contrite look on her face. I guess it was her way of saying she was sorry for last night's fiasco with Larry.

"I forgive you," I said.

She perked up immediately and twirled around in another floral dress that still looked as if it were an overgrown garden. It had a solid-colored chartreuse jacket with piping in the same floral pattern.

"How do you like my new outfit? Our old neighbor, Evelyn Bell, and I went out to that new Park Meadows Mall today, and I couldn't resist it."

I said it was definitely *her*.

We went to a restaurant on the other end of town, up close to the mountains near Golden, that suited Mom, if not her dress, much better than the previous night's microbrewery.

I knew she'd like the place. It had a cathedral ceiling,

dark wood paneling, and a wide expanse of windows that looked out on the foothills. Unfortunately, storm clouds were gathering over the mountains, and the view might soon be obscured by rain.

One of the perks of the restaurant was that it served an appetizer tray—shrimp, caviar, and a variety of cheeses and crackers—with every meal. Mom was suitably impressed.

After we'd ordered and the server had brought our drinks, I asked, "So what did you and Larry decide to do about the murder investigation?" I was trying hard to keep the sarcasm out of my voice. "Wasn't that what you said the purpose of our getting together last night was?"

"Well, yes," she said, sounding disappointed, "but Larry just wanted to keep a low profile about it."

"Good, and I assume he wants you to do the same."

"He didn't say." I could tell she was getting irritated.

I decided to drop the subject and move on to something more important. "I was wondering, did you and Larry run into one of his friends last night—a woman named Karen Westbrook?"

Mom looked puzzled. "No, we didn't run into anyone."

So that meant that Karen's encounter with Larry hadn't been at Home Run Henderson's. It could have been before Larry met us at the restaurant, but I would lay odds that it was later.

"And you said that he dropped you off back at the hotel about ten? Did he leave right away?"

Mom nodded, still puzzled, but when I didn't enlighten her, she asked about Betty instead. "What did you say her name was?"

"Florence Lorenzo, but she goes by Betty."

"And what did she do before she worked for you?"

I took care as to how I answered that. "She traveled around a lot, but she and her husband had a tailor shop at one time in New York City."

"Oh." Mom was unusually quiet after that, and we ate our dinner in relative peace, although she did ask about the "man in the alley" that Betty had made reference to when she said we helped the cops solve another case.

I gave her an abbreviated version of the story of how the police had actually come to me for help in identifying a shooting victim whose only identification was a laundry mark on a shirt. When I concluded, I said, "I'm sorry, Mom, but I'm not going to be able to stay at the hotel with you tonight."

"That's all right, Amanda. I understand."

Since Mom and I seldom understood anything about each other, that surprised me.

"And—" She curved a hand around her mouth and leaned toward me. "—I've decided to treat myself to a trip up to Black Hawk tomorrow. I probably won't be back to the hotel until late."

Ah, good. Stan and I could go out to dinner together, and I wouldn't have to feel guilty about Mom.

She and her former neighbor, Evelyn Bell, had gone up to the mountain town, a mini-Las Vegas, to gamble at one of Black Hawk's small-stakes casinos the last time she was here. Mom had won.

"But I thought Mrs. Bell had a gambling problem," I said.

Mom shrugged a chartreuse-covered shoulder. "Oh, she has it under control now. She only goes gambling once a month, and she limits herself to one hundred dollars that she can lose."

"Well, just see that you don't get her hooked again."

The rain held off until we were almost through with dinner, and I told Mom to wait in the lobby while I got my car. After all, her new multi-colored outfit might not be colorfast, and then she would wind up looking like the leftover oils on an artist's palette. I found a scarf in my purse and put it over my head as I made a dash for the parking lot.

Usually we get our summer rains in the afternoon here in Colorado, but this was one of those late evening thunderstorms. Lightning lit up the sky and thunder boomed. I hated thunder, but I suppose it was the lightning I really disliked.

By the time I collected Mom, the rain was coming down harder, but it let up by the time we reached her hotel. We were apparently just ahead of it. I dropped her at her hotel and headed home. I couldn't believe my good fortune when she didn't insist that I come in for awhile. I guess she was still trying to make up for the night before, and I was anxious to get home to assure myself that my apartment was all right.

The storm was rumbling across the city right behind me, and I hoped I'd get home before it hit on Capitol Hill. I drove around the block a few times looking for a parking place near my building. No such luck. At one point, a cat darted out from between two parked cars and raced across the street. I slammed on the brakes and narrowly avoided hitting it. It was an orange tabby that looked like Spot. If I didn't know better, I'd have thought it was him.

Then I had an awful thought. I squeezed into a parking place a couple of blocks south and ran all the way to my building. The rain had begun to splatter on the sidewalk and soak into my linen suit by the time I got there. I charged up the stairs two steps at a time to the third floor.

The door to my apartment was closed, just the way it had been the night before, but when I got inside, Spot was missing.

CHAPTER 15

The phantom intruder had struck again. I felt it in my gut, but I tried hard to reject the idea. I spent a long time looking for Spot in all his favorite hiding places, but I finally had to admit he wasn't in the apartment. I didn't see anything else missing, but so what? My cat was gone. I wanted to sit down and cry, but I couldn't afford the time. I had to find the damned animal before he got himself killed. I was sure now that Spot was the cat that had darted across the path of my Hyundai only moments before. Who knew if he would be that lucky the next time he tried to play tag with a car? I needed to find him quickly.

Why didn't I confess to Mack that the locksmith couldn't get here until tomorrow? Mack would have come earlier today and replaced the locks. He might even have caught the intruder in the act. Then again, he might have been killed by that person.

Obviously, the intruder had made a duplicate set of keys and let himself back inside my apartment. I wondered if he'd deliberately let Spot out or if the cat had escaped. Try telling either scenario to the police. They would probably say that Spot had scooted out around my legs this morning when I left for work. I'd departed in a hurry, and the patrol cops from the night before would no doubt assume that the cat had hidden in one of the hallways until I left and then made his break for freedom when some other tenant of the building went in or out. But I knew it hadn't happened that way. Spot had been here when I left for work this morning. I was sure of it. Or almost sure.

Rain was pounding on the roof by then. It might even have turned into hail. I grabbed a raincoat from the closet, slipped it over my already damp suit, and pulled up the hood. Then I closed the door, careful to lock it behind me, and went back down to the street. I called Spot's name, but it didn't do any good. It was like yelling into a Black Hole because the sound was lost in the torrent of rain. I whistled, and then called Spot again.

I went over to where I'd seen the cat dart across the street and under a parked car. I rolled up the sleeves of the raincoat, hiked up my skirt and got down on my knees. One of the knees in my panty hose popped as I looked under the car. The cat wasn't there anymore. I got up and I felt the other knee of the panty hose go.

"Here, Spot," I yelled as I continued on down the street.

A man approached me on the sidewalk just as a bolt of lightning hit somewhere in the neighborhood. "You looking for your dog, lady?" The flash lit up both our faces, and I cringed as the boom of thunder followed. Too quickly. The strike was somewhere very close.

"No, I'm looking for my cat," I yelled over the noise.

Another bolt of lightning. The guy gave me a strange look. No wonder. No one whistles for a cat, and besides, anyone knows that Spot is a dog's name. But Spot used to hang out around the cleaners, and my Uncle Chet had named him for the stains we were famous for removing from clothes. My uncle's idea of dry-cleaning humor.

"Want some help?" the guy asked over the rumble of thunder.

Until then, I'd been focused on the storm and the need to

find the cat, but suddenly I was overcome with the same fear I'd had when Ryan jumped out at me on the street the previous night.

This man looked to be about forty, and I doubted that he was Ryan's friend who'd waited in the car when Ryan had approached. But I wasn't taking any chances.

I recoiled at his offer. "No," I snarled over the pounding of the rain and continued on down the street. I guess the man was harmless. When I glanced back in his direction, I saw that he was hurrying away, perhaps afraid of thunderstorms himself or else of a woman who would have a cat named Spot. Now I was alone again.

I was too shaken to continue. I needed to go back to my apartment and call someone, maybe Stan, to help me look. No, not Stan. He didn't even like Spot, and besides, we needed to get our problems resolved before I asked him for any favors. Perhaps it would be better to call Nat, but I didn't know if the nosy reporter would go looking for a cat the way he did for clues. Maybe Mack, although I hated to wake him up, and besides, then he would know I'd lied about having new locks put on the door. But what about Betty? She related to Spot better than anyone because she said they were both "tough old alley cats."

I rubbed the rain away from my cheeks as I trudged up the steps to the front porch of the old Victorian house. No, dammit, the drops on my face were tears. I hadn't realized I was crying until then, and I closed my eyes to squeeze them out so they wouldn't blur my vision.

When I opened them again, I spotted the missing feline. He was one drenched kitty, but even so, he was sitting by the front door with a Cheshire-Cat smirk on his face. I swooped him up before he had a chance to know what happened and carried him inside the building.

"Bad cat," I said as we dripped our way up the stairs.

He retaliated by slashing me across my arm just above the wrist. I was so mad I was almost immune to pain. Spot squirmed and meowed all the way up to the third floor, but I never loosened my grip on him until we were locked safely inside my apartment. We both looked like pathetic versions of our former selves, but Spot was more indignant about the whole thing than his traumatized owner. I let go of him, and he reacted the same way he had the previous night. He hissed at me and went tearing off into my huge walk-in closet. I loaded up his cat dish with food, probably the only thing that had lured him home, and carried it to the closet, but he bounded back out and went behind the sofa.

I guess maybe I should have waited for him to return when he got hungry, but for a panicky few minutes, I hadn't even been sure that he would come back. After all, I turned a grouchy but free-wheeling dry-cleaners cat who came and went as he pleased through my uncle's office window, into a grouchy apartment-dwelling cat who never went outdoors. I hadn't even been sure if he knew how to find his way back home. All the Victorian buildings on the block looked more or less alike.

"Dammit," I yelled toward Spot's hiding place behind the sofa, "how did you get out? I want you to tell me about it right now or I'm going to dump your food in the trash." I was all bluff, of course, and I set his dish down in its usual place on the kitchen floor. "All right, don't tell me," I continued, "but you're in big trouble for running away and then having the audacity to scratch me."

The wound had begun to bleed, and it also stung like a painful paper cut. I took off my raincoat and went to the bathroom to treat it with rubbing alcohol. I stopped when I reached the door and peeked around the corner. I'd already checked there for Spot, and I knew there was nothing inside the bathroom except my paranoia from the previous evening.

I took the alcohol out of the cabinet above the wash basin and rubbed it on my wound. It burned as it touched my skin, but it was probably nothing compared to the pain

I'd inflicted on poor Spot when I'd picked him up. I guess I shouldn't have grabbed him the way I had. Uncle Chet had always insisted that Spot had arthritis or some deformity, and that's why he didn't like it when a person tried to hold him. That's probably why he'd scratched me on our trek up the stairs.

Lightning flashed through the window above my tub, followed by a sharp crack of thunder. It was as if the storm were the intruder trying to get into my apartment. I hurried back to the front door, grabbing my dinette chair as I went. I put the chain across the door and jammed the chair under the knob. I checked the windows to make sure they were locked. Then I searched the apartment for signs of something missing. Again, there was nothing obvious.

The storm rumbled away toward the east, and I finally decided it was safe to take a shower. I locked myself in the bathroom and stripped out of my wet clothes, showered quickly with the curtain open, and put on another oversized T-shirt. I applied more alcohol to the scratch, put a Band-Aid over it, and opened up the Hide-a-Bed.

Spot went streaking back to the closet, but I let him go and crawled into bed with the lights still on. I began to relax a little. The man hadn't attacked me. Neither Spot nor I had been struck by lightning or a passing car. We were both safely tucked away for the night and only slightly worse for the wear. I couldn't say the same for my panty hose or my linen suit.

The storm passed, and the water dripping off the eaves must have lulled me to sleep.

The next morning I called the cleaners and told Mack I'd be late.

"Bad night, huh?" he asked.

"What do you mean?" I wondered if he could hear my jagged nerve endings through the phone line.

"I was just curious how dinner went with your mother."

I was relieved. "Oh, that. It went surprisingly well, actually."

Mack gave a snort, either because he couldn't believe that I could forget a dinner with my mother, or else because I said it had gone surprisingly well.

"Oh and Mack, I found the tuxes. They were rented from Tony Marcano, and Phil is going to bring them in right after he picks them up, so I'll be in about ten."

"Great," Mack said and hung up.

While I waited for the locksmith to arrive, I took a quick poll of my neighbors, none of whom I knew very well. That's what I got for being a reluctant workaholic.

I was the only renter on the third floor, and my neighbors on the floors below me—the few who were home when I knocked—said they hadn't seen or heard anything suspicious on the previous two nights. I told them I thought someone had been messing with the locks on my door and I was having them changed today.

A man on the first floor said, "That's what we get for living in this neighborhood. I'm moving out next week."

The elderly woman in apartment twenty-one looked so frightened I almost wished I hadn't asked her. "I don't hear so good," she said. "The place could blow up, and I wouldn't know it."

When the locksmith arrived, he changed the locks in record time while I kept an eye on Spot to make sure he didn't escape while the door was open. Then armed with new keys, a new sense of security, and the knowledge that Spot was safely locked inside, I headed for work.

Mack hailed me as soon as I walked in the back door. "Betty called in sick this morning. She won't be coming in today."

"What's the matter with her?"

"She didn't say. Just that she ought to be back tomorrow."

I guess I was surprised she was ill because she seemed to have the constitution of a wild and stubborn mule. I made myself a mental note to call her later in the day and see how she was feeling.

"By the way, give me that maid-of-honor's dress, and I'll take a look at it," Mack said as I started to leave.

I grabbed it for him out of my office, then went up front to help at the counter. When I returned to the back of the plant, Mack came over to me. "I didn't find anything on the dress, either." He sounded disappointed.

I took over for the missing Betty in the laundry until Mack yelled at me an hour later. Phil had shown up with the clothes from Tony's Tuxes, and I was hoping we'd have more luck with them.

While Kim handled the cleaning machines, Mack and I went over to the mark-in counter by the back door. Fortunately, Juan had already finished tagging the orders that Phil and I had unloaded from the van the previous night, so we had the counter to ourselves.

Neither one of us found anything unusual until we got to the final black tux of the groomsmen. I'd even wondered if Ryan's tux was here. Probably not, but I couldn't be sure. I reached down in one of pockets of the last jacket in the order and felt a tiny slip of paper inside. I didn't say anything as I pulled it out. It was probably one of those "Inspector" identifications that we find inside clothes sometimes to indicate the person at the manufacturer who had signed off on the garment.

I stared down at the scrap of paper. "Look here, Mack." I said. "This looks like a phone number."

Mack glanced over my shoulder. "Shall we try dialing it and see who answers?"

The number seemed familiar. "Just a minute. Let me check something." I went to my office and pulled my scratch pad out of my desk drawer. I'd been right. I copied down the number and returned to Mack.

"Look at this." I held the paper up for him to compare the numbers. "It's the phone number for Charlotte Horton, the gofer girl at the wedding. She gave it to me Monday, and I thought I recognized it—our prefix and then 3456."

"That's interesting," Mack said. "So she was giving out her phone number to one of the guys in the wedding party?"

"I wonder which one." I eyed the tuxedo suspiciously, and when I held up the pants, I thought I knew. I measured out the other pants of Larry's attendants. They all had longer legs and were not as wide around the waist as the pants with the phone number in the pocket.

"I'll bet anything that's the tux that belonged to the best man," I said. "You remember Larry's friend, Brad Samuels, don't you?"

"You mean the guy you always said reminded you of Woody Allen with a weight problem?" Mack asked.

"That's him." I was embarrassed that I'd actually described him that way to Mack. I preferred to think I always referred to him only as Brad the Cad when I verbalized my feelings about him. But he was definitely short and wide around the middle.

"So I wonder why she gave him her phone number at the wedding," Mack said.

"I don't know, but it's interesting."

"Speaking of interesting . . ." Mack thrust a white vest at me. "This must be from the groom's tux. The other vests are all black. What do you notice on the front?"

I didn't have to study it for long to see the stain. "There's a lipstick smudge on it."

"Do you think this means he went in the room and kissed his fiancée just before he killed her?" Mack asked. "Didn't one of the bridesmaids claim she saw him come out the door?"

I felt this horrible need to tremble, and I gave a little twitch. The lipstick was so incriminating. At least it was to me. I wondered if the police could get IDs from lip prints. I knew they could from bite marks, but I didn't know about lips.

If Larry hadn't kissed his bride-to-be, then he'd been up to no good with someone else. And it suddenly occurred to me that it probably hadn't been Olivia, unless she'd applied her makeup in the time I'd been out of the room. I'd been prepared to have her blot it off before she put on the gown, but I remembered she hadn't been wearing any when she slipped it over her head. The cops would know if she had been wearing makeup when she was killed. I couldn't remember.

"Hold the shirt up to you," I said to Mack. "Then add a couple of inches." Larry was several inches taller than Mack, who was about six feet.

"Ah-ha," I said. "Olivia was shorter than I am, and that lipstick mark is even above where my lips would have been if I'd given him a hug." But I knew who might be about the right height to have left a lipstick stain on the front of the vest—Olivia's tall friend, Karen, who'd exhibited such an unusual interest in Larry just yesterday.

I told Mack my thoughts as we bundled up the clothes. Of course, the kiss could have misfired from a lot of people I didn't even know, or could have been planted by Mrs. Torkelson, the never-to-be mother-in-law of the groom, but I doubted it. Besides, Larry had been wearing his jacket when I saw him.

Once we had the tuxes bagged up again, I hauled them into my office. This was definitely something I thought Perrelli should see before we cleaned the clothes and removed all evidence of the lipstick from Larry's vest.

I called the detective, and a patrolman showed up about three o'clock for the vest. If Tony's Tuxes didn't get it back, I'd buy Tony another one, but it was a relief to know that this was something that was now in the hands of the police.

Once the policeman left, I tried to call Betty to see how she was feeling, but she didn't answer her phone. I thought about calling her boyfriend, Arthur, but it would probably irritate her if she thought I was checking up on her. I decided to let it go.

I worked at the counter until it was time to go home to change for my date with Stan. I didn't have to worry about Mom, and the new locks made me feel as if I were no longer at the mercy of some ghostly intruder. I went to my office to grab my purse, ready to head home to change for the date, when Theresa transferred a call to me from the counter. I hoped it wasn't Stan canceling out on dinner. That happened with surprising frequency with the two of us.

"Hello," I said cautiously.

"It's me, Betty," the voice at the other end of the line said.

"Are you feeling better?" I started to say that I'd tried to call her earlier that day, but I was cut off by a recording.

"This is a collect call—" The words were followed by another snippet of recording. This time it was from the irritated ex-bag lady herself. "Just say it's Betty." The recording switched back to the first voice. "Will you accept the charges?"

"Yes," I said, squeezing the phone so hard it's a wonder I didn't break it. Betty had called in sick this morning, so where the devil was she now?

"You may go ahead now," the recording said.

There was silence on the line.

"Betty, are you still there?"

"Is that stupid woman done talkin' yet?"

"Yes, Betty. Are you all right?"

"I'm fine, but we got big trouble up here, boss lady."

Up here? "What are you talking about? Where are you?"

"I'm with your ma, least ways I was until she got hauled off to jail."

CHAPTER 16

My mother in jail?

She must have been arrested by the casino cops for getting in a fight with a change lady or stealing money out of someone else's slot tray. After all, she was spending the day in Black Hawk, the gambling capitol of Colorado. She'd told me so, but it didn't make sense. What was Betty doing with her? Betty of all people.

"You mean you're up in Black Hawk with her?" I asked in confusion.

"Black Hawk?" Betty sounded equally confused. "No, we're in Aspen, and I gotta tell you it's so fancy up here that there ain't even no poor people for me to mingle with."

Aspen? I was getting really bad vibes about this. In fact, I felt as if I'd fallen off a ski lift and was plummeting down a steep, rocky slope with no snow to break my fall.

"What are you doing in Aspen?" I was afraid I knew. Aspen was where Larry's other ex-wife and former law partner, Patricia Robertson, lived.

Betty snorted. "That mother of yours got some wise-ass bee in her bonnet to come up here and buzz around that fancy-smantzy lady lawyer to see what she'd been up to on Saturday."

KABOOM. I bounced into a tree and came to a dead-stop on the plunge down my own personal mountainside. "And what are *you* doing there?" I kept waiting for the world to quit spinning.

"Well, the plan was that your ma was going to take this Pat person out to lunch and question her, and seeing as how I got more street smarts, I was going to sneak in her office and search the place."

If that was the plan, why wasn't Betty in jail and Mom the one making the distress call?

Betty answered my unspoken question. "But things got a little messed up, so I guess you better get your butt up here and try to bail her out."

My first thought was to let Mom rot in jail and Betty get back to Denver any way she could. My second thought was to find out what got them in this predicament in the first place. "So why did Mom get arrested?"

"It's a long story. I'll tell you when you get here."

"No, tell me now."

"Look, I gotta go before the cops come sniffin' around."

"Where'll I meet you? It'll take me four or five hours to get there."

"Don't worry about it. I'll find you. Don't go looking for me because I gotta keep movin' so the cops won't spot me."

"Okay, but I still need to know what happened."

But Betty had hung up. Damn.

I needed someone to go with me for moral support, and I ran through the whole list of people I'd been thinking of calling the night before when Spot was missing. Mack would worry the whole trip, and besides, I might need him to open up for me tomorrow. Who knew when I'd get home? Nat would be hot to trot, as he liked to say, but he would be wearing his reporter's hat, and I didn't need that. Stan would be mad and think I'd put Mom and Betty up to whatever nefarious scheme they'd been up to. I even considered asking Larry's best man, Brad the Cad. He was a criminal lawyer, after all, but if he thought the incident with me in the elevator had been funny, he would wet his pants at this.

No. It was probably wise to go alone. I called Stan at work and at home and left messages on his answering machines that I was going to have to break our date. Unfortunately, he was probably already waiting for me at my apartment, but I certainly didn't want to call him on his cell phone. This was not something I wanted to talk about right now.

"If Stan calls here before you close," I told Theresa at the front counter, "tell him an emergency came up with my mother."

I thought about trying to get a flight to Aspen, but that might take just as long by the time I called the airlines and got to Denver International Airport, better known as DIA. Better to just get in the car and go.

I changed clothes, stopped for gas, and set off to conquer the mountain passes of Colorado. Oh, sure, in a Hyundai. The car crept up the first major pull out of Denver, Mount Vernon Canyon, a stretch of interstate that's so steep on the downhill side that the road has runaway truck turn-offs at frequent intervals. I wished they had runaway turn-offs for out-of-control people.

What the hell had Mom and Betty been up to that would land one of them in jail? Surely they had to be the most unlikely criminal duo in the annals of recorded history.

Up and down. Up and down. The Hyundai and I struggled to the top of each pass and then plummeted down the other side as if we were both semis that had lost our brakes. Every landmark seemed like a metaphor for how I felt. The highest peaks still had snow, but the Loveland ski area, now that it was June, was nothing but an elongated clear-cut stripped bare the way I felt I'd been by events of the last few days. The Eisenhower Tunnel was so long that I couldn't see the light at the other end.

Signs to other ski areas and occasional denuded ski

slopes dotted the landscape as I drove toward Vail Pass, the high point of the trip, but only in a physical sense. The sun descending beyond the mountains blinded me so that I could hardly see. I felt as if the glare had worked its way into my brain, numbing me of the ability to think.

The Hyundai developed what I feared was a death rattle as it struggled to the summit. A sign said we were 10,662 feet above sea level. At least now I had an excuse for feeling dizzy and short of breath. We both seemed to be hyperventilating as we descended to the Vail Valley that had become nothing so much as urban sprawl since the development of the popular ski area.

I patted the dashboard of the Hyundai. "I know I promised you only city driving when I bought you," I said, "but it won't be so bad from now on."

Engelman spruce, lodgepole pine, and aspen gave way to sagebrush as we reached the Eagle and then the Colorado River which had cut a swath through Glenwood Canyon thousands of years ago.

The canyon had been a gigantic stumbling block to the completion of the interstate through Colorado. Finally, a two-tiered road was designed to keep from gouging out any more of the cliffs, and the double-decker section of the interstate was considered a masterpiece of engineering. I hadn't seen it since its completion, and maybe the view would have taken my mind off my personal problems, but it was dark by now. Clouds shut out the stars and hung over my head like an omen of things to come.

When I finally reached the town of Glenwood Springs, a few stragglers were still in the larger-than-Olympic-size hot springs pool off to the side of the road. I would have loved to stop for a while and rest my tense and aching body in its therapeutic waters, but there was no rest for the wicked—or at least for those related to, or employers of, the criminally suspect.

But what if Betty had flipped out and sent me on a wild

goose chase? What if Mom was happily ensconced at one of the slot machines at Black Hawk, unaware of the bag lady's prank?

I needed a break and a reality check. I pulled off the road just past the Glenwood pool and stopped at the drive-through window of a local fast-food restaurant to pick up coffee-to-go and a burger and fries. I slugged down half the coffee right there in the parking lot while I considered Betty's wild tale. It had to be true. Betty would have had no way of knowing that Mom was incommunicado unless the two of them had gone off together. Betty and Mom together? It was a concept my mind couldn't quite grasp. I should have at least tried to call the jail before I left Denver.

I shook my head at the whole mess as I nibbled on the burger and continued the forty miles on up Highway 82 to Aspen, the winter playground of the rich and famous. When I reached it, I cruised the town to get a feel for the layout. It had changed so much since I'd been there as a teenager that I hardly recognized it; but despite the wealth, some of the rustic charm of the earlier Aspen remained.

I spotted the old and stately Pitkin County Courthouse on Main Street, which was quiet now that it was nearly midnight. The action seemed to be up the hill at the Hard Rock Cafe, the Red Onion, and the Acme Bar and Grill. As I drove back down the hill I spotted the city hall on a side street. I got out and circled the building, looking for the police station and my mother's partner in crime.

There was no sign of either, but I spotted a young couple on a sidewalk across the street and made a dash for them. "Excuse me, but I wondered if you could help me," I said.

The man was wearing a T-shirt that said "Life's Too Short to Smoke Cheap Cigars." Easy for him to say. Right now I would settle for an off-brand cigarette. Too bad I'd quit smoking too long ago to start in again.

The guy was probably filthy rich and afraid I was a mugger after his money. He drew back from me, stepping behind the woman, and eyed me suspiciously. "What do you want?"

"I'm looking for the police station."

Relief spread over his face as if someone looking for the police couldn't be all bad. Little did he know that I consorted with middle-aged mobsters.

"Oh, good," he said, pointing back to Main Street. "It's down there—in the basement on the north side of the courthouse."

I thanked him, darted back across the street to lock my car, and started walking toward the courthouse. I was passing a church when I heard a rustling sound nearby.

Either Mr. "Life's-Too-Short" was right and Aspen was a hot-bed of crime or else I'd found Betty. I slowed my pace, but I didn't hear anything else.

"Psst." The noise sounded like Spot's hiss.

I stopped.

"PSST." The hissing was louder now, and it seemed to be coming from a bush in the church yard.

It had to be Betty, but I didn't want to play games with her. I started to cross the street to the courthouse.

"Damn it, Mandy. It's me." She finally emerged from the bushes wearing burglar black instead of her usual bilious green pants suit.

I turned around. "Okay, Betty, before we do anything else, I need the full story."

"Now?"

"Now."

Betty glanced around uneasily. "Not here, boss lady. The cops been patrolin' around here all night, and I had to be wily to keep them from spottin' me."

"What if we go to my car?" When she nodded, I led the way back up the street and unlocked the car door so Betty could get in the passenger side, then went around to the driver's seat. "All right, let's hear it."

Betty took a deep breath. "Okay, here goes. Your ma called

me last night. Said she found my number in the phone book—"

So that was why Mom had seemed to have an unusual interest in Betty during dinner the previous evening.

"She asked if I wanted to help her by getting somethin' on this lawyer gal. I said sure, anything for the boss lady. She said she'd pick me up this morning, but I didn't know she was goin' to come all the way up here to hell and gone. We even saw a herd of buffalo, if you can believe it."

Before she gave me a blow-by-blow account of the buffalo park at the top of Lookout Mountain, I interrupted. "Just get to what happened when you got here."

"Anyways, I already told you the plan, but turns out this Patricia gal was out-of-town on some lawyer stuff when we got here. End of plan. I said maybe we could wait until this Pat person's secretary went home, and then we could both sneak into her office."

I was shaking my head in shock. "And my mother went along with that idea?" Mom, who was the epitome of her own peculiar form of propriety.

"She didn't come up with nothin' better, so along about five o'clock the office gal goes home, and we sneak in and—" Suddenly, Betty slid down in her seat as some sort of SUV went by. Jeeps and other four-wheel-drive vehicles, instead of luxury cars, were the transportation of choice in Aspen. "Duck, it could be the cops."

"Oh, good grief, Betty." I gripped the wheel in an effort to keep my composure, which was already in shreds. "How'd you get inside?"

Betty raised up. "No sweat. I know a thing or two about pickin' locks."

Dear God. If I'd had her with me that time I locked myself out of my apartment, I never would have had to put a duplicate set of keys above the door, and I wouldn't have had a phantom intruder sneaking into my place the last few nights. I might even have suspected Betty if the person hadn't gotten in with a key. But that was a whole other problem. Right now I had a more immediate concern with a couple of real, if inept, break-in artists.

"Anyways, we get inside, and we're searchin' the place pretty good when this office gal comes back for some reason." Betty ducked, then popped up again as if she were a jack-in-the-box puppet at the mercy of every passerby. "The gal must have heard us inside the place and called the cops. Pretty soon all hell breaks loose. I do a quick skedaddle out the window to the fire escape, and when I get to the ground, I look back and see your ma trying to pull her fancy dress loose from where it's caught on the window ledge."

"Oh, swell." It was a pretty pathetic response, I admit, but it was the best I could do.

"She's a tuggin' and a yankin', but she can't get away, and there ain't nothin' I can do to help her." Another car went by and Betty slid down in her seat, or maybe she was just trying to demonstrate her actions earlier that night. "So I hide behind a Dumpster and watch the pigs haul her off to the Big House. Then when I figure the coast is clear, I call you. End of story."

I wanted to bang my head against the steering wheel. This was worse than I thought.

"We'd a both made a clean getaway if your ma hadn't been dressed to the nines, and I gotta tell you, even if she hadn't got caught on the window ledge, she'd a never got down that fire escape in those fancy shoes of hers."

Ah, yes, my mother, the well-dressed crook.

"Okay," I said in more of a sigh than an actual sound. "Let's get to the police station and see if we can bail her out."

"Huh-uh. No ma'am. I ain't goin' nowhere near that place."

"Very well. You sit here and wait for me. Don't go wandering off someplace. Do you understand?"

"Gotcha, boss lady, but I sure could use some food."

I thrust the cold, limp french fries at her that were left from my meal-on-the-run. "We'll have something else later."

She grabbed one of the fries and stuffed it in her mouth as she took another dive into the seat. "There was one other—"

"Later, Betty. Let me see if I can get Mom out of jail first." I climbed out of the car and headed for the courthouse.

I followed a sign to the police station and took a short flight of stairs down to the entrance. Locked. A sign said to use the phone.

"I'm here to see about a prisoner named Cecilia Smedley," I said. "Can you let me in?"

"You'll need to go over to the county jail," a voice answered, and directed me back up the steps. "Turn right and keep veering right on the sidewalk. It'll take you to the jail."

I did as instructed and wound up at another building with a locked door and a telephone. I picked up the receiver and explained about my mother again.

Someone unlocked the door, and I entered a hallway that dead-ended at a window, probably bulletproof, with a cashier-like tray underneath. As I walked the short distance to the window, I passed a dark-haired woman sitting on a chair against one wall. She was working on a bunch of papers on top of her briefcase and didn't look up at me.

I waited, and finally a deputy came to the window. "I'm here about my mother, Cecilia Smedley. I understand you're holding her here."

At that point, I was vaguely aware of the woman watching me.

"She's about to be released," the cop said. "Why don't you have a seat out there? She'll be along soon."

The other woman got up and approached the window. "You must be Mandy Dyer," she said. "I think we have something in common."

I turned and looked her up and down. She was about my height and size with the same dark hair, only hers was longer than mine. She was wearing a long-sleeved navy-blue suit with shoes to match. Both looked expensive.

I decided to take a shot. "Are you Patricia Robertson, by any chance?"

She nodded. "Yes, another of Larry's ex-wives."

I guess I should have been able to take some comfort in the fact that Larry had chosen a second wife who looked a little like me, but at the moment, I was too puzzled. "Are you acting as Mom's lawyer, Patricia?"

She smiled. "Please, just call me Pat, and no, the charges are being dropped. Luckily, I was able to reach someone in the district attorney's office or she would have had to stay here overnight for an advisement hearing tomorrow morning."

So why was Pat being so nice? I tried not to squint suspiciously as I waited for her to continue.

"I guess my secretary forgot to lock the door when she left," Pat said, "and because your mother thought I'd be stopping by the office when I got back to town, she decided to wait for me inside. It was all quite innocent, and it apparently scared her to death when the police showed up. She thought the place was being burglarized and tried to get out a window."

Was Patricia really buying Mom's story? I couldn't believe it, but I sure wasn't about to do anything to upset whatever dream world she was living in.

I was spared the need to respond because Mom appeared right then from the back of the jail, popping out of a double set of doors to the right of the window. When Betty had said Mom got "a bee in her bonnet," she hadn't been far wrong. The bee seemed to be the only thing missing from Mom's flower-bedecked hat, which sat slightly off-center on her head.

"I'm sorry about the mixup, Cecilia," Pat said, going over to her. "And I'm glad that I got here in time to clear things up and get you released."

I was sure now that Patricia was playing along with Mom's story for some devious reason of her own.

"Thank you, Patricia," Mom said, more ruffled now than the floral dress she was wearing. "I know the whole thing sounds farfetched, dear, but I'm so glad you believed me." She started to center her hat, then noticed me. Her face ran the gamut of emotions from relief to irritation and then to all-out fear. Maybe she thought I would give away her innocent act.

She finally regained her composure. "Oh, Mandy dear, I had hoped to avoid involving you in this. How did you hear about—?" She must have realized the moment she asked that the only possible way I could have gotten wind of the situation was through her cohort in crime. "Well, never mind. I just want to get home and forget this whole dreadful experience."

"I was hoping I could take you—and your daughter, too—out to get a bite to eat," Pat said, glancing at her watch.

Mom started to shake her head. "Oh, I don't think so."

"Why not, Mom?" I asked. "After all, you must be hungry."

"Most of the restaurants quit serving at ten," Pat continued, "but I know a bar that has food service later."

Mom glared at me, but I didn't want to let her off the hook that easily. I wanted to see her squirm a little at what she'd put me through, and besides, I thought it might be interesting to have a chance to ask Patricia a few questions.

Mom finally turned to Pat with a feeble smile. "I suppose I could eat something."

There was one small problem. Betty. I had a feeling she would be no more anxious to associate with a lawyer than she was with the police, but you could never tell about her. And Betty might be tight-lipped with the cops, but who knew what she'd say in a social situation with Pat. Still, I couldn't very well ignore the hungry woman who was eating cold french fries as we spoke.

"I have a friend with me," I said. "I hope you don't mind if I ask her to come along."

Mom opened her mouth, then closed it again.

"Of course not," Pat said. "There's a place called the Slalom within walking distance of here." She pointed up the hill in the general vicinity of where the Hyundai was parked. "Let me put my briefcase in the car, and I'll meet you right back here." With that, she put the papers in her briefcase, snapped it shut, and went out the door.

"Why'd you have to accept her invitation?" Mom demanded the moment Pat was gone. Then she looked around guiltily in case the place was bugged and continued in a whisper, "And why'd you have to invite Betty along?"

I escorted Mom through the door. "She's hungry."

Mom kept her voice low even when we got outside. "Did Betty tell you about her ill-conceived plan to search Patricia's office?"

"Yes, she did."

"Did she also tell you how she abandoned me there? It was only my quick thinking that enabled me to get out of a very awkward situation."

"And it was only Betty's quick thinking that got me up here in the middle of the night to bail you out in case the police didn't buy your story." I dropped my hand from her arm. "Wait here while I go get Betty."

"Do you have to?"

"Yes." I turned and headed out to the street and across to where my car was parked. I knew I was going to have to make Betty promise to keep her mouth shut if she were going to have dinner with us.

When I got to the Hyundai, I couldn't see her. She had scooted down in the seat again, but she was still nibbling on the stale french fries. "Okay, Mom's out of jail," I said, "and we're going to go have something to eat with Patricia."

Before I could even go into my spiel about watching what she said, Betty snapped to attention. "No, siree. No way. Not me. I ain't going to break bread with no *murderer*."

I was so surprised by the vehemence of Betty's response

that I stepped back in astonishment and tripped over the curb. Fortunately, I regained my footing before I sprawled on the sidewalk.

Lawyer, yes, but murderer? Okay, suspect maybe, but actually Patricia was way down at the bottom of my list. In fact, I'd put her there mainly because of wishful thinking. She was still "the other woman," after all.

I bent down to get a better look at Mom's accomplice in crime. "We don't know that for sure, Betty."

"I do," she said. "That's what I was going to tell you when you lit out of here in such an all-fired hurry to spring your ma. I got the goods on that lawyer lady, and I don't care what she says. She went down to Denver on Saturday, and I can prove it."

My legs were shaking, and I had to grab the car door for support. "What the devil are you talking about?"

Betty reached into a pocket of her black polyester pants, pulled out a piece of paper, and handed it to me.

"What's this?" It looked like a credit card receipt, but I couldn't read what it said because it was so dark on the street.

"I found it in that Pat-person's wastebasket. It's a bill from where she bought gas in Denver on Saturday afternoon just after the murder."

CHAPTER 17

I strained to see if the receipt really was from a gas station in Denver. Finally, I reached in the glove compartment and pulled out a flashlight.

Darned if Betty wasn't right. The credit card receipt showed that Patricia had purchased gas in Denver Saturday afternoon, and what's more, the gas station was only a couple of blocks from the hotel. The time that was imprinted on the ticket listed the transaction as taking place shortly after I walked into Olivia's room and found Larry bending over her body.

This seemed like a smoking gun to me, and I'd have to give Betty a pat on the back for her burglarizing skills. But not now. I put the flashlight back in the glove compartment and stuck the charge receipt in a zippered pocket of my purse.

"Okay, Betty, if you're sure you don't want to go with us, here's a twenty." I handed her the money and hoped there was another place in town besides the Slalom that still served food. "Grab yourself something to eat and meet us back here in an hour."

"You still goin' to eat with that murderer?"

"That's all the more reason to talk to her. Besides, I can't let Mom go off with her alone." I started to leave, then leaned down again. "Incidentally, does Mom know you found the receipt?"

"Weren't no time to tell her. That's just about when the cops started poundin' on the door, and it was every man for hisself."

I glanced in the direction of the jail. "Look, I better go." I stood up and started to shut the car door.

Betty caught it before it closed. "Where'd you say you were goin'?"

"Some place called the Slalom. It's just up the street apparently."

"Okay, that's good—just in case I change my mind and decide to join you."

I hoped that was Betty's idea of humor.

"I'm sorry but my friend is too tired to join us," I said as I rejoined Mom and Patricia outside the jail.

I could see the relief on Mom's face.

"She wants to grab a nap in the car before we start back to Denver," I continued.

It was just a little fib, but nonetheless my nose began to itch. Fortunately, Pat didn't know that the itch was a sure sign I was lying. I rubbed my nose surreptitiously as we made our way up the hill to the restaurant. There was no sign of Betty as we passed the car. Either she had ducked down in the seat again or she had gone looking for food now that she had money to spend.

"I always wondered what you were like," Patricia said, breaking the silence. "Larry told me your marriage was over in all but name long before he met me."

I didn't answer.

"I doubt if that was true," she continued. "I think he told Valerie, the ski instructor, the same thing about us when he fell head over heels for her. Literally, I might add."

I glanced over at her. "Valerie, the ski instructor?"

Pat nodded. "Except she met a millionaire from Argentina and decided to marry him instead. For once, Larry was the one who got the boot along with a broken leg. That's when he moved back to Denver."

We'd reached the Slalom Bar and Grill at the edge of the mall, and I'd been so intrigued with the information about Larry that I'd forgotten all about my itching. Maybe Patricia wasn't such a bad sort after all. Just one of the countless victims who littered Larry's path like uprooted trees on a mountainside after an avalanche.

The Slalom turned out to be a rustic bar with crossed-skis on the walls, wooden booths, and limited food service. It obviously wasn't one of the "in" places in town, and there were only a few customers on stools at the bar and a table up front.

I could see Mom wasn't happy about something. Maybe in Aspen—even after midnight—she'd expected haute cuisine; then again, maybe her feet were hurting after the walk from the courthouse in her high-heeled shoes.

Patricia led us to a booth in the back. "I'm so sorry you had to stay in jail for even a short time," she said as she settled in next to Mom, who was busy fanning herself.

"It's warm in here, isn't it?" Mom said. "And it was even worse in that jail. They make the women wear sweatpants and these awful orange sweatshirts that are really hot. It doesn't seem fair because the men get to wear T-shirts."

Patricia smiled over at her. "I think the deputies feel it might be too provocative for the male inmates if the women wore the T-shirts. They're very thin."

"Oh, my," Mom said, probably torn between the injustice of it all and the idea that she still had the power to be provocative.

She perked up even more when she noticed someone at the bar. "Isn't that—" She let out a little gasp, but she apparently couldn't think of the name. "Oh, he's a movie star who used to play in those Doris Day–Rock Hudson kind of movies."

Patricia glanced at him and shrugged. "Could be. We have a lot of Hollywood types here winter and summer."

I could tell Mom liked the Slalom better now that it had the celebrity seal-of-approval.

Pat turned to me. "You must really have been upset when your mother called and told you what happened."

"She's a wonderful daughter," Mom said before I had a chance to answer.

"And it was nice that you had a friend to drive up from Denver with you," Pat continued.

Mom gave me a nervous look and wiggled on the uncomfortable wooden bench.

"Yes, it was," I lied.

My nose started to tickle again, and it turned into a full-body itch as I looked toward the front of the bar. Betty burst through the door and headed for our booth. Damned if she wasn't going to join us after all. And what would happen now? I'd never gotten around to warning her to keep her mouth shut.

But miracle of miracles, she gave no sign that she even recognized us, much less planned to join us. She plopped down at a table just out of sight of Mom and Patricia. That's why she wanted to know where we were going. She wanted to spy on us.

"I'm so sorry I wasn't here earlier today," Patricia said, turning to Mom. "Was there anything in particular you wanted to see me about, Cecilia?"

"No, I was just passing through town on the way to be with my daughter." Mom reached across the table and patted my hand as she lied far better than her offspring. "You did hear about that terrible incident with Larry's fiancée, didn't you?"

Pat nodded. "I heard about it on the news."

I wanted to confront her with the fact that she'd also been in the vicinity when it happened. But how could I do that without producing the stolen gas receipt? And that, of course, would make a sham of Mom's story that she had merely been passing through Aspen en route to Denver. Never mind that Aspen wasn't exactly on a direct route from Phoenix to the Mile High City.

Besides, I was sure the credit card receipt would never be admissible as evidence, seeing that it had been obtained under questionable circumstances by the charter members of the Middle-Aged Meddlers From Hell.

The waitress arrived to take our orders. We ordered steaks, which were the only thing on the menu except for burgers. Mom and Pat ordered drinks—Mom a glass of wine and Pat a scotch on the rocks. I ordered coffee since I was still hoping to drive home that night. I presumed Mom intended to drive her car down from the mountain tomorrow.

"The same as those people are having, but skip the booze," Betty said from the nearby table and winked at me. Any hope that she couldn't hear us was lost at that point.

Mom looked ill-at-ease, apparently recognizing the voice out of her criminal past.

"Have the Denver police made an arrest in the murder yet?" Pat asked.

Mom fell silent, too overcome with fear to answer.

"Not that I know of," I said. I tried to look Patricia in the eye, but I was having difficulty because of Betty's pantomime in the background. She was pretending to pull her napkin out of her pocket, probably to indicate that I should produce the credit card receipt.

"Is it true that you were the one who cleaned and delivered the wedding gown to the hotel?" Patricia asked.

"Yes," I said as I shook my head.

The gesture probably confused her, but I was trying to get Betty to quit waving her napkin around like a white flag of surrender.

"It must have been terrible," Patricia continued, a puzzled look on her face. "Why do you think Larry's fiancée brought her gown to you in the first place?"

The lady lawyer, as Betty called her, was good. She was quizzing me a whole lot more adeptly than I was quizzing her.

"If I knew that, maybe I'd know who killed her," I said, then took a deep breath, and with Betty as my cheering section, plunged headlong down a slippery slope. "Someone said you were invited to the wedding and that they saw your car near the hotel that day."

Pure fabrication, of course, but I reasoned that some of Larry's friends—Brad the Cad, for instance—could have recognized her.

Mom let out a little gasp, but Betty gave me a high sign for a job well done.

The confident lawyer-look on Pat's face collapsed. "Oh, my God," she said. "So that's why the police questioned me."

I didn't want to lose the advantage so I kept talking while the waitress delivered our drinks. "So you *were* there?"

Pat's face had turned an ashen shade of white. "No, it wasn't me."

She was lying. I was sure of it, but short of producing the receipt from the gas station I didn't know what to do about it except to pull another itch-inducing bluff.

"I believe the person said he saw you using your credit card at a service station in the area." I was running on pure octane now.

"Oh, my God," Patricia said again, then made an effort to pull herself together. "Well, it certainly wasn't me."

I rubbed the side of my nose and wished Pat had some sort of body language that would indicate she was lying, too.

"I'm sure you have nothing to worry about, dear," Mom said, apparently having decided Betty wasn't going to blow her cover. "The police will check your credit card charges and know the person who identified you made a mistake."

Pat gave Mom an appalled look, the way I do sometimes

when she's being too motherly, but for once, I was happy. Not only was the attention not directed at me, but Mom had zeroed in on the one thing that could hang Patricia.

At the other table, Betty gave me an A-OK, forming a circle with her thumb and forefinger.

"Do you—I wonder if someone dressed up like me to set me up?" Patricia said.

She was quick on her feet. I'd give her that. She was already trying to concoct a story to explain what could have happened, but there was still the credit card receipt burning a hole in the pocket of my purse.

The waitress delivered our steaks to the table, balancing the three plates up her arm.

Pat took a drink of Scotch and pushed up her jacket sleeve just enough to expose her watch. "If you'll excuse me, I think I better go home and call the police to clear this up." With that, she got up from the table and stuck me with the bill. For a minute, I thought she was going to turn around and offer to pay, but instead she said, "I never even thought about going to Larry's wedding. I swear."

Oh, yeah, she was lying, even if she didn't have the body language to prove it.

We watched her hurry out of the bar, and for once, Betty had the good sense to wait until she disappeared before joining us in the booth. She sat down in the seat vacated by Pat.

"I knew that was you," Mom said icily, moving as far away from her co-conspirator as possible.

The waitress returned with Betty's dinner and looked around in confusion to see where she'd gone, then spotted her and brought her meal to our table.

"Is that true, Amanda—that someone saw Patricia near the hotel?" Mom asked when the waitress left. "If you'd told me that earlier, we wouldn't have had to come up here to Aspen." Oh, yeah, now it was my fault.

Betty was only too eager to claim responsibility for the

information. "Mandy didn't know nothin' until I found the credit card receipt in that lawyer-lady's office."

"You didn't tell me that. If you had, we could have gotten away before the police came." Now Mom was making it sound as if the caper were entirely Betty's idea.

"I didn't have time. You were too busy trying to get untangled from that window ledge, and I've got to tell you, Cece, if you plan to go into this line of work, you're going to have to get yourself a whole new wardrobe."

Mom winced at Betty's nickname for her, then turned back to me. "Is that true about the receipt?"

Betty wasn't through talking yet. "Yep, but Mandy pulled a pretty good bluff. That Pat-lady is running scared now, and I gotta hand it to you, boss lady."

Somehow my heart just wasn't in it to take credit for what I'd done. Maybe I'd goofed by tipping Pat to the information we had on her. She'd probably gone home to figure out some story that the police would buy.

And much as I wanted to yell at the two mismatched meddlers, my heart wasn't in that, either. Still, I felt as if I had to say something. "Why did you come up here, Mom, after you promised me you wouldn't contact Patricia?"

Mom took a delicate little bite of steak. "I didn't promise that. I promised I wouldn't call her. I didn't say anything about coming up here to see her."

"She's got you there, boss lady," Betty said as she slid Pat's steak onto her plate and began to scarf them both down. "And I gotta tell you, Cece—we make a pretty good team. We'll have to do this again sometime."

Mom didn't say anything, but I could almost hear her thinking *not in this lifetime*. At least, I hoped to God that's what she was thinking.

And if politics makes strange bedfellows, it's nothing compared to what crime does. In fact, our stay in a motel for the rest of the night was a fitting climax to the day from hell.

CHAPTER 18

It was impossible to find a room in Aspen after midnight. I finally dropped Mom off at her car. By then, I figured that the effects of her glass of wine had worn off, although Betty offered to drive just in case. Since Betty had no driver's license, I suggested that she ride along with Mom instead. The two of them followed me down to Glenwood Springs where I finally located a motel with an all-night attendant and a room with two double beds. I charged it on my credit card.

As soon as we entered the room, Mom looked around with distaste. "I can't sleep with anyone, except in a king-size bed."

Betty gave her a dirty look and said in a mocking voice, "Well, I certainly can't either." This from a woman who'd slept in God-knows what kind of conditions in her life as a bag lady.

I was way beyond caring. I'd had it with both of them, so I called and asked the desk clerk for a rollaway. When he brought it, I gave him a generous tip, left a wake-up call for six-thirty in the morning, and turned to my companions who had established their territories on the respective double beds. Mom, I noticed, had grabbed the one by the window which she seemed to think was a more desirable location.

"I'll sleep on the cot," I said, as if I had a choice.

"But what are we going to do for nightgowns and toothbrushes?" Mom asked.

"You should have thought about that before you set out on this ill-conceived little adventure," I said.

Betty pulled off her shoes and rolled under the covers of her bed, fully-clothed in her burglar-black outfit. "Cece, you got to be less particular if you're going to be a crook."

Mom sniffed haughtily as she removed her hat. "You should have let me be the first one out that window. Then you could have helped me untangle myself from the ledge."

"Age before beauty, Cece," Betty said.

Well, Mom wasn't about to argue with that. She carefully removed her dress and hung it on a hanger. Then she climbed into bed in her slip. "Will you open the window for me, Amanda?"

I remembered Mom's desire for fresh air from my other stay with her in a hotel. If she weren't hermetically sealed under air conditioning in Phoenix, she needed fresh air because of her ongoing battle with hot flashes and night sweats.

I opened the window, and went in the bathroom where I took off my slacks and blouse. Before I went to sleep, I was hoping to figure out a way to tell Detective Perrelli about Patricia. Should I use my name or make an anonymous phone call to suggest that the police look into her charge account bill for this month? Better yet, I could let Mom do it since she'd seemed hurt to be out of the loop about the credit card receipt. Besides, if we were going to call anonymously, she wouldn't have to disguise her voice when she talked to the cops.

By the time I got out of the bathroom and turned off the light, Betty had begun to snore.

That was all it took. "Amanda," Mom said, "I'll never be able to sleep with Betty making all that noise."

I felt my way to my cot. "Then tell her to roll over on her side."

"You do it, dear, since you aren't settled in yet. I'm just getting comfy, and I don't want to get out from under the covers."

It wouldn't do any good. I knew that from the two occasions when Betty had bunked at my place, but to pacify Mom, I went over and gave Betty a shake. "Betty, turn over on your side."

She gave a startled snort and rose up on one elbow, obviously dreaming about her and Mom's earlier brush with the law. "Run for it, Cece. It's the cops."

"It's all right, Betty," I said. "It's just me. You were snoring."

She sank back down on the pillow, and turned over on her side. "Boy, I thought they were going to get me for sure this time." A minute later, she was snoring again.

"I know I won't be able to get to sleep," Mom said. "She sounds like a sick goose with that honk."

I ignored the remark and fumbled my way back to the cot.

"I wish I had some ear plugs and my eye shades," Mom said a few minutes later. "I can't get to sleep without them."

I got up, turned on the light, and went in the bathroom where I grabbed some tissues from a box. "Here. Stuff these in your ears." I shoved them at Mom, and for good measure, pulled the second set of drapes across the window to shut out the light. "This is as good as it's going to get."

Mom was silent at last. She always knew just how far she could push me before I blew my top. And soon she was asleep and snoring herself.

Betty's night sounds had an erratic rhythm: a snore, a snort, and then silence for so long a person might wonder if she'd died, only to have the snoring start again. Mom, on the other hand, had a delicate little snore that was more like a sigh or a whimper. Unfortunately, the snoring snoops weren't in sync. Snore, whimper, snort, sigh, silence, whimper, and then snore again. They were like a couple of wind instruments that were badly out of tune.

And why was I the only one being driven crazy by the sounds? It wasn't fair, but I tried to look on the bright side. At least it gave me time to think. First, I thought of poor, hungry Spot waiting for me at home. I should have returned to Denver that night if for no other reason than that the present situation was unsatisfactory. I knew Spot wouldn't starve overnight, but for a moment, I thought of calling Mack and asking him to go over to my apartment and feed my cat. Nope, that wouldn't do. There was no longer an extra set of keys above my door, and the spare keys I'd given Mack wouldn't work now that I'd changed my locks. I made a mental note to have a duplicate set made for him first chance I got.

I turned my thoughts to Patricia. We knew she was lying. If someone else had dressed up to look like her, then she wouldn't have had the credit card receipt. But how to prove it without giving my associates away? If worse came to worse, maybe I could claim I snuck a look in her purse at dinner.

And if she'd been in the vicinity of the murder site, did that mean she'd killed Olivia? It sounded like it to me. I wondered if she was busy at this very moment arranging an alibi with a friend who was willing to lie for her.

But what about the break-ins? Had she come down to Denver on two other and separate occasions to sneak into my apartment? If so, why? I couldn't help thinking that the break-ins were related to the murder, and it was possible that Larry had told Patricia at some point during their marriage about the spare set of keys I kept above my door. Still it didn't make sense that Pat or anyone else would go to the trouble to break into my apartment and not do anything to it. Not unless the person was looking for evidence against me or trying to make me look like a paranoid ex-wife who was crazy enough to kill. And I hadn't even been crazy until I'd spent this night with the snoring snoops.

At some point, I drifted off to sleep. I was startled awake by a shout from the bed nearest to the door.

"Scram, Cece. It's the pigs."

Mom had been jolted awake, too, although I couldn't see her. "Amanda, can't you get that woman to keep quiet. And what's she mean about pigs?"

"It's a seventies term for the police." Although that was Mom's generation, not mine, she'd led a sheltered life. "Are you all right, Betty?" I added.

"Of course, I am," Betty mumbled, "but I wish you two would quit talking. You're keeping me awake."

"I told you I wouldn't be able to sleep with her making all that noise," Mom said.

A moment later, Betty resumed snoring. Mom got up and went to the bathroom, turning on all the lights as she went. When she returned, she left the bathroom light on. "It's too dark in here without at least one light on," she said and sat down at the foot of the rollaway.

"Fine," I said with my eyes closed. Never mind that she was the one who wanted it pitch-black.

"That Betty is a strange duck," she continued in a whisper. "I probably shouldn't have asked her to come up here with me, but Nat said she had street smarts."

I opened my eyes and stared at her. They were certainly getting to be pals, considering that she'd never liked him when we were back in school. "When did you talk to him about Betty?"

"After our dinner last night. I wanted to find out something about her before I asked her to help me, and I figured he would know."

"You told him about your plans?" He must still be chuckling, and I was going to kill him for not tipping me off. Still,

Mom and Betty had turned up the credit card receipt, and so there was a part of me that was glad about their foray to Aspen.

"Well, no, I didn't tell him the plan," Mom said. "I just inquired about Betty. After all, I thought it made sense for her to come along since it was her idea to find out what the other suspects were doing at the time of the murder."

I gave up. "Try to get some sleep, Mom."

"It's too cold in here."

I rolled out of the rollaway and closed the window, and Mom returned to her bed. Snore, whimper. The cacophony of disparate sounds resumed. It reminded me of the cuckoo clocks at Greta's.

Finally, I gave up on sleep. I got up, dressed, and snuck out of the room. I canceled the wake-up call since it was nearly six already and went looking for a pay phone. I found one near a convenience store and used my calling card to dial Mack who had just arrived at the cleaners.

"Where are you?" he asked.

"I'm in Glenwood Springs."

"What the hell are you doing there?"

"I had to go up to Aspen to bail Mom out of jail."

It sounded as if there'd been an explosion in the cleaners the way Mack erupted. "What the devil was she doing in jail?"

"It's a long story." I gave him an abbreviated version. "I'll be back as soon as I can."

When I managed to get Mack off the phone, I took a deep breath and called Detective Perrelli's direct line at the police department. If I were going to do this, I'd decided to give my name, but I figured the one thing I had going for me was that I wouldn't actually have to speak to him at this time of day.

"Detective Perrelli here," someone said.

Damn. Not his voice mail. Maybe I should go for "anonymous" after all. I tried to disguise my voice. It wasn't hard to do. I squeaked when I spoke, probably from a combination of fear and exhaustion.

"I have a tip," I said. "Patricia Robertson, Larry Landry's second wife, was seen near the hotel on Saturday when his fiancée was murdered."

"Who is this?"

Panic overtook me. I couldn't have told him if I'd wanted to. "Someone saw her at the gas—"

"Who is this?" he yelled.

I slammed down the receiver, but it was a few more seconds before I could release the phone from my sweaty palm.

Why had he been more interested in the messenger than the message? I hadn't even been able to tell him about the service station or Patricia's credit card receipt. Maybe he thought I was a crank caller, but I didn't think the police treated anonymous tips that way.

Still puzzled, I wrenched my hand away from the pay phone receiver, went inside the convenience store, and bought three toothbrushes and a tube of toothpaste. On the way back to the motel, I thought of another possible explanation for Perrelli's attitude. What if he already knew about Patricia's visit to Denver? Maybe someone actually had seen her at the gas pump, and life had imitated my made-up version of it. The idea gave my heart a lift as I reached the motel.

A continental breakfast had been set up in the lobby by the time I got there. Since it came with the room, I grabbed some doughnuts and three cups of coffee, put them in a cardboard container along with my convenience store purchases, and headed upstairs.

"Breakfast," I said as I entered the room, feeling more optimistic than I had in days. If the police really were onto Patricia for reasons unknown to me, then it had nothing to do with me and my two irritating roommates.

Mom groaned, but Betty didn't stir.

"Here are a couple of toothbrushes and some coffee. I'm heading back to Denver now."

At that, Mom shot up like fireworks on the Fourth of July. "Don't you want to take Betty with you?"

"She might as well ride back with you since you came up together." Besides, the two of them deserved each other.

"But I thought we could all drive back at the same time. Then we could stop along the way for a nice lunch."

"No, thanks. I have to get to work."

"But doesn't Betty need to get back to work, too?"

Betty opened an eye and gave me an evil grin. "I think I'll just hang out with Cece if you don't mind me taking the day off." I decided she was enjoying her role as Mom's tormentor. Good.

"Sure, it's fine with me, Betty."

"Are you sure you don't want to go back with Amanda?" Mom asked.

"Naw, I'll wait for you." With that, she closed her eyes as if she'd gone back to sleep.

Mom went over to the bureau and looked at the doughnuts. "Is that all they have? I always eat bran for breakfast."

"Sorry, that's it, but maybe you and Betty can go out for a *nice* breakfast later." I went in the bathroom and brushed my teeth, then grabbed a doughnut and a napkin, plus one of the coffees to take with me. "Bye. See you later."

Both of the snoops gave me strange looks. Mom's was one of annoyance and Betty's was one of pure delight—like Spot when he sees a person who hates cats.

I drank the coffee on the way downstairs, then grabbed another one for the road.

Now that it was light, I was able to see the towering cliffs of Glenwood Canyon and the roadway carved into it. I decided I was entitled to a break halfway through the canyon and pulled off at a roadside park along the banks of the Colorado River.

I settled down at a picnic table with my doughnut and coffee and turned my head up toward the sky that was like a blue streak above the canyon walls. Unfortunately, the sun hadn't reached the bottom of the canyon yet and I felt cold. I took the lid off the coffee and took a sip of the now cool contents as I let my mind soar up the rock walls of the canyon toward the sky.

Had Perrelli known about Patricia and her trip to Denver before I tipped him off, or was I imagining things? And then it occurred to me. Maybe the police had already checked everyone's credit cards and phone bills to see what people had been up to before and after the murder. Oh, damn. They were probably still checking them, and I'd left a paper trail as long as the Colorado River on its way to the Gulf of California. Not only had I used my credit card for the motel, but I'd used my calling card to phone the detective from the pay phone nearby.

My stomach rumbled the way the river was doing down below, and I climbed back in my car before I drowned in my own anxiety. I should have given my name. No, I shouldn't have. I should have waited to make the call from a pay phone back in Denver. I argued back and forth with myself as I drove the rest of the way back to Denver without stopping. My car lugged on the uphill grades and zoomed ahead when I dipped down on the other sides. It almost didn't make it up to and through the Eisenhower Tunnel, but this time I tried to tell myself that there was light at the other end. The police were on to Patricia, and that's what mattered.

The Hyundai and I continued our up-and-down journey to Denver that was a match for my shifting moods of optimism and depression. We'd finally reached Genessee Park and were on the final approach to Denver. I began to relax as I looked over at the side of the road and the buffalo herd that Betty had talked about the day before.

It was all downhill through Mount Vernon Canyon after that, and as I dropped toward Denver, I sped past the runaway truck turnoffs. I wondered if I needed a graveled off-ramp to stop my personal descent.

When I reached my apartment, I pulled myself up the

stairs at the human equivalent of how my car had taken the hills. I was tempted to take a nap before I went to work, but I knew I better not risk it or I'd sleep until the next day.

I turned my new keys in the locks with some difficulty and entered my personal sanctuary. I didn't see the destruction until I rounded the corner into the kitchen. My first thought was that someone had broken in again, new locks or not, but then I took a better look at the carnage.

A roll of paper towels that I kept on the counter was unfurled across the floor. The trash can had been tipped over and its contents scattered, a cupboard door beneath the sink was open and a ten-pound bag of Purina Cat Chow was turned over.

I examined the evidence with a detective's eye. "Bad cat," I said, stomping my foot.

Spot wasn't spooked this time. He gave me an indifferent look as if to say "This is what you get for leaving me alone for over twenty-four hours."

"So you're proud of yourself for being able to open the cupboard door, huh, Spot?" He'd done it once before, but that time I'd thought it had been an accident. Somehow I couldn't get mad at him any more than I could at Betty and Mom. I must be too exhausted to care.

I cleaned up the mess, filled Spot's dish with fresh water, opened a can of cat tuna, and put it in the other side of the bowl. Then I hit the replay button on my answering machine, which was flashing that I had three calls. I wanted to find out if Stan had called and how he'd taken the news about my standing him up the night before.

"This is Stan," the object of my off-and-on-again affection said. "I got your message, but not until I checked my machine after waiting for you for forty-five minutes." Whoops. He sounded a little irritated. "But I'll overlook it, considering that you had to break your date because of your mother. I'm curious to know what's up with her. Call me when you get home and maybe we can get together tomorrow."

He was talking about tonight, of course, and I decided maybe I should take him up on the offer and see if I could pry any information he had about Patricia out of him.

Beep. The answering machine moved on to the next message without waiting for my response to Stan.

"It's me," Nat said, and luckily I knew his voice. He never bothered to give his name. "I called you at work. What you doing playing hooky?" Obviously, the call had come in this morning. "I got some news that will blow your mind—"

Okay, tell me what it is, I urged the recorded Nat, or I'll wring your scrawny neck.

He paused for so long it was as if he'd heard me and had deliberately decided to withhold the information. I hoped it wasn't just to tell me about Mom making inquiries about Betty. If that were it, he was a few days late with the information.

"What say we get together tonight and go out for a beer?" he continued. "I'll drop by your place when I get off work. Ciao."

Wasn't that just like the egotistical reporter? Thinking I would drop everything to go out with him. Besides, I wasn't about to wait to find out what his mind-blowing news was. If necessary, I would storm the *Trib*'s editorial room in person.

The answering machine moved on to the third message. It was just as interesting and frustrating as Nat's because the caller didn't say what she wanted either.

Beep. "This is Karen Westbrook," Olivia's fast-talking maid-of-honor said. "I need to ask you something *really*, *really important*. Can you call me as soon as possible? It's urgent." She gave me her number.

I wrote it down on a scratch pad, then picked up the phone and dialed it. Her line was busy.

CHAPTER 19

When I finally dragged into work it was after two o'clock. Mack had everything under control in the cleaning department. Just a few more loads to do and he and Kim would be through for the day. It was wonderful to have him back from Alabama, but he wanted the long version of the trip to Aspen as soon as I walked in the door.

I told him I had a couple of calls to make and then I'd tell him the whole sordid story.

I went to my office, stashed the credit card receipt in a desk drawer and locked it. Then I tried to call Karen again. Her line was still busy. I would have thought she'd have had call waiting, as much as she liked to talk on the phone. Maybe she'd heard about Richard Willis being seen at the hotel Saturday and was telling all her friends about it. Perhaps that's even why she'd called me—to tell me that Willis could, in fact, have been the person who'd recommended, either directly or through a friend, that Olivia bring her gown to Dyer's Cleaners.

Nat was usually out of his office this time of day, but I tried his number anyway. My luck was getting better. He answered his phone.

"This is Mandy. How dare you leave me a message that

you have some mind-blowing news and then not tell me what it is." If it were about Mom's unexpected interest in Betty, then I'd really chew him out. Nope, come to think of it, I couldn't do that without telling the nosiest reporter in the world about their trip to Aspen.

Nat gave a sadistic chuckle. He liked to torment me, and I wasn't even sure he'd tell me now. Usually, he "played it close to the vest," as Uncle Chet used to say, when it came to hot news stories, preferring to share them with all of Denver before sharing them with his friends.

"Okay, Nat, give—or our friendship's over."

"You'll have to buy me dinner tonight."

"I thought it was just a beer."

"The price just went up."

"First tell me the news. I have to see if it's worth it or not."

"You drive a hard bargain." He paused, but this time I could hear him flipping pages in his ever-present notebook. "Seems you weren't the only ex-wife at the crime scene Saturday." Another pause, but this one was for dramatic effect.

I wasn't sure the information was worth a beer, much less a dinner, since I already had the goods on Patricia, but at least I was happy to hear that Perrelli knew about her trip, whether it was from my anonymous tip or not.

But Nat wasn't through yet. "Seems Patricia Robertson called the police in the wee hours this morning and 'fessed up to being in Denver last Saturday."

"Would you mind repeating that?"

"She called the police." Nat turned more pages in his notebook. "She says she even drove to the hotel but chickened out and didn't go inside. Claims she turned turkey and went home instead."

"I think it's 'turned tail,' " I said, annoyed at him for his everlasting and, in this case, inaccurate use of clichés.

"Whatever. But ain't that a kick in the pants?"

Except for his mixed metaphors about barnyard fowl, it really was. In fact, I was having a hard time taking it in.

"I thought you'd be more excited," Nat added. He actually sounded hurt.

"I am. I'm practically speechless."

I could tell I'd finally made Nat happy with my reaction. "I knew that would blow you away."

"Right out of the water," I said. "But she didn't confess to stabbing Olivia, huh?"

"Not yet, but she came down to Denver this morning, and they're talking to her about it right now."

"Okay, Nat, that's definitely worth the price of a meal, but not tonight. I have a date with Stan." Maybe—if I ever called him back. "How about waiting until after Mom goes home?"

"I guess—if that's the best you can do." Nat sounded disappointed.

"It's a deal. Bye now." All I wanted to do right then was get off the phone and process this new information. Luckily, Nat was in a hurry, too.

"See you later, alligator," he concluded, using one of his typical reptilian goodbyes as he hung up.

I sat back in my chair. So that's how Detective Perrelli had known about Patricia being near the hotel. Not her charge-account records or an actual eyewitness—or even my anonymous tip. It must have been the bluff I ran with my made-up story in the bar last night. God bless Betty for egging me on; I was still stunned that my fictional tale had caused Patricia to confess, at least about being in Denver last Saturday. I even felt a little guilty about it, but not too much if it would solve Olivia's murder without me having to produce the credit card receipt.

More to the point, was Patricia telling the truth, or only half-a-truth? Lawyers are so careful in their use of words. If she said she hadn't gone to the wedding, so what? No one had gone to the wedding because it never took place. The question was, had she gone inside the hotel and killed Olivia?

Now that I knew Nat's news, it was no wonder he hadn't been able to keep the information to himself until the paper came out the next day. He'd heard enough about Patricia back when I was picking up the pieces after my divorce from Larry. Nat and I tended to share our broken romances with each other even if we didn't share a lot of other things. Much as I loved Mack, I couldn't turn to him in the romance department. He was always more like a worried parent than someone you could commiserate with about your failed relationships.

And speaking of romance, or what was left of it, I called Stan's voice mail and left a message that I was free for dinner tonight and would be home by seven-thirty.

I reminded myself that I'd have to be careful of what I said to him about Mom, and I would have to do the same thing when I saw Nat. I couldn't risk telling either one about the part Betty and Mom—okay, and even I—had played in Patricia's confession. And of course, there was also the problem of what to do with Mom while I was otherwise occupied tonight. It was all too much.

I tried Karen one more time. Her line was still busy. Then I checked the front counter where Elaine, Theresa's afternoon assistant, had called in sick. Julia from the morning shift had agreed to work until four. I promised to be back by then, and finally Mack and I went over to Tico Taco's so I could give him the unabridged version of the dastardly deeds of the menopausal mischief makers. Mack was the only one I dared tell about the break-in up in Aspen, the stolen credit card receipt, and the bluff I'd run on Patricia.

That's when it occurred to me that I also needed to tell Betty and Mom to keep quiet about their Aspen antics. I figured Mom would be happy to stay mum about her evening in lock-up, but I wasn't so sure about Betty. She could be the soul of discretion when she wanted, but her ethics were based on a street person's code of never squealing on a pal. I just wasn't sure that Mom and Betty were that good of friends.

Manuel, the owner of Tico Taco's, wasn't at his normal post so we ordered cokes from a waitress and I described the trip in detail. "And this will blow you away," I said, saving the best for last. "Apparently, Patricia decided she better come clean about her whereabouts Saturday. According to what Nat said just a few minutes ago, she called the police this morning and admitted that she'd been near the hotel that day."

"Then you won't have to show them the charge receipt from the gas station," Mack said. "That's good."

I didn't have the heart to tell him about the anonymous call I'd made from Glenwood Springs to Perrelli that would stand out like Pike's Peak on my telephone bill if the police ever got around to looking at it.

"Do you think she murdered Olivia?" Mack continued.

"I don't know. I keep thinking the break-ins at my apartment were connected, but maybe I'm wrong. I sure can't imagine why Patricia would come all the way down from the mountains to sneak into my apartment."

It's funny how Mack can pick up on every little thing I say, including the pluralization of break-in.

"Break-ins?" he yelled. "I thought there was only one."

Then, of course, I had to admit to the incursion Tuesday night after he got home from Alabama.

"You should have let me come over right then and put new locks on your door."

He fussed about it until I diverted his attention by telling him about poor Spot being outside when I got home and how he'd scratched me when I finally caught him, then hissed and hid in the closet.

"So that's where you got that cut on your arm?"

I nodded, thinking about how the cat's reaction afterwards had reminded me of the time Stan sat on him accidentally.

Spot had hissed and raced for the closet once he got through gouging a trail up Stan's back.

"Oh, my God," I said, almost jumping out of my seat. "Spot acted the same way when I got home Monday night. As soon as I turned on the lights, he hissed at me and went streaking off to the closet. What if it was because my phantom intruder tried to pick him up." I pointed to the remains of my scratch. "Spot could have scratched the person the same way he did me."

Mack's eyes lit up. "And that could be a tip-off to the identity of the burglar."

"Exactly. So maybe we should be looking for scratches on body parts instead of clues in clothes."

"Unless the person is covering up the scratches *under* his clothes," Mack said.

I had a sudden flashback. "You know, Patricia was wearing a long-sleeved jacket last night when we talked to her. Maybe she did come down to Denver and break into my apartment, and the long sleeves were to hide a scratch she got from Spot."

"You should tell the police about it."

"I probably should, but then I'd have to tell them about Mom and Betty's escapade in Aspen."

"Then just tell them Spot might have scratched someone."

We finally headed back to the cleaners, but not until I promised Mack I'd call Perrelli to give him my cat-scratch theory. First I needed to get to the counter so Julia could go home.

"I don't mind working until seven," she said, always eager for overtime.

I said fine. I could use a nap before Stan came over to pick me up that night. Before I left, I went over to the phone at the end of the counter and called Betty to warn her to keep her and Mom's mountain mishaps to herself. No answer. I prayed they weren't up to any more shenanigans.

Then I tried Karen one last time. Her phone was still busy, and I was getting irritated. But maybe I'd copied her phone number down wrong.

I depressed the receiver and glanced over at Julia who was just closing out a customer's transaction on our computer. Maybe Karen had been on her computer all day, but I felt sure she had enough money to afford a separate line. "Would you check the records to see what phone number we have for Karen Westbrook?"

"You mean that girl who was in here Tuesday?" Julia asked. "She called this morning and wanted to talk to you."

"What'd she say?"

"I don't know. Ann Marie took the call and asked me if it would be okay if I gave her your home phone number. I told her it was against store policy." Apparently, Julia had typed in Karen's name as we talked. "Here's her number."

She read it to me, but it was the same one I'd copied down from the answering machine. While Theresa had the name pulled up, I went over and checked Karen's address. It sounded as if it was in one of the many new condos that were being built just north of the Cherry Creek Business District. I could be there in five minutes.

"Okay," I said. "As long as everything's under control, I'm leaving." On the way home, I could stop by Karen's condo.

I walked back to the cleaning department to make sure Mack was gone for the day. Then I grabbed Karen's freshly pressed maid-of-honor gown and went out the back door. If Mack had still been at work, he would have wanted to know where I was going and would have had a fit when I told him. And if I'd lied, he would have caught any slight twitch of my nose. He was as sensitive to my unfortunate body language as if I'd been Samantha on the old TV show *Bewitched*.

It was a hot afternoon with no thunderclouds in sight, and I was sweating by the time I got to the address I'd copied down. All I wanted was to make a quick stop to satisfy my curiosity before heading on home. The idea of a nap was looking better all the time.

When I found the correct address, I climbed out of the car with the gown and went up the few steps to Karen's front door. I'd been right about where she lived. It turned out to be a fancy new condo that probably sold for four or five hundred thousand dollars. It had its own double-door entrance, and I spent a long time ringing the bell. I tried banging on the door, too, but there was no answer. I gave a furtive little twist to the knob. The door was locked.

I put one hand up to the front window and peeked in the living room. It looked like the showroom of a fancy furniture store window, but I was getting bad vibes about the place and I wasn't about to give up yet.

Maybe she'd accidentally knocked the phone off the hook before she went out for an afternoon of tennis. Or maybe she was sitting out in her mini-backyard talking on the phone. Any of the above sounded good to me. I hiked down the block and around to the rear of the connecting row of condos. They each had their own little private patios, divided from one another by redwood fences. It took me awhile to figure out which one was Karen's, and when I did, I tried the latch on the gate. I expected it to be locked the same as the front door, but to my surprise, it opened. Just one quick look inside and then I'd drop the whole thing, I promised myself.

I went through the gate and saw that the sliding glass door to the back of the unit was open. I suddenly felt afraid. This was too much like déjà vu of the time I'd found my friend's body in the apartment above her vintage clothing shop. But surely it couldn't happen again. It would be the same as being struck by lightning twice.

I hung the poly garment bag with Karen's dress in it over the top of the redwood fence. I would go over to the door, I told myself, but under no circumstances, would I go inside the condo.

"Karen?" I called softly, and then again louder.

I edged closer to the door, and then with a giant effort, I grabbed the door frame and looked inside. I didn't have to look any farther.

Karen was lying on her kitchen floor with the telephone near her outstretched hand. The long phone cord was wrapped around her neck.

CHAPTER 20

Once I saw Karen's body, I had to force myself to go the few steps into her kitchen. I knelt down beside her, but I knew she was dead. Still, I reached for her hand and tried to find a pulse. There wasn't any.

Lightning did strike twice, and I felt as if its current was running through my body and had welded me to the floor. Karen's eyes were staring up at the ceiling, her face swollen almost beyond recognition, but I knew it was her.

I got up and willed myself not to be sick, at least not before I called for help. I felt no impulse to pick up the phone—not with the cord wound around Karen's neck and embedded into her flesh so that I could hardly see it. There was dried blood on the side of her head.

All I wanted was to get out of there, but as I turned, I almost tripped over something, which went clattering across the floor. Off balance, I ran out the back door and through the opening in the redwood fence. I slammed the gate shut behind me.

Damn. I'd sworn I was going to get a cell phone. It was still on my to-do list.

I rang the doorbell on four other condos in the complex,

but no one was home. I finally found an elderly white-haired woman who answered my knock at a small brick house across the street, one that hadn't been torn down yet to make way for the glitzy, super-expensive condos.

The woman opened the door but didn't open the screen. In fact, she made a point to reach over and see that it was locked. "I don't want any solicitors. Go away."

"I'm not selling anything, honest." I probably sounded like one of those magazine salespeople who said she was working her way through college.

The woman's faded blue eyes narrowed with suspicion, and she started to close the door.

I was drenched with perspiration, and I tried to dry the sweat off my face. "Look, I need help. I need you to call 911 for me."

She stopped with the door half shut. How could I keep from scaring her when I told her someone had been murdered across the street?

I tried to soften my words, but it didn't work. "There's been a death at one of the condos over there." I pointed in the direction of Karen's unit. "I wondered if you could call the police. Ask them to come to—" I took the piece of paper where I'd written down Karen's address and pushed it toward her. I realized she wasn't about to unlatch the screen so I read her the number. "I'll wait right here. Okay?"

She looked at me as if she were thinking about calling 911 to report a berserk magazine salesman at her door.

"Please." I pointed at the logo on my uniform blouse. "I'm from Dyer's Cleaners, and I was making a delivery when I found the body."

The woman finally left, shutting the door and locking it behind her. I heard a deadbolt fall into place, but I didn't know if she would call or not.

She returned a minute later and unlocked the door. "What did you say the address was again?"

I told her.

The woman started to close the door, then stopped. "And what's your name? The lady on the phone wants to know."

I gave her my name, but I couldn't hide my irritation. "Will you hurry, for God's sake. This is an emergency."

She gasped and shut the door again. I heard the lock being turned a second time. I wished I could have asked her to explain that the "emergency" was connected to the murder of a bride at a hotel the previous Saturday, but it was probably just as well to wait and tell it to the first patrolman on the scene. In fact, I was afraid she would have forgotten the street address again by the time I gave her my name.

After a few more minutes, the woman returned. This time the deadbolt turned, but she only opened the door to the length of a chain. "They said they'd be here in a few minutes. Now leave. I don't want to be involved. I knew those fancy condos over there would be nothing but trouble." She closed the door for good.

She must have hung up on the dispatcher, too. I knew from past experience that the 911 operator wanted the caller to stay on the line until the police arrived.

I crossed the street, and when I looked back at her house, I saw that the drapes were open a crack. She dropped them back in place as I glanced her way.

I waited by my car, but it was too hot to get inside. Finally, a patrol car showed up. The two cops who got out looked young enough to be in high school. One was black and the other was fair.

"This is Officer Jackson, and I'm Officer Larkins," the blond one said. "Are you the lady who called about a body?"

I nodded. "Actually, I had a neighbor do it." I pointed across the street. "It was a woman in that house over there." The drapes fell into place again from where she'd been watching us. "And the person who's dead was murdered."

"How do you know?" Jackson asked.

"She was strangled."

He asked me to show them where I'd found the victim, and I led them down the sidewalk and around to the alley. I knew which condo it was this time. It was the one with the bridesmaid dress hanging on the patio fence.

"Do you know the woman's name?" Larkins asked.

I told him it was Karen Westbrook, and suddenly my words began to tumble out the way Karen's once had. I explained about the urgent message on my answering machine that morning and how I'd tried to call her but her line was always busy. I hadn't even gotten to the part about the connection to Olivia Torkelson's murder when he stopped me.

"I'll get all that information later," he said. "Stay here while we take a look inside."

Gladly. I began to tremble as if I'd come down with a sudden chill. It was a weird feeling as hot as it was. The temperature must have been nearly ninety degrees in the alley. I waited for several minutes as Jackson stood at the gate, apparently not willing to let me out of his sight.

When Larkins returned, he was on his radio calling for the paramedics and all the other people who would have the place marked off with crime-scene tape in a matter of minutes. He looked almost as pale and ill as I felt, although my face was probably beet-red from the heat.

"I need to tell you something," I said, but he waved me off.

In fact, he stepped back into the enclosed patio so I wouldn't bother him. When he reappeared, he was off the phone. "Now, what was it you wanted to say?"

"I'm sure this is connected to the murder of Olivia Torkelson, the woman who was killed Saturday just before her wedding. Karen was her maid-of-honor."

He started writing something in a notebook.

"What I'm trying to say is that I think Detective Perrelli should be notified."

He put in another call from the privacy of the patio, and

when he came back out, he was finally ready for me. "What's your name and your connection to the victim?"

I started to explain the whole complicated thing.

"Officer Jackson will take your statement."

So I started over with the other cop. I wasn't even halfway through when the paramedics arrived, followed by two more uniformed officers. One of them even looked old enough to vote.

Larkins and the new arrivals went back inside the fence while Jackson continued to write down what I was saying. We'd just finished and I'd signed the statement when the first homicide officer arrived on the scene. I knew I was in big trouble because it was Stan, looking for all the world like a kinder, gentler Dirty Harry. Only trouble was that he tensed up the moment he saw me. This was sure to set our relationship back a notch or two.

"What are you doing here?" He ran his hands through his curly, blond hair in a gesture of frustration, or perhaps disbelief.

"I—I found the body."

"Damn it, Mandy. No one said you called in the report. It was a—" He flipped through his notes. "It was a Mrs. Landis."

Apparently, she forgot my name between the door and the phone, but at least she got the address right. "She must be the woman across the street who made the call for me."

I could see his jaw muscles tighten which is what he does when he gets upset. "Stay here. Don't move."

Boy, was I getting used to that, but I was going to get sun stroke standing out here with the heat burning into my body. No one seemed to care. I didn't even care. I was going to get sick, and I did care about that.

"I'm going to go over there," I said to Jackson who had resumed his position at the gate. I pointed across the alley and moved over to where an elm tree provided a patch of shade.

I'd been going on instinct at first, but now I was flashing back to Karen's body. I remembered the dried blood on her temple. I'd been trying so hard not to look at her, but it hadn't worked. The graphic images were sure to haunt me for months.

And there'd been the thing on the floor that I'd kicked. A mallet of some kind. Maybe something to pound meat. I wondered if Karen had been hit over the head with it, then strangled. She'd seemed like an athletic person, and I couldn't imagine her being killed without a fight. Yet there hadn't seemed to be a struggle in the room.

The nausea passed, but then I began to feel dizzy, as if I might pass out right there in the alley. There was a rock garden outside the picket fence that surrounded another small house, this one a single-story white frame building just up the alley. I moved there and collapsed on one of the rocks. I would have put my head between my legs to ward off a fainting spell but I was wearing a skirt, part of the uniform from the cleaners, and it didn't seem like a good idea.

I took deep breaths and tried to think of something else: the blue satin dress hanging from the top of the fence. What should I do with it now that Karen was dead? Damn, maybe her killer was the mysterious Richard Willis, who'd once been one of our customers. He'd been engaged to both women, but he'd only been spurned by one. Olivia. Why would he kill Karen? Unless he'd tried to win her back after Olivia had dumped him and she'd rejected him, too.

And then I thought of Patricia up in Aspen. She'd been at the hotel the day of Olivia's murder. And she was in town today. Nat had just told me that on the phone. But again, why would she kill Karen? Olivia maybe, but why Karen? Except that Larry might be seeing Karen on the rebound from his fiancée's death and Patricia could have gone into a jealous rage because she wasn't going to get him back after all. Nothing made sense, and I had the feeling I was getting delusional from the heat.

I closed my eyes, but there was Karen again. I opened them to find Stan towering above me. I tried to get up, but I was too low to the ground to do it gracefully. Not in that silly skirt.

Stan gave me a hand. "Look, I'm sorry I was upset when I saw you here. I know this is even worse for you, but it drives me crazy when I see you getting more and more involved in another murder case. I'm already having a hard time persuading Perrelli not to put you at the top of his suspect list."

Gratifying as it was to know that Stan was on my side, it was really scary to hear that Perrelli thought I could have killed Olivia.

For a moment Stan looked as if he wanted to hug me, but all he did was give my shoulder a squeeze, which wasn't nearly comforting enough. "Let's go out front to your car." He started walking down the alley.

I stood still. "You mean I can leave now?" I pointed to the dress hung over the fence. "Should I take that with me? I was delivering it to Karen."

He stared at me and then at the gown, his eyes the same cool blue as the gown shimmering through the garment bag. "No, leave it there, and no, you can't leave yet. We're going to go out front to wait for Perrelli so he can talk to you."

"Why don't I give you my statement?"

That was wishful thinking. I knew that our romantic involvement would probably preclude him from interviewing me, and he might have to withdraw from the case entirely. I wished he would. I didn't want this to come between us, and actually, it already had, from the moment Olivia's brother had been arrested for kidnapping me and my delivery truck.

"Just tell me one thing," he said. "Why did you think you had to deliver it to her personally? I thought for a change you were managing to keep out of a police investigation."

Oh, if he only knew. I didn't dare tell him about Mom and Betty and their escapade in Aspen. I supposed he'd find out soon enough, but I wasn't going to be the one to tell him.

He started to walk down the alley.

I hurried after him. "Would you wait so I can explain." He stopped. "I got a call from Karen this morning, but I wasn't available to take it. I kept calling her, and her line was always busy so I came up here. I thought I might as well bring the dress while I was at it."

"How did she happen to bring the dress to you?" Then he turned and continued down the alley. "Never mind. You can tell Perrelli, and we'll talk about it *later*."

Yes, we definitely needed to talk, but I wasn't sure I could suppress my feelings of anger and hurt until later.

When we got to the front of the condo complex, he took me to my car and opened the door for me to get inside. "Wait here. I'll go get Perrelli."

The detective with the basset-hound look was just getting out of his car up ahead. Stan went up to him, and they talked for a long time, with Perrelli giving angry glances in my direction more often than I liked. They seemed to be arguing.

I started the car and turned on the air conditioning, but it had no effect in the heat which seemed to be soaring like their tempers. I checked my watch. It was after six. I would have thought it would have cooled down by now.

Finally, Stan came and got me. "You can talk in Perrelli's car." I hoped it had better air conditioning than mine.

Call me a masochist, but I had to find out something. "I know dinner's out tonight, but when is later?" I put the emphasis on the final word, the way he had.

Stan gave me a look I couldn't decipher. "I don't know. In fact, it might be better if we don't talk at all right now."

I felt a chill run up my spine even as the sweat ran down it. I wondered if Perrelli had ordered Stan not to see me, but I didn't think one homicide detective had that authority over another one. Maybe the order had come down from someone higher up in the department. Or what if Perrelli was about to arrest me and Stan didn't want to be the one to tell me?

CHAPTER 21

It was the interrogation from hell. Perrelli had an officer take me by my apartment to retrieve the tape from the answering machine. Then we went down to police headquarters where the detective talked to me in one of the little interview rooms with another detective present.

I wondered how a man with the soulful eyes of a basset-hound could suddenly turn into a crazed rottweiler. Everything I told him was met with disbelief. He made me tell my story so many times that it began to sound phony even to me.

"So where were you this morning?" he asked for a fifth time.

"I told you. I was up in the mountains. That's why I wasn't home to get Karen's message. I was by myself, and I didn't stop for gas or anything to eat."

"Why did you suddenly just up and decide to take a trip?"

I was afraid if I told him about Mom and Betty's junket to Aspen it would only muddy the waters which were already running at flash-flood stage. The last thing I wanted was to have the middle-aged madcaps hauled into the police headquarters. Betty might very well go berserk, never mind what Mom would do. I wasn't going to bring them into this except as a last resort and after I warned them about it. And I could only assume that Patricia hadn't mentioned the trip to Perrelli when she'd come in earlier that day or he would have hit me with it by now.

"I needed to get away," I said. "I stopped at a roadside park, but no one else was there." I didn't even pause for breath as I changed the subject. "I wanted to mention the break-in at my apartment that I called 911 about—"

I knew that Perrelli had heard about it, but he was quick to point out that it wasn't theoretically a break-in if someone got in with a key. I told him my theory, anyway, that the burglar might have been scratched by my cat. He rolled his eyes as if I were hallucinating.

"But there was a second break-in Tuesday night," I said, "and the person let my cat out of the building."

"Was this with a key as well?"

"Yes," I admitted. "I guess they had a duplicate set made."

"And did you report a second entry?"

"Well, no, because the policemen who came about the first one didn't seem to believe me because I couldn't find anything missing." I was beginning to think it had been a mistake to even mention the no-theft incursions, but I kept going.

I tried to explain how I'd grabbed Spot when I finally found him after the second break-in, and how the cat had reacted the same way he had the previous night. "That's why I think someone must have tried to pick him up on Monday, and it's very possible that he scratched the person the way he did me." I held up my arm to show him the slash that still hadn't healed. "Maybe the person even came back a second time to get even with the cat. I know it sounds crazy, but so does going in and not taking anything."

"What makes you think these alleged entries had anything to do with the murder of Olivia Torkelson?"

"Because I never had one before." Then I had to retract

that statement. "Well, actually I did have one last summer, but that was connected to another murder." Too bad I'd brought that up because then I had to explain about how the burglars had ransacked my apartment looking for a valuable dress. "All I'm saying is that you might look for someone with a scratch on his hand or arm."

Perrelli stared down at my scratch as if he thought maybe he'd found that person, and I was tempted to point out the long sleeves that Patricia Robertson had been wearing when I saw her the previous night. I didn't. That would have revealed a whole lot more about my activities in the last twenty-four hours than I cared to make a part of the record. But surely he would make the connection if Patricia had shown up in Denver this morning in one of those power suits that lawyers wear. Or would he?

He finally let me go, but he seemed about as reluctant to do it as a guard dog would be to let a trespasser escape from a salvage yard in the middle of the night.

A patrolman took me to my car, still parked in front of Karen's condo, and I headed home where I no longer had a tape in my answering machine. Now I had no way of knowing who might call when I wasn't home, but I didn't care. It would have been a good thing if I hadn't gotten the call this morning.

I fed Spot, but not myself. All I wanted to do was stare off into space and try to make sense of what was happening. It seemed too coincidental that Patricia had been in Denver on the two occasions when someone connected to her ex-husband was killed. I probably should have told Perrelli that I thought Karen might have had an interest in Larry herself. I wasn't about to call him tonight, not when one more word from me might make the basset-hound-turned-rottweiler put the bite on me.

My stomach growled, and I finally pulled myself together and whipped up some scrambled eggs. I'd just sat down at the table to eat them when someone knocked on my door.

Maybe it was Stan, and he'd taken himself off the case. That's what he should do if he really cared about me. Right now I needed a friend.

"Who is it?" I yelled as I headed for the door.

"It's me—Larry. I have to talk to you."

I cringed. This was not a friend, and I didn't want to talk to him again. On the other hand, maybe I could find out what had been going on between him and Karen before she was murdered. It wasn't until I opened the door that I considered the possibility that he might be a homicidal maniac who could have killed Olivia and Karen both.

One look at him, and I rejected the idea. He looked too listless and un-Larry-like to have killed anyone. He'd even forgotten to comb his geled hair and it stood out in gluey strands all over his head.

"Have you heard about Karen Westbrook?" he asked, his face a grim reminder of the once devil-may-care womanizer. "She was murdered today—just like Olivia. What is someone trying to do to me—kill off the whole wedding party?" He started to sob.

So this was all about *him*, huh? It was so typical of Larry to take that attitude.

Apparently, he didn't know I'd found the body, and I wasn't about to tell him. "Why don't you come over to the table and I'll fix you a cup of coffee?"

"It's so terrible. Olivia's funeral was yesterday, and now it's happening again." He put his head down on the table, and when he finally quit sobbing, he sat up and looked at me. "They took me down to the police station again and grilled me about it. Fortunately, I had an alibi. I was tied up in court all day."

Lucky for him. I wished I had an alibi.

I came back from the kitchen where I'd put a mug of water in the microwave. "Were you involved with Karen?" I know it sounded slimy, but I had to ask.

He acted shocked. "What do you mean?"

"Just what I said. Were you seeing Karen?"

He couldn't look me in the eye. "Well, I'd been going over to her condo to talk to her, if that's what you're asking, but it was no different than the way I'm talking to you."

I decided to go for the whole package. "What about your little tête-a-tête with her before the wedding?"

Larry got up angrily. "I don't know what you mean."

"Didn't she kiss you that afternoon?"

He crumbled back into his chair just as the buzzer went off on the microwave. "I didn't think anyone saw that. It was a congratulatory kiss, that's all."

"Yeah, right." I went over and poured a spoonful of instant coffee in the mug and brought it to him. I'd be damned if I'd fix him anything to eat.

He didn't even seem to notice the coffee. "It was more of a hug than anything."

So I'd been right about the lipstick on his shirt, and I suddenly had another thought. What if this actually was about Larry after all? What if someone hated Larry so much that they were killing anyone he had anything to do with? Did that mean I was next? I tried not to think about it.

"That must have been why the police asked me about my relationship with her," Larry said. "I couldn't even remember the hug at first."

While we were on the subject of what Mack and I found during our tuxedo detecting, I asked him if he knew if his best man, Brad, might be dating Charlotte Horton.

"Lord, no. Why would you think that?"

I explained to him that we cleaned the tuxes for the company where he and his groomsmen rented them. "We found her phone number in his pocket."

"That's strange. I'll ask him about it."

"Did you ever date her?"

"What would make you ask something like that?" He suddenly seemed ill-at-ease, and it made me wonder if he had and didn't want to admit it. Maybe she might even be in danger now, too. Either that or perhaps I should put her higher up on my list of suspects.

"You didn't answer my question," I said.

Before he could, there was another knock on my door. He looked relieved.

"Who is it?" I yelled.

"It's your mother. I've been worried about you. Your answering machine doesn't seem to be working."

I opened the door and she entered in her usual swirl of colors and Chanel No. 5 perfume. "Have you forgiven me yet?" she asked, giving me a hug.

"No, but come on in." I was afraid she'd blurt out something about the trip so I added quickly, "Larry's here."

"Oh, you poor dear." She went over to the table and gave him a hug, too. "I heard on television that the maid-of-honor for your wedding was found dead today. Surely, it doesn't have anything to do with your fiancée, does it?"

Larry shook his head as if it couldn't possibly be connected. In your dreams, fella.

"Good, I was so worried when I heard about it." She turned to me. "That's why I've been calling ever since I listened to the news. I called the cleaners, but they said you had gone for the day." She looked from me to Larry. "Maybe we could go out for dinner. You both look as if you could use something to eat."

"No, I have to get going," Larry said, apparently anxious to get out of here before I cross-examined him any more about Charlotte. He looked over at Mom. "Maybe we can get together again before you leave, Cecilia." Well, that was better than when he used to call her Mother Cilia.

Mom gave him another comfort hug and glanced down at the table and my now-cold dinner.

"Oh, that looks good," she said. "I've been too upset to eat all day because of, well, you know . . ." I gathered that "well, you know" would forever be her euphemism for her incarceration in Aspen.

"Do you want some eggs, too?" I asked reluctantly.

Larry sat back down, looking equally pathetic. "Yeah, that would be nice."

I guess I deserved that. I should have been more specific when I made the offer. I went to the kitchen and started banging pots and pans around. Good thing I'd just bought a carton of eggs before the whole world fell apart on Saturday.

While Mom consoled Larry, I dished up my specialty for them. It was about as far as my culinary skills went. I came back over to the table with the two plates and set them down in front of Larry and Mom. Well, actually, I slammed them down so hard it's a wonder they didn't break. Then I picked up my own eggs and went back to reheat them in the microwave.

"I'll take some tea if you have any," Mom said.

What made her think I'd have it now when I hadn't had it the last time she was here? She finally settled for coffee, and Larry chimed in that he'd take a cup, too. I pointed out that he already had one that was untouched on the table.

"Where's Spot?" Mom asked, looking around the apartment.

Spot, hearing his name, emerged from the closet and headed in her direction.

"Shoo," she said as he approached, then looked surprised. "Well, isn't that interesting?" She sniffed several times, then smiled. "Here he is, and I'm not even sneezing. That new allergy medicine must be working."

Pleased as I was that she'd found something for her overactive sinuses, this might not be a good thing for me.

"Maybe I could stay here with you after all, dear."

Rap. Rap. Rap-a-tap-tap. Another knock at the door, and this time I knew who it was. That was Nat's signature knock, but what was he doing here? I'd already told him I had a date with Stan—back before I found Karen's body. And even though I'd been feeling sorry for myself and in need of a friend earlier in the evening, right now my plate was full, so to speak. Which reminded me of the eggs in the microwave. I went back and retrieved them before I went on over to the door. By then, Nat had knocked a couple more times.

"I know you're in there," he yelled.

I opened the door, and my skinny reporter friend barged on inside. "Why don't you come in and join the crowd?"

"Hello, Nathaniel," Mom said, but I could tell she wasn't pleased to see him. Maybe she thought he'd been talking to the bag lady.

But Nat was too busy casting eager eyes on Larry. He'd never liked my former mate, but that didn't stop him when he was looking for fodder for a story.

"So, Larry," he said, slipping into the fourth chair at the table. "Tell me what you know about Karen Westbrook, the woman who was just murdered."

"It was a terrible tragedy." Larry gulped his eggs and got up from the table. "I'm sorry, but I have to go now. Thanks for the dinner, Mandy."

"No, wait," Nat said, but Larry was racing for the door.

"I have to go, too," Mom said. "I'm very tired. I didn't get much sleep last night." She cast an irritated look in my direction as if Betty's snoring had been my fault.

Nat was as good as an insect repellent when it came to getting rid of unwanted house guests.

"Larry can walk me to my car, and I'll talk to you later," Mom said. I was relieved to know she'd decided not to sleep over, despite the discovery that she seemed to be allergy-free. Maybe she was afraid Nat would turn his inquiring mind on her and ask why she'd wanted to know about Betty the other night.

"Hey, that looks good," Nat said, noticing my plate. "Got any more eggs?"

I handed him the ones I'd never touched. They were probably cold and rubbery, anyway.

Mom was still standing by the door. "Goodbye, Amanda." I went over to give her the expected hug, and she whispered in my ear, "Just so you won't worry, I wanted to let you know that Mrs. Bell and I really are going to Black Hawk tomorrow." With that, she joined Larry on the landing, and he escorted her down the stairs.

When I returned to the table, Nat swallowed a forkful of eggs and glanced at me. "If you don't mind my saying so, Mandy, you look like something the cat dragged in."

"A dog's more like it." I was thinking of Rottweiler Perrelli, but when Nat looked puzzled, I shook my head and sat down across from him. "Never mind. It's a long story. Besides, what are you doing here? I told you I had a date."

He looked around the room. "Yeah, I noticed."

"So how'd you know I'd be home?"

"I saw Stan down at the police station."

"Oh."

Nat waved his fork as he swallowed another bite of eggs. "What's this I hear about you finding the body?"

"Stan told you that?" I was hurt that he'd tell Nat about me when he wouldn't even talk to me.

"It was off-the record." He winced at the dreaded word. "So what's the scoop?"

"You tell me."

He reeled off his information. "The victim was the maid-of-honor at Olivia Torkelson's wedding. It appears she was hit over the head with a heavy object, perhaps a mallet found at the scene, then strangled with a telephone cord." He paused. "But I heard she called you this morning and said she needed to talk."

"And that's all I know. I tried to call her all day, and her line was busy, so finally I went over to her condo and found her body. It was awful."

Nat reached over and tousled my hair. "I'm sorry, kid."

I jumped up and went to the kitchen because I was beginning to feel as if I might start crying, or else pass out. I couldn't handle his sympathy, and besides, I needed something to eat.

"Say, what's with your mother?" Nat said. "She called me the other night and asked me a lot of questions about Betty."

I broke two more eggs in the pan, glad for a change of subject even if I didn't want to get into the Aspen adventure. "Really," I said. "Why didn't you call me about it at the time?"

"I was on deadline, and I didn't think about it again until I saw her just now. So what gives?"

Instead of lying, I turned as I scrambled up the eggs and told him about Betty and Mom's first encounter during my meeting with the crew. He laughed through the whole story, and it seemed to satisfy him as to why Mom was so curious about the bag lady.

I waited for Nat to say something else, but when he didn't, I turned back to the eggs. Then with my back toward him so he wouldn't see the tears that had sprung up, I steeled myself to ask about Stan. "What did he say about me?"

"He seemed worried about you. He said you might need someone to talk to tonight."

I slammed the skillet down and turned around, fire now mixed with the moisture in my eyes. "Then why the hell isn't he here? He could have withdrawn from this case. In fact, he should have since we're supposedly—" I put my fingers up in the air to indicate quote marks. "—'involved.' "

Nat shook his head. "Maybe he got Perrelli to let him assist so he can stay on top of things. From what I hear, you're in deep doo-doo, and Stan's probably having to walk a tight rope right now between you and his job."

I didn't want to hear about the trouble I was in or even a justification for Stan's behavior. "I'm about ready to throw in the towel." Another expression Uncle Chet was fond of using. "This thing with Stan never seems to go anywhere."

"Tell me about it," Nat said. "Remember that beautiful blonde kick boxer I was telling you about? Well, she dumped me."

I scooped my eggs onto a plate and came back over to the table. "Why?"

"Oh, I got all bent out of shape the other night when we went to a bar down in LoDo." He wiped his mouth on a napkin and fell silent.

"What about?"

"Will you promise not to tell anyone?" When I nodded, he looked around the room as if someone else might accidentally overhear the conversation. "Okay," he continued in a whisper, "it was like this. We're sitting in this booth, and I have to go to the head. I get up for a minute, and when I come back, this big burly biker guy is hitting on her.

"I tell him to leave the lady alone, and he says who's going to make him. I say 'I am,' and he says, 'You and who else, stick boy.' Well, he gets up, and he's about a foot taller and a hundred pounds heavier than me, but I figure I got speed and mobility on my side. I begin dancing around and then Tanya—that's her name—gets up and quick as anything decks the guy in some sort of fancy-dancy karate move."

I had to laugh at the picture Nat was painting, but I stopped when he looked hurt.

"It was a humiliating experience," Nat said. "Here I am, still prancing around, and my date swings the guy over her shoulder, and kerplop, he's down on the floor, her foot at his throat, and he's begging for mercy."

I couldn't resist. "So first she decked him, and then she dropped you?"

Nat bowed his head. "Yeah, that's about the size of it. She said the guy would have killed me if she hadn't come to my rescue, and if I couldn't appreciate that, she didn't want anything more to do with me."

I, for one, was grateful that Nat had shared the story with me. I wondered if he would have told me about it if he didn't think I needed cheering up. Who couldn't help but love a guy like that, even if he was impossibly irritating at times?

I had another thought. What if some deranged person was going around killing women Larry was associated with because they wanted to protect him? It was an even scarier thought than if someone hated him.

CHAPTER 22

Mack called after the ten o'clock news that night. He'd heard about the latest murder and was worried about me.

"Damn it, why didn't you call me?" he demanded. "I could have been over there in five minutes."

"I had my hands full with Mom and Larry and Nat," I said. "But I'm sorry I didn't call you."

"Want me to come over right now?"

"Nat's still here, so I'm doing okay. I'll see you at work tomorrow. I don't even want to think about finding her body right now—"

"What?" Mack yelled.

I guess the TV report hadn't mentioned that I was the one who discovered the body.

"Okay, come on over and I'll tell you about it." Besides, I still had a few more eggs left in my refrigerator.

We were up until after one reviewing what we knew about the case. We didn't have any sudden inspiration, especially as the night wore on.

"I thought for sure it was that Karen woman who killed Larry's fiancée," Mack said. Fortunately, he didn't say anything about our earlier suspicions that it had been Patricia. Mack is always good that way about not revealing confidences. In fact, I'd have loved to talk to him about my predicament with Perrelli as far as establishing an alibi for earlier that day, but not in front of Nat. My nosy reporter friend didn't need to know about Betty and Mom's kamikaze attack on Aspen.

I yawned and knew I'd better try to get some sleep.

"Yeah, it's getting late," Nat acknowledged. "I guess we better call it a day. Want me to sleep over?"

I could see Mack turn into the protective parent. "If anyone's going to stay on Mandy's rollaway, it's me," he said.

"Both of you—out. I'll be fine now that I have new locks on my door."

"New locks?" Nat asked. "Why?"

Then, of course, I had to tell him about my phantom break-ins, which took another half-hour.

I didn't have any nightmares about Karen that night, and I was grateful to Mack and Nat for that. I was not so grateful the next morning when I forced myself to get up and go to work. Now I did feel like something the cat dragged in, just the way Nat had said the night before.

I was late, so I didn't have time to pick up the morning papers on the way to the plant. I stopped at the cleaning machines and grabbed Mack's copies instead.

"No mention of you in the stories about Karen Westbrook," he said, reading my mind. "Not even Nat's."

That was good enough for me. I didn't feel like reading about the murders right then, so I handed the papers back to him, checked to see if Betty was in the laundry department yet—she wasn't, and continued to the call office.

"You're wanted on the phone," Julia said as soon as I got there.

I took the receiver and gave the standard hello as suggested in the manual set up by my late uncle. "How may we help you?"

"This is Larry."

I hoped this wouldn't become a regular thing.

"I wanted to call you and tell you about Brad," he said.

"I just got through talking to him, and I asked him what Charlotte's phone number was doing in his pocket."

"And what did he say?"

"He said she slipped her phone number to him after the murder because she was worried about handling the scissors and thought she might need an attorney."

I was disappointed, especially because now she probably had dibs on Brad, and I was the one who might need a good criminal lawyer.

"He advised her to go tell the police about it," Larry said.

"Okay, that answers one question, but you never did tell me whether you'd dated Charlotte or not."

He seemed irritated that I was bringing that up again. "No, I never dated her."

I knew Larry's way with words. "Okay, but did you ever take her out?"

"All I did was take her home from work once when she locked herself out of her car, and we had coffee a couple of times so she could fill me in on the office politics. She knew where all the bodies were buried . . ." He stopped, apparently appalled at what he'd said. "I didn't mean that the way it sounded. Honest."

"I hope not," I said, but I wasn't about to be diverted. "So did you sleep with her?" His idea of dating and sleeping with someone weren't necessarily the same thing.

There was a sharp intake of breath on the other end of the line. "Of course not." He hung up on me.

I didn't know how much his denial was worth. He'd told me the same thing about Patricia just before our marriage ended.

"Where's Ann Marie?" I asked, turning to Julia.

"She called in a few minutes ago. She won't be here until ten. She forgot she had a dental appointment."

That was typical of the absent-minded teenager. By the time I talked to her, I hoped she could still remember what

Karen had said when she'd called the cleaners the previous morning. That is, if Ann Marie even remembered talking to her.

I stayed and helped at the counter until after nine when the work-bound customers quit coming. I told Julia that I'd be in my office if she needed me and slipped back to the plant.

Lucille stopped me at the mark-in counter with a complaint about the missing Ann Marie. "She keeps forgetting to put red tape on the garment when customers point out stains," she said.

"I'll talk to her about it as soon as she comes in." I was always having to remind Ann Marie of little details that slipped in and out of her memory bank. It wasn't the first thing I would be talking to her about, though.

"I think that ponytail she wears sometime cuts off the circulation to her brain," Lucille added as I continued back by the pressing equipment.

I hoped Betty had made it to work by now. I detoured through the laundry and spotted her at her customary place by the washers and dryers.

She looked a lot more perky than Mom had the previous night. "How's Cece?" she said. "You know, that whole thing was kind of a kick. But when I told Artie about it, he was real upset. He said your ma is a bad influence on me."

I wasn't sure who was the bad influence on whom, but I said, "Your boyfriend seems to be the only one with common sense, and I want you to promise me that you won't go blabbing about the Aspen trip to anyone else."

Betty made a big production out of running her hand across her lips as though she were zipping them shut, then locking them and throwing away the key. "Mum's the word," she said and guffawed, apparently at what she thought was a clever reference to my mother.

I decided to drop the subject and went to my office where I pulled out the note with Richard Willis's phone number on it. I took a deep breath and dialed the office number for Olivia and Karen's old boyfriend.

"Torkelson, Martin and Emory Law Firm," a female voice said.

I slammed down the receiver. Since he hadn't been into the cleaners for more than a year, I should have thought that the business number he'd listed might have been from when he worked for Olivia's father.

Worse yet, the person on the other end of the line sounded like Charlotte Horton. Thank God I hadn't said anything, but I hoped the police weren't tracing incoming calls to the law firm. Detective Perrelli would be sure to wonder why I'd been calling there, and he might not take kindly to the fact that I'd been trying to track down the two murder victims' old beau.

It took me a while to summon up the courage to call Willis's home phone number, but I was in so deep at this point that I figured I might as well plow ahead.

A man answered the phone with a simple hello.

"I want to speak to Richard Willis."

"You're speaking to him."

Now is when things got tricky. "My name is Mandy Dyer, and I'm calling from Dyer's Cleaners. We routinely go through our list of customers who haven't visited us for more than a year. We like to find out why they quit using our service, and in appreciation for answering a few questions, we'll send you a fifty-percent-off coupon the next time you bring in an order for more than twenty dollars worth of cleaning." I'd been talking so fast poor Richard might have been afraid I was Karen's ghost.

"Who'd you say you were?"

I repeated my name.

"You're that asshole Larry's ex-wife, aren't you?"

Obviously he'd been listening to the news coverage about Olivia's murder—but had he known about me earlier?

"Yes, I am," I admitted, "and I really would like to offer you a fifty-percent-off coupon to encourage you to return to Dyer's Cleaners, but that isn't the whole reason I called."

"So what is it?"

"Okay." I made an effort to speak more slowly. "Perhaps you know that Olivia Torkelson came to my cleaners to have her wedding gown cleaned and altered. The police want to know why she chose to bring the work to the ex-wife's plant, and I don't know. You see, I didn't have any idea who she was marrying when she first came here."

"So what's that got to do with me?"

"I'm desperate to find out who might have recommended us, and I was wondering if it might have been you since you'd been one of our customers until last year." And secretly, I couldn't get over the idea that the person who did it was also the killer.

"No, it wasn't me. Olivia and I didn't part on the best of terms, and yet the crazy broad sent me an invitation to the wedding."

I took a deep breath. "Did you go?"

"I started to, but I got sidetracked when I ran into her brother, Ryan. Lucky for me, we were both trashing Larry down in the hotel bar when Olivia was killed."

So that's why Ryan apparently wasn't a suspect in his sister's death, and I guess that meant that Richard also had an alibi. At some level, he'd been my top suspect in the death of the two women. After all, he'd been engaged to both the victims.

"Do you know anyone else who might have hated Larry enough to kill his bride-to-be?"

"Personally, if I were the cops, I'd look for someone who had a thing for him. He was always coming on to anything with boobs."

That had been my second choice, but it didn't get me any closer to a suspect.

"Well, thanks," I said, and always the dry cleaner, I continued, "Why did you quit coming to Dyer's Cleaners, if you don't mind my asking?"

"I quit working at the law firm and started law school. You don't have to dress up for that."

"I'll send you the coupon, anyway, for when you start practicing law."

"Swell."

I was sweating when I hung up. Betty picked that moment to come rushing into my office.

"I just heard that you found another body."

"Did Mack tell you?"

"No, it was on TV."

I guess it had been too much to hope that my name would be kept out of it indefinitely. After all, Nat had known last night, and besides, I was Larry's ex-wife. But not the only ex-wife, damn it.

"You gotta real bad habit for doing that," Betty said. "But at least you got an alibi for the time of the murder. You were on your way back from Aspen."

I glowered at her. "For all the good it'll do me. I can't very well say anything about that unless I get into the whole thing about you and Mom."

"Whoops," Betty said, but she had one of those strange, pensive looks on her face that she gets sometimes.

"Don't you dare do anything more to help me out," I yelled as she left the room.

Mack must have heard me on his way to the break room. "Having trouble with Betty?"

I slumped down in my chair. "It's everything."

"I have a quote for you," Mack said, settling into a chair across from me. "I bet you don't know who said it."

I suppose he was just trying to cheer me up so I nodded my head for him to continue.

" 'How loosely woven is the fabric of our lives,' " he said. "Do you know who said that?"

I frowned at him because I didn't understand it, much less know who said it, and besides, my life seemed too tightly woven at the moment with people I didn't even know but who all seemed to be connected to Larry.

"So aren't you even going to try and guess?"

"If you'll pardon the expression," I said, getting up to check on whether Ann Marie had arrived yet. "It sounds like some 'stuffed shirt' said it."

Mack laughed. "You're closer than you think. It was Kelsey Grammer on *Frasier*."

I gave him a dirty look. "That's cheating. We're only supposed to use quotes from movies, not TV."

"Look, things are bound to start getting better. Patricia has to be the cops' prime suspect now that she has admitted coming down from Aspen."

"I suppose." So why wasn't there something on TV about her? I headed for the door. "I have to go up front now."

Ann Marie had arrived when I reached the call office, but she sounded like she had a wad of gum in her mouth. It was the novocaine from where she'd had a tooth filled.

"Listen, Ann Marie, this is very important. Julia said you were the one who took a call from Karen Westbrook yesterday morning. Do you remember?"

She frowned and held her jaw.

"Karen Westbrook," I repeated. "She said she had something urgent she wanted to talk to me about."

"Oh, yeth, now I 'member." Ann Marie touched her lip. "It's all numb. I can'th feel a thin'."

I hoped the shot hadn't also numbed her brain. "Think very carefully. What did she say?"

"Tha' she wanted to talk to you."

That's what I'd been afraid of. Apparently, Karen hadn't been any more specific with Ann Marie than she'd been on the answering machine.

Just when I'd given up hope, Ann Marie continued, "She wath really weird. She askth if that note you menthioned was on blue paper. She was so weird about it tha' I gave her your home num'er." Ann Marie gave her co-worker a nervous look for disobeying orders, and with a supreme effort, attempted to speak so I could understand her. "She kept saying 'I got one, too. I got one, too.' "

CHAPTER 23

I still hadn't found out if someone had recommended Dyer's Cleaners to Olivia, but at least I knew why her maid-of-honor had called me. It was really scary to think that both women had died after they'd received notes on blue paper. I wondered if Karen's note had been a warning, too, and if its message had been formed with words cut out of newspapers.

I relayed the information about the note to Detective Perrelli's voice mail, but I couldn't help thinking about it as I drove home from work Friday night. Normally Stan and I went out on the weekend, but I'd heard nothing from him since his maybe-it's-better-if-we-don't-talk remark. Frankly, I was so upset with him I was beginning to think it might be better if I never heard from him again.

Even Mom was otherwise occupied. It seemed she really had gone up to Black Hawk today with her friend Evelyn Bell. I'd checked with Mrs. Bell to verify it—just in case Mom was planning on any more snooping. Apparently, she wasn't.

Meanwhile, I'd decided to tackle something I'd meant to do a long time ago: make a list of all the suspects and what I'd learned about them since Monday. At this point, all I'd written down were their names, courtesy of Charlotte, keeper of the guest book and all-round gofer girl.

It was another hot day without an afternoon or evening thunderstorm, but I was too tired to take advantage of it. As soon as I got home, I changed into jeans and a T-shirt, fed Spot, and scrambled up the last two eggs of the dozen I'd bought the previous week. I was glad for the window air conditioner that I kept on for Spot, but soon I'd be able to open up the place to the night breezes. It was one of the things I always liked about Denver; it cooled off at night.

I finished eating, moved my plate aside, and pulled out the scratch pad I'd brought from work so I could study the list I'd made. I transferred each name to a larger sheet in my sketch book and left space between the names to list what I'd found out about the people.

Karen might have had a reason to kill Olivia for stealing her old boyfriend, Richard Willis, and she'd been in the hotel so she'd had the opportunity. Only problem was, she was dead now, too, but I wrote her name down anyway.

> KAREN WESTBROOK: *Could she have killed Olivia for stealing her boyfriend or because she had fallen in love with Larry? And then could someone else have killed her? Or maybe she'd been murdered because she knew who the killer was, but she'd given no indication that she knew anything.*

I moved on to Larry's second ex-wife:

> PATRICIA ROBERTSON: *Still in love with Larry? Was in Denver when both women were killed; bought gas at a service station near the hotel; could have come down to Denver and broken into my apartment, but why?* AND WHY HAVEN'T THE POLICE ARRESTED HER*????*

As far as I was concerned, she had means, motive, and opportunity. I starred her name and continued:

> RICHARD WILLIS: *Dumped by Olivia, but* WHY KILL KAREN? *He'd dumped her—unless he tried to get her back*

and she rejected him. Supposedly has an alibi because he'd been drinking in the bar with Ryan Torkelson.

RYAN: *Brother of the bride*—WHY KILL HIS SISTER? *Has the same alibi as Richard Willis. Could they be covering for each other? Had other people seen them in the bar? Maybe he secretly hated his sister even though she was the only one who accepted him.*

LARRY: *About to marry Olivia and had a good future with her father's law firm*—WHY KILL HER? *Been talking to Karen, but only the way he talks to me or so he says.* WHY KILL HER? *Blackmail maybe—if she saw him kill Olivia? Says he has alibi for time of Karen's death.*

When I finished writing down the information on Larry, I turned off the air conditioner and opened the windows, all except the one by the bathroom door that led to the fire escape. The phantom intruder wasn't going to gain access that way.

The sofa looked so tempting that I moved over to it with my pad and pencil and stared down at the names of the only two other people on the list: Victoria Burnett, the dark-haired bridesmaid who'd pointed an accusing finger at Larry, and Charlotte Horton, who'd backed him up. I continued to write:

CHARLOTTE: *She'd been concerned about handling the scissors. Seemed resentful of Olivia when she told me about the wedding invitations. Larry said he'd taken her home one time when she'd locked herself out of her car and also out for coffee a few times. Could she have read more into this than there really was?*

VICTORIA (VICKY) BURNETT: *Supposedly hated Larry because he hit on her once; didn't think Olivia should marry him, but why kill her? What if she'd said that because she'd developed a fatal attraction to him? Not a customer, but could she have recommended us to Olivia anyway?*

I stopped writing as I thought about all the other people—members of the wedding party and invited guests—whom I didn't know and had no way of finding out about. I did know Brad the Cad who, besides being a lawyer, seemed to have developed a second career being Larry's best man. For good measure, I added his name to the list, but I couldn't think of anything to put under it.

I leaned my head back against the sofa, closed my eyes, and tried to think of any motive he might have had for wanting Olivia and Karen dead. A knock on the door jarred me out of my thoughts. Or maybe I'd gone to sleep.

I jumped. "Who is it?"

"It's Charlotte."

"Just a minute."

Damn, why hadn't I kept my mouth shut? Maybe the gofer girl would have thought I wasn't home. I really didn't want company, but once I asked who it was, I didn't know how to get out of answering the door. I started forward, then gave a guilty look at the suspect list with Charlotte's name on it. It wouldn't do for her to see that.

I grabbed the papers, went to the kitchen, and stuffed them in a drawer.

"Please, Miss Dyer, I don't know where else to turn."

"I'm coming." I hurried to the door and opened it.

Charlotte looked as if she'd just come from the office. She was still wearing her work clothes, although the brown suit somehow didn't give off the "power" image that Patricia's had. It was gabardine, and with it, she was wearing a white blouse with a prim Peter-Pan collar.

"I'm sorry to bother you, Miss Dyer," she said, licking her lips in that nervous way she had. "But I've been so upset all day. I don't know if you knew, but Olivia's funeral was a couple of days ago."

"Yes, I heard it was."

"Well, the office reopened yesterday, and we're so far behind that I had to work until six-thirty. I tried to call you before I stopped by, but your answering machine didn't come on."

"Sorry. I don't have a tape in the machine at the moment. What can I do for you?" I didn't really want to invite one of my suspects inside right then.

"It's—" She gulped and started over. "You remember how we both probably left our fingerprints on the scissors—"

"Yes, but we had a legitimate reason to use them and we've admitted it."

"I know." She started to cry, and I hated to leave her standing out in the hallway.

"Come on in, and I'll get you something to drink."

She accepted with the same reluctance I'd had in making the invitation. "I really hate to bother you." She stabbed at the tears on her cheeks with her hand.

"I suppose you got my address out of the phone book."

She nodded. I really needed to do something about that because, once people came to my building, it was no problem to find my apartment number on the mail boxes down in the lobby.

"You can have a seat over there." I motioned to the dinette table, then moved to the kitchen counter, grabbed a tissue, and handed it to her. "So what's the matter?"

"Well, I—" She sniffed, then blew her nose, and stuffed the tissue in a sagging pocket of the suit jacket. I handed her a couple more tissues. "Maybe I could use a cup of coffee—"

I'd forgotten all about the offer of a drink. I grabbed my dirty dinner plate and cup from the table and went into the kitchen. I filled both my cup and another one with water and put them in the microwave to heat. "All I have is instant," I said.

Charlotte nodded. "That's okay. It's very kind of you to talk to me." She twisted the tissues in her hand, then looked over to where Spot must have come out of his closet hiding spot. "Oh, you have a kitty. I love kitties."

She got up and started toward him. Spot hissed.

"I wouldn't do that. He's not very sociable."

She stopped and came back to the chair. Spot must have ducked back inside the closet.

The microwave beeped and I grabbed the cups from inside, put heaping teaspoons of coffee in them, and brought them over to the table.

"Did you ever find out anything more about that note that you said Olivia received?" she asked, perhaps trying to work up her nerve to tell me what she'd come here for.

I certainly wasn't going to tell her that Karen had received one, too, but just in case she might get one in the future, I said, "All I heard is that it was written on blue paper and there were cut-out words pasted on it."

She shuddered. "That's really scary."

I agreed, but now that she seemed to regain a little self-control, I thought it was safe to ask her why she'd sought me out at home. "Do you feel up to telling me what's wrong?"

She nodded and put Sweet 'n Low in her coffee, then stared into the cup. "I couldn't believe it when I found out about Karen Westbrook. And then I heard you were the one who found her body . . ." Her voice faded away.

I nodded and waited for her to continue.

"Well, the TV said the police think she was hit over the head with something from the kitchen, and I was—I'm—" Again, she couldn't continue.

"But what does that have to do with you?" I asked.

Charlotte made an effort to pull herself together. "Well, Karen was the maid-of-honor, you know. She held a bachelorette party for Olivia a couple of nights before the wedding, and she asked me to help." A bitterness had crept into her voice. "Apparently, she knew that Olivia's father had said I was to do anything Olivia wanted to help with the wedding preparations."

I shook my head. "I still can't believe that."

"Believe it," she said, suddenly more angry than upset. "Anyway, the party was at Karen's house, and she asked me to help. She had me doing a lot of things in the kitchen. I'm afraid the weapon may be something I touched, and—" The tears began again. "And then the police will find my fingerprints on that, too." She wiped her eyes with one of the now-shredded tissues in her hand.

"I'm sorry." I patted her hand the way Greta the waitress had patted mine in the German restaurant Saturday night. Unfortunately, I didn't feel I was giving her nearly as much comfort as Greta had given me with her men-are-scum remark. "I'm sure there'll be a lot of fingerprints in the kitchen if there was a party there."

"I was wondering if you saw what it was?"

"Didn't it say in any of the news reports?" If it hadn't, I wasn't about to mention it.

Charlotte looked around the room, then jumped up abruptly and went over to the pile of newspapers I'd been planning to tie up for Mack's recycling efforts. "Here, let me read you what the article said." Before I could stop her, she started going through the stack. "It was right on the front page . . ."

"Don't bother, Charlotte. I didn't get a newspaper this morning. Those are old papers from the last few weeks."

Charlotte stopped mid-search and came back to the table.

"Anyway, I don't know what to do. It—it was so terrible." She started turning her cup around and around in her hand. "They had a male stripper and played all these raunchy games, and all I wanted to do was get out of there."

I couldn't see what that had to do with anything, but maybe I should put the male stripper on the suspect list, too.

Suddenly, Charlotte jumped up. "Uh—well, thanks for the advice."

What advice? I hadn't given her any advice, and before I could, she was on her way to the door.

"I have to get going. I've probably taken up too much of your time already."

"But you haven't touched your coffee," I said, puzzled.

"That's okay. I have to leave now." She was at the door before I could stop her.

Not that I wanted to stop her, but something about the male stripper seemed to have set her off. Had something weird gone on at the party that she didn't want to talk about, or was she simply uncomfortable with discussing such things?

"Look, just tell the police about helping at the party," I said, going to the door after her. "I'm sure there'll be a lot of fingerprints in the kitchen besides yours, so I wouldn't worry about it."

Charlotte was halfway down the stairs by then, and I'm not even sure she heard my feeble attempt at advice. I guess I should stick to dry cleaning.

But what had just happened here? One minute she was seeking my words of wisdom because she was afraid the police would find her fingerprints on the weapon. The next she was hell-bent to get out of here. It was as if the reminder of the male stripper had sent her off in a completely different direction. But why had she acted as if she were so frightened that she didn't want to stay in my apartment a minute longer?

I went back inside and grabbed my suspect list out of the drawer. The only thing I'd written about Charlotte on Monday was "Why is she telling me all this?" I still wondered about it. But wasn't that the same thing Olivia had done when she'd told me about the threatening note she'd received? I'd even justified Olivia's behavior to Detective Perrelli by saying that sometimes it's easier to talk to a stranger than it is to a friend. I seemed to have answered my own question about why Charlotte had come to me. Besides, we were the only two who'd had the problem with—and a legitimate reason for using—the scissors.

So what about tonight? She'd certainly had a strange reaction to the mention of the male stripper and the raunchy games, and she did seem bitter about Olivia's father giving

Olivia carte-blanche use of poor Charlotte during the wedding preparations. I imagined this put Charlotte far behind on the chores she normally did at the law firm—whatever they were.

What about the male stripper? Did her reaction indicate something about her mental stability—or was she a prude like Lucille at the cleaners who wallowed in the office gossip, but reserved the right to be offended by it. I made another note under Charlotte's name—"uncomfortable at mention of male stripper."

Could she be unbalanced and so embittered by people like Olivia and Karen that she'd killed them?

CHAPTER 24

For good measure, I added "embittered" and "unbalanced???" to the list. I knew that didn't necessarily mean Charlotte had killed anyone, but it still made me nervous.

In fact, I was so shaken that I had a hard time getting back to work. I thought about Victoria—Vicky for short—Burnett, the bridesmaid with the dark hair who'd accused Larry of killing Olivia. All I knew about her was that she'd disliked Larry, and according to Karen, she claimed he'd hit on her. Could she have confronted Olivia with this information on her wedding day? Could it have led to a fight?

In Vicky's defense, it didn't look as if Olivia had fought with anyone; it looked as if someone had snuck up behind her and stabbed her in the back. But what better way to make herself look innocent than to claim she'd been in the hall and seen Larry at Olivia's door? I wrote "What if Vicky had been inside the room and heard Larry call Olivia's name?" I decided that could work for Charlotte, too, and I drew an arrow to her name.

It was too bad I didn't have some way to talk to Vicky, but I didn't even know where she lived. Her name wasn't in the phone book the way mine was, and she'd apparently never been to our cleaners. But hadn't Karen said something about her working at the family shoe store this summer? Maybe I could follow up on that.

I reviewed the list with a niggling feeling that there was something here that was important—either something I'd written down or something I'd forgotten to include. The bottom line was that I was at a dead-end—except for the incident with Charlotte, which had unnerved me more than I realized.

I went to the closet where Spot was staring at me with more hostility than usual, as if I'd somehow betrayed him. Strange, but I couldn't figure out the cat any more than I could the "clues" on my list. Maybe I'd interrupted one of his grooming sessions instead of just a nap. I changed into another of my oversized T-shirts, converted my sofa into a bed, and hauled the list over with me in case I had any brilliant ideas. No ideas came, brilliant or otherwise, but even though I was exhausted, I was too wired to go to sleep. I finally threw back my sheet, climbed out of bed, and grabbed Charlotte's cup off the table, leaving mine in case I wanted to reheat it later. Charlotte hadn't even touched her coffee. I dumped it down the sink, and then began to wash several days' accumulation of dishes, putting them in a drainer to dry.

Still wide awake, I stared over at the pile of papers which was so high it was beginning to look like a miniature Leaning Tower of Pisa, especially after Charlotte had started to thumb through it. I wished now I'd brought home a copy of today's paper so I could have tried to figure out what she'd wanted to show me. In lieu of that, I decided I might as well bundle up the pile for Mack. I got some twine out of the closet, bent down in a squat, and began to stack the papers neatly in two bundles to carry down to the car on Monday.

I lifted the papers off one at a time, separating out a few glossy magazines which the recycler wouldn't take. I was only three or four issues from the top when I rocked back on my heels. I couldn't believe what I was seeing.

Something had been cut out of the front page of the

Tribune. Not one of the articles I sometimes rip out, then can't remember why I've saved a few weeks later. This was something from the headline—a single word.

I shook my head as the horror of it hit me, but I checked the date just to be sure. This wasn't even a paper from the last few weeks, which was all that should have been in the pile. It was an issue back in April. I dug down through the rest of the papers in a manic burst of energy. I found another word cut out of a headline from another front page—still back in April—but in a smaller size and different type face. I didn't even take time to analyze what the missing words could have been.

My breath was coming harder now as I kept going through the stack. And then I found the clincher. Hidden away between two papers at the bottom of the stack was a blue note pad with several sheets of paper torn off. I withdrew from it as if it had the power to physically burn me.

Then I fell back on the floor and covered my face with my hands. I didn't need a homicide detective to tell me the significance of what I'd found. I was sure the missing words had been pasted on a piece of the blue paper and sent to Olivia to warn her off marrying Larry. Karen had received a note on the same kind of paper.

After a few minutes, I jumped up and began to pace, even though what I wanted to do was cuss and stomp and kick something. Instead, I felt myself begin to shake as the realization hit me that my phantom intruder hadn't entered my apartment to steal from me or to search for something to incriminate me in Olivia's death—the way Betty and Mom had done with Patricia. No, the person had come here to plant evidence against me.

I needed to turn the papers over to the police, and I started to the phone. I came to a stop before I got there. How could I go to the police without achieving exactly what the intruder intended: Make me look guilty in the eyes of the law?

Oh, sure, I'd reported a break-in Monday night, but as the officer had pointed out, it wasn't a break-in. There'd been no evidence of forced entry, nothing reported missing—only the upraised toilet seat that was sure to make the cops who'd come to the door remember my hysterical claims. Who was going to believe me if I suddenly came up with the tools used to produce the threat to Olivia and claimed they'd been planted here?

I began pacing again, and suddenly I knew what I had to do. It probably wasn't the right thing to do, but I couldn't think of anything else. I had to get rid of the evidence before it burned me all the way to the electric chair or the Colorado equivalent.

I ran back to the closet, incurring Spot's wrath again, and threw on the jeans I'd discarded just minutes before. Grabbing a sweatshirt, I pulled it over my head, returned to the front room and tied up the papers in two sloppy bundles.

When I was through, I grabbed a stack in each hand and took a quick survey of the floor. There was an indentation in the rug where the newspapers had been. I stopped to scuff up the nap. Then I hauled the papers down to my car, stopping only long enough to glance up and down the street to make sure no one was around to spot me in my panicked departure from the building. As I drove away, I was careful not to exceed the speed limit, lest a cop stop me and discover my contraband. I watched out the rearview mirror to make sure I wasn't being followed.

My paranoia consumed me, and just a short time before, I'd thought Charlotte was the one who was unbalanced. I headed down toward Cherry Creek and the cleaners as if I were on automatic pilot. Halfway there, I thought better of it. I didn't want the papers to be found anywhere near my place of business.

I considered heading for downtown Denver. Surely I could find a Dumpster in one of the alleys where I could get rid of the incriminating evidence. Then I remembered how a homeless man had been sleeping in a downtown alley when the husband of a friend of mine had been killed. The homeless person, a guy named Honest Abe, had seen enough to help solve the murder. I didn't want to run the risk of someone spotting me in one of those over populated alleys as I shoved the papers in a waste receptacle.

I kept heading toward the cleaners, getting more and more upset the closer I came. Was I out of my mind to head for work, like a missile heading for its target? I didn't dare get rid of the papers in the Dumpster behind the plant. I knew I wasn't thinking clearly, so when I reached First Avenue where I would normally turn to go to the plant, I continued south on University Boulevard. The street led to the University of Denver, and a small campus business district. Not a good place to find a Dumpster away from the prying eyes of students. I headed west over to Broadway where there were more small businesses—antique shops, used book stores, and here and there a vintage clothing store which would be closed at night.

Finally, when I reached the area on Broadway, I drove through the alleys looking for a suitable Dumpster. One had a car parked beside it. Apparently, an owner was working late at his store the way I should be doing. I pulled the Hyundai out of the alley, drove across a side street, and into another alley. For a moment, I wondered if I should go on south to Englewood. In my muddled state of mind, it seemed like it might be wiser to dump the "proof" of my culpability in a different jurisdiction from Denver. That way there'd be less chance of the police knowing what they had if they found the papers with the gaping holes in them.

Jeez, I had to get a grip, plus I didn't have the energy to keep going. I finally spotted a lone Dumpster in an empty expanse of alley. Not even a marauding cat to break the silence. Still, I circled the block to make sure none of the store fronts had lights in them. Everything seemed calm, even in a coffee shop that was closed for the night. On the second go-round, I cut the engine as I turned into the alley, then coasted to a stop in the shadow of the coffee shop, which was next to the Dumpster.

Grabbing the first bundle of papers from the car, I ran to the Dumpster and tried to lift the heavy metal lid. Nothing doing. I had to put the bundle down as I struggled to raise the lid. The smell of rotting food, courtesy of the restaurant, assaulted my nose. Then I stretched down with my free hand for the pile of newspapers. I had to let go of the lid. It slammed down with a crash that echoed around the neighborhood. The noise radiated up to my brain, and it finally brought me to my senses. What the hell was I doing? I shouldn't be destroying evidence. I didn't have the guts to take the papers to the police right now, but all the same, I shouldn't get rid of them.

I had to think of an alternative. Next, I had to find the killer. Only then would it be safe to produce the papers. I wasn't entirely sure I was thinking clearly even now, but suddenly it all seemed so logical.

Maybe I'd even had it in my mind subconsciously as I drove to this location. I was only a couple of blocks from where Betty lived, and if ever there was a person who had reason to keep her mouth shut, it was the bag-lady-turned-Aspen-accomplice.

I hoisted the bundle of papers back in the car with its mate and spent a few minutes with my head resting on the steering wheel as I tried to recover from the big mistake I almost made. What if I dumped the papers and then realized I shouldn't have gotten rid of them? I would have had to climb into all that rotting food inside the Dumpster to retrieve them.

When I'd gotten a second wind, I started the car and headed over to Betty's. She lived in an apartment that was as wide as it was high and reminded me of a child's building block. I'd found the place for her, mainly to get her out of my apartment when I'd feared she was going to take up permanent residence on my rollaway bed.

The building even had a security system of sorts, buzzers by each name so that the person you'd come to see or anyone else dumb enough to answer your buzz would let you in the entry door. Well, that was a whole lot better than my own place.

I put down the papers and leaned on Betty's buzzer for what seemed like an eternity. Oh, please, let her be home and not out cavorting with her boyfriend, Arthur Goldman, the doll doctor.

Finally, when I'd almost given up, she answered. "Yeah, who is it?"

"It's Mandy. Let me in."

"What do you want?" She seemed unnecessarily reluctant to buzz me in.

"Look, this is important. I need to talk to you."

A long pause. "Okay, I'll come down there."

"No, I want to—" But she'd cut off the connection to the intercom. I leaned on the buzzer, but she didn't answer.

Finally, I saw her coming down the hall through the glass pane in the door. She was wearing her bilious green polyester pants suit which, like my basic black dress, served as her all-occasion outfit.

She opened the door a crack as if she didn't plan to let me inside. I picked up the papers and pushed my way through to the hallway.

"This is a little late to come callin', don't you think?" she asked. "Me and Artie might have been makin' out."

It was always difficult for me to think of them having sex, not so much because of their ages, but because they seemed so totally unsuited for each other. What's worse, I'd been the one who'd introduced her and the doll doctor, but it had been my plan to hook Arthur up with a neighbor of Betty's, a round, cheerful woman who looked like Mrs. Santa Claus.

I still couldn't believe that Cupid's arrow had gone so completely awry.

"Look," I said, "you're fully dressed so don't give me that crap. Besides, I have a tremendous favor to ask you." I motioned down to the bundles dangling from my hands. "I want you to store these papers for me for awhile, but don't tell anyone about them, okay?"

Betty looked relieved. "Sure, no problem, but why don't you let me have them? I'll take them on up. No need for you to come, too."

"I'm taking them upstairs." I didn't want to risk having her toss them in the nearest trashcan, and besides, she was acting so strange that I wanted to see what was going on.

She gave in, but not graciously, and followed me through the hallway and up the stairs.

"I don't see why I couldn't just take the papers," she grumbled from behind me.

It was all I could do to hold on to them as we got to the second floor hallway. The twine was slicing into my palms like razor blades.

At the door, she made one more attempt to grab the papers, but I held on to them, and she let me in. She opened a closet door just inside the entrance, and I set the papers on the floor.

"What's so all-fired important about them, anyway?" she asked.

I came out of the closet and saw Arthur on the couch.

"How are you tonight, Miss Dyer?" he asked, standing up to address me. He looked every bit like a gentlemanly Kewpie Doll with his pudgy body, ruffled white hair, and courtly manners.

"Just fine, and you?" I surveyed the rest of the living room and kitchen. Everything looked okay.

"What about the papers?" Betty said.

"I'll tell you later." I gave a little flick of my head toward

Arthur as I addressed Betty. I hoped she'd think it was because her boyfriend was here.

"Gottcha, boss lady," she whispered and opened the front door for me.

I was almost as eager to leave as she seemed to be to throw me out. "And remember, don't say anything about this or Aspen to anyone," I said.

She went through the same gesture she'd used at work, running her fingers across her lips as though she were zipping them shut. "Mum's the word," she said again.

I thought I heard Arthur snicker in the background. It wasn't like him. I came back in the room where he seemed to be having a hard time controlling himself. That's when I caught the scent of perfume.

"What's that smell, Betty?"

She sniffed dramatically. "It must be that perfume Artie gave me. I spilled some awhile ago."

"What kind is it? I think I recognize it."

She looked over at her boyfriend for help. "What was the name of it, Artie?"

"Uh—" he said, "Lilac, I think it was."

If that were lilac, then I'd been badly misled by my mother all these years into thinking it was Chanel No. 5. I went over to Arthur. "My mom's here, isn't she?" He refused to make eye contact with me. "Is that why you laughed when Betty said 'mum's the word'?"

Arthur turned red in the face.

"Cece," Betty said, "the jig's up. You might as well come out here. Mandy's on to you."

With that, there was a rustling in the bedroom, and my mother emerged in her usual haze of perfume and swirl of colors. She was wearing another flower-garden dress, more suitable for teatime than an evening with Betty and her beau.

But perfume and pastel colors aside, I couldn't believe my mother would actually make a social call on the bag lady. "What are you doing here?" I demanded.

Mom lifted her nose in the air. "I have every bit as much right to be here as you do, Amanda. In fact, *I* was invited."

Chalk one up for Mom.

"But why aren't you in Black Hawk?" I protested. "You were supposed to be gambling up in Black Hawk. You lied to me again."

"I certainly did not." She seemed outraged at the accusation. "Evelyn Bell and I went up to Black Hawk for the afternoon, but if you must know, I was so nervous about—well, you know—that I couldn't even enjoy myself. As soon as I got back to Denver, I came over to talk to Betty to make sure she would keep the whole unfortunate incident in strictest confidence."

"Mum's the word," Betty repeated.

This time Arthur couldn't contain his giggles.

"I would have told you my concerns last night," Mom continued, "but I couldn't very well do it in front of Larry and Nat."

"Right," I said, not sure whether to believe either one of the middle-aged meddlers, so I looked to the doll doctor. "Is that true, Arthur?"

"Yes," he said, still not making eye contact. "I told Betty it was a foolish thing to go gallivanting up to—"

"So," Mom said, "maybe you could walk me to my car, Amanda. Arthur was going to do it, but now he won't have to."

I grilled her some more about her visit with Betty and Arthur as we walked to her car, but she turned the tables on me.

"So why were *you* there, Amanda, so late at night?"

"The same reason you were. I was trying to make sure Betty was going to keep quiet about your big adventure."

CHAPTER 25

I yanked off my jeans and sweatshirt as soon as I got home and flopped on the bed, not even bothering to pull the sheet up over me. I was exhausted, and I needed to get to sleep. Most people have nightmares when they sleep, but mine had been following me around all evening. I wanted to fall into a state of blissful unconsciousness where they couldn't get to me. I did sleep for awhile, but then something awakened me.

I didn't know what the sound had been or even what time it was. All I knew was that it was still dark outside, and I'd jumped up from the bed and was standing in the middle of the room groping for a light.

The sound came again. It was a banging at my door, and it was followed only seconds later by a guttural voice, "Open up. It's the police."

I continued to stand like a statue in a sleep-induced stupor. Why would the police be at my door? I hadn't called them, so they couldn't really be here. This had to be a nightmare.

More banging, and again, "This is the police. Open up."

I wondered if someone had noticed my suspicious behavior a few hours before when I'd tried to unload the newspapers in the Dumpster. Had the person copied down the number of my license plate? My guilt returned. Fortunately, I still had enough sense to turn on the lamp by the side of my sofabed. I ran to the closet and yanked a flannel bathrobe off a hanger. I normally only wore it in the winter, but it was all I could find.

"I'm coming," I yelled.

When I reached the door, I turned on the overhead light in the entryway. I blinked at the sudden brightness and tried to rub the sleep out of my eyes as I opened the door to the length of its chain. There were two men standing on the other side, but only one of them was in uniform.

"Are you Amanda Dyer?" the plainclothes one asked.

I nodded but kept on the chain. "What do you want?"

"I'm Detective Sampson and this is Officer Langford." He pointed to the man beside him, and they both flashed their badges. "We have a warrant to search the premises." He shoved a piece of paper at me.

"Just a minute," I managed to squeak as I closed the door, took off the chain, then opened it again. "I'm sorry, but I don't understand."

"We have a search warrant," he repeated, enunciating each word carefully as if he were speaking to someone who read lips.

"You'll have to move aside so we can come in."

I moved. "But I still don't understand."

I was remembering back to when Stan had wanted to search the cleaners after my competitor was killed inside the building. He'd said he could get a search warrant or I could allow the police to search the plant voluntarily. I'd opted for giving my permission, but I didn't seem to have a choice this time.

"What are you looking for?"

Neither cop answered, and I followed them into the room.

"Does this have something to do with the report I filed

about an intruder?" I asked. If it wasn't because of my suspicious behavior at the Dumpster, that's the only thing I could think of, but it didn't make sense.

"Ma'am, maybe you'd like to go to a neighbor's while we carry out the search."

I shook my head. That's what I got for not being friendly enough with my neighbors that I could pop in on them in the middle of the night. And downstairs the other inhabitants of the building were probably wishing I didn't even live here.

"If you want to stay, you'll have to sit over there while we carry out the search." He pointed to the chair that had been occupied by Charlotte earlier that night—before she made her mad exodus from the apartment.

I put my hands on my hips, mainly so I wouldn't wring them in despair. "I demand an explanation." I hoped they couldn't hear the tremor in my voice.

Langford, who had thinning blond hair and a gap between his front teeth, turned to me. "We have reason to believe that there may be evidence here pertaining to the murder of Olivia Torkelson. A judge swore out a warrant giving us permission to search the premises." He escorted me to the chair.

"I know what a search warrant is," I said, "but don't you need a really good reason to burst into a person's home in the middle of the night?"

"We do have reason. The judge wouldn't have issued the warrant unless he thought there was just cause."

If they weren't here because of my foray into the alleys on South Broadway or because of the break-in Monday, then I could think of only one reason they were here. It had to be because of the newspapers that I'd gotten rid of in the nick of time.

I'd run out of anger and was left with only a numbing anxiety. I collapsed on the chair and dropped my hands to my lap, where I began to wring them the way I'd been afraid I would.

Langford headed to my closet and turned on the overhead light, scaring Spot out of his sleep. The cat raced out from his hiding place, as upset as I was by these unexpected visitors.

"Damn," the man said. "Where did he come from?"

"It's all right, Spot," I said, although what I wanted to do was tell him to run for his life.

The cat scrambled behind my bed. I'd have liked to crawl in with him—if only his hiding place were big enough for me, too.

Detective Sampson, who had brown hair and a tiny mustache that reminded me of Hitler, looked around my all-purpose living quarters, and his gaze settled on the spot where the pile of newspapers had once been. I glanced away, trying not to show any emotion, but I couldn't help myself. I looked back at him and I thought he was studying the rug. Thank God, I'd taken the time to scuff up the nap before I left.

I wanted to admit what I'd done and scream that somebody had set me up, but I stopped myself. I was sure I could never make them understand that my phantom intruder had planted the evidence against me. And the fact that the person had left me hints he'd been here meant that he was not only shrewd, but totally deranged.

I bent forward in the chair as if I had a stomachache. I tried to catch my breath, which was stuck somewhere near my vocal cords.

"May I say something?" I asked when I could finally speak.

"Not now."

I said it anyway. "I want to call my attorney. I think he should be here." I remembered Charlotte's phone number in the pocket of Brad the Cad's tux, and I could only hope that she hadn't sewn up his services so that it would be a conflict of interest for him to represent me.

The detective gave me a scathing look, made even scarier by that tiny mustache above his lip. "There'll be plenty of opportunity for that later."

Not a good sign. And I even wondered if Brad the Cad's own presence at the hotel when Olivia was murdered would preclude him from accepting either Charlotte or me as a client.

Thank God, I'd locked Patricia's credit card receipt in a drawer at work. I wondered what the police would have made of that if they'd found it here.

Sampson went into the kitchen and began to look in my drawers. For the first time, I wondered if the phantom intruder had planted some other evidence against me. I should have looked around the place more carefully when I got home. What other suspicious things could be hidden here?

I looked over toward my fold-out bed and saw the edge of my sketch book sticking out from under the sheet that I'd thrown back when I got up to wash the dishes hours ago. It had my list of suspects on it. I became fixated on that corner of white paper.

If Sampson and Langford didn't find anything else, I was sure they'd read something ominous into my list. I didn't want them to take my list. I had a manic feeling that somewhere on that list was something that would point me in the direction of the real killer. I began to obsess that it was the only thing between me and death row. If the police found it now, it would only be further proof of my guilt.

While the two officers tore my place apart, I sat at the table, not moving, just staring at the tiny piece of paper sticking out from under the sheet. How should a person act who's trying to look innocent? Especially when she knows damned well what the cops are looking for and aren't going to find because she just removed it?

As far as I could tell, they weren't finding anything else. I tried not to watch, afraid there was something I didn't know about that would incriminate me. I finally looked over to where Langford had joined Sampson in the kitchen. They seemed to be reorganizing the meager supply of cereals in my cupboard.

I glanced at my watch. It was three forty-five in the morning. I planned to go to work in a few hours, although I don't always go on Saturdays. In fact, the previous Saturday I'd planned to take the day off—until I had to make the delivery of Olivia's wedding gown to the hotel. It seemed like an eternity ago. I wondered if I'd be able to go to work now, or would the cops produce an arrest warrant as soon as they completed their search?

Langford went over to my bed, threw back the covers even more than they'd already been, so that I could no longer see the sketch book. He looked in the opening where the bed folded up on itself to become a sofa. I presumed all he saw was Spot and some dust bunnies behind the bed. He got up and proceeded to the bathroom, and I felt a ridiculous relief. He hadn't spotted my suspect list, and I was beginning to come down from the fantasy world where I'd thought it mattered.

I wanted to run after him to the bathroom. After all, that's where the intruder had left the hints of his presence. Had he planted something in the back of the toilet? Isn't that where junkies liked to hide their drugs? Maybe that's even why the intruder had lifted the lid—to point to the place where he'd stashed some more phony evidence.

Langford finally returned empty-handed and joined Sampson who was going through my desk drawer by now. Together they searched every nook and cranny of the desk. Then they huddled for a few minutes and consulted in hushed tones.

I couldn't hear what they were saying, but finally Sampson turned to me. "We'll be going now, Miss," he said, coming away from the desk. "We're sorry we interrupted your sleep."

Sorry? Sorry. Was that all they were going to say?

My guilt had turned to a strange euphoria that I'd found the newspapers and hidden them someplace else. I was convinced I would have been under arrest by now if they'd found the papers here. The fact that the two men were leaving made me hopeful they hadn't found anything else.

"These are for you." Sampson handed me two pieces of paper. "They're a copy of the warrant and a statement saying nothing was removed from the premises."

The statement sounded like a good thing, but I stared down at the warrant. There was nothing on it saying who had signed a complaint that there might be something incriminating here.

I was sure the warrant had to come from someone, and finally my brain released some much need adrenaline. "Who gave you a tip to come here?"

"I'm sorry, but we can't say," Sampson said.

"I hope you got the person's name, and it wasn't an anonymous tip. It could have been the killer, trying to set me up."

Sampson didn't answer, maybe because my logic didn't make sense to him. After all, he and Langford didn't know what I did: that the person who had come into my apartment on Monday and again on Tuesday had actually planted evidence in my apartment. I was the only one who knew that—except for the intruder. And he had to be the killer. But of course I couldn't explain that, now that I'd removed the evidence.

I suddenly had another thought. I hoped to God I was wrong. "Just tell me one thing. Did you get a tip from someone named Charlotte Horton? Is that why you're here?"

I thought I saw a flicker of recognition in Langford's eyes at the mention of her name.

"I'm sorry, we aren't allowed to give out that information," Sampson said.

But Langford's look was all the confirmation I needed.

It was Charlotte. Damn, damn, damn. She'd gone over

and thumbed through the newspapers. She must have spotted one of the papers with the words cut out of it or else the blue notepad. And just after I'd told her about the note Olivia had received. Suddenly her strange behavior made sense, but it shot holes in my theory that the police tipster had to be the killer.

I was too stunned and disappointed to say anything as the two officers left. I followed them to the door and locked it behind them. Then I went back to bed, grabbed my suspect list, and stared at the word "unbalanced???" under Charlotte's name.

What if it hadn't been the memory of the male stripper or the raunchy games at Olivia's bridal shower that had made Charlotte go ballistic on me? What if it had been my stack of newspapers? One moment she'd been crying and wanting my advice and the next, it was as if she were a crazy person who was hell-bent to get out of my apartment.

I couldn't say I blamed her for her weird reaction. If I'd spotted such obviously incriminating evidence in a stack of newspapers, it would have sent shock waves through me, too. I don't even think I could have walked back over to the table as calmly as she had and made conversation—about male strippers or anything else. The discovery would have sent me yelling and screaming into the street. And would I have gone to the police with my discovery? Damned right I would have.

Begrudgingly, I had to admit that Charlotte probably wasn't the mad homicidal maniac I'd been contemplating when she tore out of the apartment. She was a person scared to death of what she'd found and afraid for her life.

I scratched "unbalanced" from under her name. It was too bad. She'd zoomed to the top of my list because of her strange reaction to the mention of the male stripper, and now she'd dropped way back down to the bottom again.

And where did that leave me? Just because the police

hadn't found anything in my apartment didn't mean they wouldn't be back soon with an arrest warrant. I felt myself getting claustrophobic, as if the invisible hand of the phantom intruder were cutting off my air. I had to get out of here. I got dressed in one of my uniforms and left the apartment, racing down the stairs even faster than Charlotte had a few hours earlier.

CHAPTER 26

I didn't know where else to go at this time of the morning, so I went to the cleaners and let myself in through the back door. I flipped on the lights in the cleaning department, but it only lit up the back of the plant. Between there and the call office, which we kept illuminated all night as advertising, the equipment rose up like ghostly images of robotic beings with metal body parts. The Suzie for steaming wrinkles out of garments looked much like a dressmaker's form by day, but now it seemed to be a person with no head.

I hurried around the corner of the cleaning machines to my office, went inside, and closed the door. I tried not to think of murders or headless equipment. I set to work in a frenzy, attacking my computerized business records with an energy I usually reserved for things I liked.

It's surprising how much work a person can get done when she's avoiding thinking of something else. By seven o'clock, when I heard Julia and Ann Marie enter the back door, I'd almost caught up with everything I'd let slide for the last week.

"I'm already here," I yelled, going to the office door and pulling it open.

"We saw your car," Julia said. "I didn't think you'd be in today."

"I changed my mind. I have a lot of work to do." I didn't bother to explain that I'd arrived before dawn because it seemed like the only safe place to be, the one that was not tainted by the alien presence of the phantom killer. "I'll be up front by nine o'clock to help on the counter." On Saturdays, we didn't get the before-work traffic that there was on weekdays, so the call office didn't get busy until later in the morning.

I continued to work on the books. I even made a few calls to customers with problem garments. It's usually a little easier to find people home on the weekend.

When I got to the call office, Ann Marie had an excited look on her face. "Jason Hendrix just called again." That was the TV guy she thought had a real cute butt. "He wanted to come down and talk to you, but Julia said to tell him you weren't here." Ann Marie glanced over at Julia as if the older woman were putting a serious crimp in her social life.

Julia shrugged. "I knew you wouldn't want to talk to him."

I nodded. "I guess Saturdays must be slow news days if he's still wanting to talk to me." Or else, something had happened—like the issuance of an arrest warrant—that I didn't know about.

I spent a nervous few hours working the counter. Even though it was summer, when we don't have as many customers as we do in the other seasons, we had a good morning. A lot of customers in this neighborhood even bring us their clothes that have to be laundered. Ah, the luxury of not having to use the washer and dryer at home.

At one point, I took a phone call from a man who wanted to speak to "Mandy Dyer." Call me chicken, but when he wouldn't identify himself, I said I wasn't there. I could hardly wait to get off the counter.

A college student I'd hired to work on Saturdays came in at eleven. His name was Aaron, and he was dark and preppie looking. Ann Marie took on a whole different and coquettish persona when he arrived. I left Julia to handle their little flirtation and said I was going back to my office for awhile and "to hold my calls". She knew what I meant.

The sofa looked so inviting that I cleared off the fabric samples on it and sacked out for a few hours. It was the first good rest I'd had in days. I must have been dreaming about the murders, though, because I woke up with the urge to do one final bit of detecting before I gave up on my suspect list.

Karen had said Olivia's friend, Vicky Burnett, was working in her brother's shoe store in Cherry Creek while she was home from college for the summer. She'd even mentioned that Vicky had gotten off work for the wedding last weekend. Maybe that meant she'd be working this weekend, too.

But where? Shoe stores always seem to flourish in shopping centers the way fast-food restaurants do along freeways. I picked up the Yellow Pages and checked for the obvious under shoe stores.

I was due for a bit of good luck, and here it was. There was a Burnett's Shoe Salon listed on Second Avenue, a short walk from Dyer's Cleaners, even if I didn't have good walking shoes. I had on a pair of flats that were getting a bit scuffed so this seemed like the perfect opportunity to pick up a shiny new pair.

I changed out of my uniform into a presentable pair of slacks and a striped cotton blouse so I'd look like a typical Saturday shopper. Only trouble was it reminded me of prison stripes, but I left it on. Then I slipped out the back door and headed the few blocks to the shoe salon.

The area is called Cherry Creek North and is an upscale addendum to the Cherry Creek Mall across First Avenue along the creek of the same name. It has all manner of high-class restaurants and stores, including boutiques, gift stores, art galleries, and the Tattered Cover, an independent book store which is so large that it's in a multi-story building that once housed a department store.

So why should I have been surprised about Burnett's? One look in the window told me this definitely wasn't the kind of self-service shoe store with racks of shoes displayed according to size.

Nope, this was a shoe store with genuine leather shoes on pedestals and names like Ferragamo on the boxes. I shuddered at the thought of how much they cost, since the store had chosen not to enlighten me with price tags, and I would probably have turned and walked away if I hadn't spotted Vicky inside. She was definitely the dark-haired bridesmaid who'd pointed an accusing finger at Larry, and she was wearing a pair of slacks and a blouse not unlike mine.

I lingered on the street until another customer, a woman about my mother's age but more tastefully dressed, came out with a bag bearing a pair of shoes that probably cost more than I allocated to my whole wardrobe for a year. I ventured into the heavily carpeted store and studied the attractively displayed shoes until Vicky came forward.

"May I help you?" she asked, giving me a perky smile that went with her upturned nose and sweetheart-shaped face.

Since Burnett's didn't appear to have a lot of low-heeled shoes suitable for us poor working women who were on our feet all day, I turned to her, then pointed to what I thought was probably the cheapest pair of shoes in the store. They were plain black pumps to go with my basic black dress-up dress. "I was wondering if you have these shoes in my size," I said, then stopped. "Don't I know you from some place?"

She studied my face for a moment. "You do look familiar," she said, then quickly asked for my shoe size and disappeared into a back room.

I went over and sat down in one of the suede and chrome chairs and waited. She returned with a couple of boxes in her hands and sat down on one of the low stools in front of me. "We didn't have that shoe in your size, but it tends to run large so I brought a half-size smaller, and I also brought a few other styles while I was at it." As she spoke, she pulled out one of the shoes from a box.

I tried for a thoughtful look as I stretched out my right foot. "Weren't you at the wedding last Saturday?" I was sure she'd know the one I meant.

She looked at me in astonishment. "Of course," she said, "That's where I saw you. You're the one who delivered Olivia's wedding dress." Her face paled, and she drew back from me. "I heard you were Larry's ex-wife. Is that true?" All thoughts of helping me into the shoe seemed to have slipped from her mind.

"Unfortunately, it is," I admitted. "But I swear I had no idea she was marrying Larry until it was too late to do anything about it."

She seemed to be stunned that I was here. The smile disappeared from her face, and the shoe dangled from her hand near my hose-clad foot.

"Isn't it the wildest coincidence that we would run into each other like this," I said. She nodded, but before she thought about coincidences too much, I continued, "It must be fate that I came in here today. Maybe you can help me with something that's been troubling me."

"Sure," she said, but she didn't sound as if she meant it. She was probably as unnerved by my being here as I'd been with Charlotte's visit the previous night.

"Well, I've been trying to find out who referred Olivia to our cleaners. She'd never been there before, and so I was wondering—was it you, by any chance? Our plant is just a few blocks from here."

She shook her head, but I hadn't really expected her to say yes. After all, she wasn't a customer. But I still wasn't willing to accept the idea that Olivia had deliberately come to me because she knew I was Larry's ex-wife.

"Do you know anyone else who might have sent Olivia to our cleaners? Someone said she might have come to me *because* she knew I was his ex-wife."

"Oh, no, I don't think Olivia would have done a thing like that." Vicky put the shoe back in the box; it was as if she'd forgotten I was a potential customer. "In fact, now that you mention it, she stopped by one day after she'd been to your place for a fitting. I think she said someone who was helping her with the plans had recommended your work. I bet it was one of those wedding consultants. I know she had one."

Why hadn't I thought of that? We had a close working relationship with several bridal shops and wedding consultants who recommended us to their customers to clean and box the gowns after the ceremonies to preserve them. I'd even advertised in a local bridal magazine this spring, but it had never occurred to me to think in that direction, probably because Olivia hadn't purchased a new gown. In a way, the possibility that Olivia had found out about Dyer's Cleaners through some professional consultant was anticlimactic, but at least it would provide me with an explanation to give to Detective Perrelli.

"Do you know the name of the consultant she used?" I crossed my fingers, but it didn't do any good.

She shook her head and suddenly seemed to remember the reason I'd given for being in the shoe store. She grabbed the shoes I'd requested and stuffed my feet into them, then insisted that I walk around in them. I winced as I hobbled over to a mirror and viewed my feet squeezed into them like sausages in too small a casing. Oh, good, that gave me an excuse for not buying them.

She got out one of the shoes from another box. It looked almost the same and fit perfectly. She insisted that I try on its mate, too, and go through the same drill. They were fine, but the price wasn't. She said they cost three hundred dollars.

I didn't even flinch. "I'm sorry. I had my heart set on the other pair."

She nodded understandingly. "I'm sorry, too. They were on sale for two hundred dollars."

Boy, did I have an eye for a bargain or what?

"I just had an idea," I said. "Where did you get the bridesmaids' dresses? Maybe that's where she heard about us."

She gave me the name of a bridal shop where I'd dropped off some of our cards one time. I was anxious to get back to the cleaners and give the owner a call, but at the same time, I would have liked to ask Vicky about the time Larry hit on her. I just didn't know how to broach the subject, so I said a quick good-bye and hurried back to the cleaners, stopping only long enough to pick up a to-go sandwich before I checked the bridal shop she'd mentioned.

The phone call was a dead-end because the owner said she hadn't given the referral, but she promised she'd recommend us in the future. So maybe the inquiry wasn't a total loss.

I spent the rest of the afternoon calling bridal shops and wedding consultants I knew. My momentary good luck at finding Vicky had turned cold again, and I didn't find anyone who'd helped Olivia with her wedding plans. I called Perrelli's voice mail at police headquarters, anyway, and told him there might be a connection between some wedding consultant and the referral.

When my afternoon counter people closed up at seven, I left with them. I didn't particularly want to go home. It was as if a black cloud had settled permanently over my apartment, and it had nothing to do with the real thunderheads that were rolling in from the west.

So I finally decided on an alternate course of action. I would drive home, feed Spot, then call Mom and offer to spend the night with her at the hotel. In fact, I wished I'd called her earlier because the plan had several things to recommend it: (1) I wouldn't be home if the police came calling again tonight, (2) It might ward off any future complaints by Mom that we didn't spend any "quality time" together while she was here, and most importantly, (3) I could question her some more about her visit to Betty's. Somehow it just didn't feel right that Mom had been there. I guess it was the part about her saying she'd been "invited" that bothered me.

My mood lifted once I decided on something to do. My apartment building didn't even have the imaginary black cloud above it when I got there, although the real storm clouds were moving relentlessly in the direction of Capitol Hill. I could already hear the boom of thunder and see flashes of lightning toward the mountains.

I found a parking spot right in front of my building, climbed to the third floor, and unlocked the door, which resisted my efforts to push it open. I noticed that something was caught under the door, and I reached down and picked it up—a bulky white business-size envelope with no writing on the front and a sealed flap on the back.

My stomach muscles tightened as I stared at it, but surely the police wouldn't leave an arrest warrant in an unaddressed envelope pushed under the door. Didn't they have to serve a warrant in person the way they did a subpoena?

More likely, someone had left me a note because they couldn't reach me on my answering machine. Maybe Mom, irritated that she hadn't been able to reach me all day. I hadn't meant for Julia to hold *all* my calls, but perhaps she had.

I took the envelope and went over to the kitchen where Spot was waiting for me. Once I fed the cat and put fresh water in his bowl, I turned the envelope over and started to run my finger under the flap.

It occurred to me that I was trying to think of an innocuous explanation for why someone had stuffed a plain envelope under my door. No name. No handwriting I could recognize. Its very blankness rattled my frayed nerves.

Go ahead, just open the damned thing, I told myself. I took it over to the table, sat down by the mug of cold coffee I'd never gotten around to drinking the night before, and ripped it open. There were a couple of wadded-up sheets of blue paper inside.

That's all I needed to see. My hands began to shake. I dropped the envelope on the table as if it were a toxic substance. I ran to the front door to make sure it was locked. My eyes swept around the apartment as I went down the short hall to the bathroom. I forced myself to look inside, but everything seemed okay. I checked the windows. Still it took me a while to come to my senses. If the person who'd delivered the note had been able to get in the apartment, he wouldn't have had to slip the note under the door.

Wouldn't it be just like Mom to write a note on blue paper and scare me to death? I went over and picked up the envelope, but my hands kept shaking. I couldn't seem to make them stop as I pulled out the two sheets of paper. I felt a momentary relief. The note didn't have cut-out words on it the way Olivia's note was supposed to have had.

Even so, I had to force myself to read the message, written in caps with what looked like a red grease pencil.

> YOU DID IT, BUT IF YOU THINK YOU CAN GET LARRY BACK—

The rest was written on the second page.

> YOU'RE CLIMBING UP THE WRONG TREE.

CHAPTER 27

The note might not sound like a death threat, but I knew better. Olivia had received a message on blue paper. So had Karen. Both were dead now, and even if Olivia's note had been composed of words clipped out of newspapers and this one was written in capital letters, the warning was just as real.

I threw the note down and wondered why I felt as if I'd heard that threat before. Olivia's note had said she'd be sorry if she married Larry. I didn't know what Karen's note had said. It didn't matter. What mattered was that I get out of here. NOW. Just because the killer hadn't gotten into my apartment this time didn't mean he wouldn't be back. Karen had died soon after receiving her message, and I knew I had to get away.

I grabbed my shoulder bag, ran to the door and locked it behind me before I raced down the stairs. This time I had a plan. I would go see Stan. It didn't matter if he wanted to see me or not. We still had a history, and that had to be worth something. I was going to tell him everything and let him try to sort it out.

The wind had kicked up, and I had difficulty opening the car door. Once the car was moving, I thought to look in the back seat. Thank God, there was no one hiding there, but someone could be following me. My eyes darted from the rearview mirror to the road ahead in a non-stop motion. It wasn't until I was several miles away that I began to calm down. No one seemed to be on my tail, but I took a roundabout route to Stan's apartment all the same.

That's when I began to have second thoughts about what I'd done. I should have called 911 as soon as I opened the note. At the very least, I should have brought the note with me. I argued with myself. No, it was better to get out of there and leave it where I'd dropped it on the counter. Less chance of smudging more of the killer's fingerprints—if there were any. Besides, I didn't need the note to remember what it said. The words were etched into my brain.

I tried to make sense of the note itself. Had Patricia written it? This was the weekend. Had she made another trip to Denver the way she had last Saturday when Olivia was killed? Or had my continued snooping—the call to Ryan and the visit to the shoe store to see Vicky—made the murderer turn his attention to me, no longer just to frame me, but to kill me? Maybe Vicky had become obsessed with Larry after he hit on her.

The sky was now dark with storm clouds, some with wind-whipped tails hanging down as if they might be spawning twisters. We got tornadoes in Denver sometimes, and I thought about turning on the radio to see if the Weather Bureau had issued a warning, but I didn't know what I'd do about it if there was one.

I drove south as if I were going to the plant, then turned east and wound my way to Leetsdale and south again on Monaco to the apartment complex where Stan lived. Be there, Stan, please be there. I didn't see his car, but I took the stairs two at a time to his apartment. It was on the second floor and had its own outside entrance with another apartment across a tiny alcove from it and a second flight of stairs leading up to more units on the third floor. I knocked on the door, and the instant I did, Stan's dog, Sidearm, started to bark.

Sidearm's a terrier mix who had disliked me from the first time we met. Stan said the dog probably smelled cat hairs on my clothes, but I personally thought he saw me as a giant cat, vying for the affection of his master. Sidearm's furious barking didn't mean Stan wasn't home; it just meant that he hadn't yelled for the dog to be quiet yet.

I kept ringing the doorbell. Sidearm kept barking. I had to face it, Stan wasn't home. I listened for any movement inside the apartment. Damn it, Sidearm, shut up. I was sure he barked only because he knew it was me on the other side of the door.

My fear had reduced me to the point I was paranoid about a dog. I slid down in front of the door, the way people were always doing at my place. I would huddle in the doorway until Stan got home, no matter how long it took.

But Sidearm wouldn't shut up. He was louder even than the thunder that was popping around me like fire crackers. The dog knew I was here. He wasn't going to calm down until I left. Of course, for all I knew, he barked all the time, but right now he was calling unwanted attention to me.

The first drops of rain splattered in my face when I scooted over and sat on the stairs. I gave up and decided to wait in my car. The sound of Sidearm's barking followed me down to the sidewalk. I was almost there when lightning zigzagged its way to the ground only a few blocks away. I stopped as though it had scored a direct hit on me.

Something was wrong. The note I'd just received said "If you think you can get Larry back, you're climbing up the wrong tree." What was the matter with that statement? My brain was churning so fast my thoughts couldn't keep up. Then I finally realized what was the matter. The expression should have been "barking up the wrong tree," not "climbing up the wrong tree."

But so what? That wasn't any more of a threat than

"climbing up the wrong tree" unless you were eyeball to eyeball with a barking dog like Sidearm. But why did I have the feeling that I'd heard the same misquoted cliché at some time in the not-too distant past and that I'd had a similar reaction then? It couldn't have been from Olivia and Karen's notes because I didn't even know what they'd said, except that Olivia would be sorry if she married Larry.

The rain was pelting me harder by the time I reached the car. I could still hear Sidearm's muted barking from Stan's apartment as I climbed inside and locked the door. In a few minutes, the rain turned into sheets of water on the windshield, and I could no longer see outside or hear the dog.

I thought about the note some more, but I felt as if I were ten feet under water, trying to force my memories to the surface. Where else had I heard someone say "climbing up the wrong tree?" Suddenly, my thoughts broke free, and I knew in what context I'd heard the phrase misquoted, and in that same instant, I knew who the killer was. It had to be.

I was remembering what Olivia had told Charlotte about helping with the wedding preparations: "My daddy said I can use you to help with the wedding, and if you think you can get out of it, you're *climbing up the wrong tree*."

The statement hadn't seemed like much of a threat when Charlotte told me about it, but more importantly, it hadn't seemed like something Olivia would have said. That's because it wasn't necessarily a direct quote from Olivia. It was Charlotte paraphrasing what her boss's daughter had said to her—the same way I'd probably just paraphrased what Charlotte had told me.

But it was too much of a coincidence that two people—both Olivia and the killer—would have misquoted the same hackneyed expression. So it must have been Charlotte, not Olivia, who had used the phrase incorrectly, not just once, but twice. Nat would have realized it in a second. He knew his clichés, at least most of them, but it took Sidearm to point this one out to me. Bless the feisty, unfriendly dog.

The rain was still coming down in torrents, punctuated by more flashes of lightning and cracks of thunder, but I couldn't wait. I started the car, turned on the windshield wipers, and headed home. My windows were closed, and they'd steamed up from the humidity and my jagged breathing. I rubbed my hand across the glass, trying to clear off the moisture. It didn't do much good. The windshield steamed up again, so I cracked a side window. Now the rain whipped in, but I kept going. I knew who the killer was and what I had to do. Tell the police and turn the note over to the them.

I squinted to see the pavement up ahead. The downpour had turned the road into a river. Trucks and SUVs splashed water up on the windshield as they roared past me. I fought to keep the Hyundai from hydroplaning.

The rain finally let up when I was almost home, but the wind was still howling. At some point on the drive, I'd even realized how Charlotte could have gotten into my apartment. That's the thing that had bothered me when I wrote down my suspect list—the thing that seemed always just beyond my grasp. I'd written down that Larry took Charlotte home one time when she locked herself out of her car. If she'd left her keys in her car, wasn't it likely that she'd also locked her apartment keys in the car? And it wasn't such a stretch from there to imagine that Larry had casually mentioned to her that she ought to keep another set of keys above her door the way his ex-wife did. It could explain how she knew where to find my keys.

I was only a few blocks from my apartment when the rain stopped and I thought of the clincher. Vicky had said she thought someone who helped with the wedding had recommended Dyer's Cleaners to Olivia. Damn, damn, damn. I should have thought of Charlotte immediately. Only problem was I'd dismissed her once I decided she'd seen what was in the stacks of newspapers the previous night, and innocent that she was, had gone running to the police. I still didn't know whether she'd simply hated Olivia and Karen or had an obsession for Larry, but at least the pieces of the puzzle were finally fitting together.

She'd known "where all the bodies were buried," Larry said, so she could have easily pumped him about me and known I ran Dyer's Cleaners. She'd obviously been in a position to send out wedding invitations to people who weren't on Olivia's list.

I turned the corner to my block and plowed through the water where the storm drains were running full. There were no empty parking spots in front of my building, and I was thinking of double parking while I ran in to get the note. Just at the last moment, I spotted a panel truck, not unlike the one we had at work. It was in the space I'd occupied earlier. Only trouble was it had TV call letters on the side for the station where Jason Hendrix worked. I didn't need that, and once I turned the note over to the police, Hendrix would drop his interest in me.

I kept driving north, turned east on Colfax, and circled back until I found a parking spot in the block behind my apartment. I backed the Hyundai into it, jumped out of the car, and snuck through a yard between the two houses on the next block, aiming for my back door.

The grass was wet from the recent downpour and squished under my feet, soaking through the soles of my flimsy shoes, as thunder still rumbled to the east. Water dripped down from an overhang of elms, and I was peppered by raindrops as the wind rattled through the leaves. But I was almost home. I launched myself across the alley and up the steps to the back door of my building.

I crept through the hallway and up the stairs just in case Hendrix was skulking around one of the corners. I glanced back when I reached my apartment, but I didn't see anyone as I dug in my shoulder bag for my keys.

I unlocked and opened the door. The lights were still on the way I'd left them, but the wind rushed through the apartment like a wind tunnel trying to suck me inside. I started to retreat.

Before I could, Charlotte stepped out from behind the door and pointed a gun at me. "I wasn't expecting you yet, but come on in. This will work."

CHAPTER 28

"How—how'd you get in here," I stuttered. I didn't know how much more I could take. I felt as if I might have a stroke at any moment.

Charlotte's face was contorted with anger and a crazed excitement, and her jeans and sweatshirt were soaking wet. "Well, after you had your locks changed, smartass, I had no alternative but to come up your fire escape and break the window back by your bathroom. Luckily, no one heard me with all the racket from the storm." She motioned with her gun. "Get inside. I mean it."

I did as she ordered, and as soon as I entered, I saw that she'd been tearing the place apart.

"I have a few questions I want answered," she said and gave me a shove. "What did you do with that stack of newspapers?"

"What newspapers?"

She motioned to the place on the floor where they'd been. "I had it all set up for you to take the fall for Olivia and Karen, so what'd you do with them?"

"I recycled them." It was the only thing I could think of to say, but I guess I shouldn't have.

"You dumb broad. You and those other rich bitches always think you're so smart, lording it over people like me and thinking you can steal my man, but I'm twice as smart as all of you."

"Are you talking about Larry? I don't want Larry." I practically spat out his name, never mind arguing the "rich bitch" thing.

"Then why did you meet him in that restaurant in LoDo?" Her eyes were wild. "I thought once I got Olivia out of the way and backed up his story that he didn't kill her, he'd realize he loved me, but he kept turning to you."

I stared at her. "What were you doing? Stalking him?"

"I was only trying to make sure he was okay, but when I saw you waiting for him, I realized you were the perfect person to frame for Olivia's murder, so while you were trying to win him back, I got into your apartment and saw how I could set you up. It was easy to come back the next night with the things I used to write Olivia a warning note and hide them in that stack of papers. Besides, you were the one who'd used the scissors."

And she was the person who'd brought them to me and realized they'd be a perfect weapon. I should have thought about that, too.

I glanced around the room. "What have you done with Spot?"

She waved her arm at me, pushing up the sleeves of a gray sweatshirt, and I could see the scratches where the cat had clawed his way up her arm. "See? Do you see what he did to me?"

"Where is he?" I'd been right about Spot marking the killer. I'd just focused on the wrong long-sleeved jacket, zeroing in on Patricia in her power suit instead of Charlotte on her way to make a condolence call on the Torkelsons and the other time when she'd said she'd been coming from work.

"I got even with him. I threw him off the fire escape." My heart did a nosedive, and I started toward the hallway and the window. "Stop right there."

I stopped. "But I have to find him."

"Don't you understand? He's dead—just the way you're going to be in about thirty seconds."

"Damn you. Larry doesn't even like you."

She shoved me so hard I almost fell. "He does, too. He made love to me."

So much for Larry's denial that he'd gone to bed with her.

"And he loved me until that rich bitch, Olivia, put her hooks in him. So I got even. I sent out invitations to all those people who weren't on her list and then told you about it, and I was the one who suggested that she go to you with her wedding gown." There was a look of pride on her face.

"But Karen didn't have her hooks in Larry."

"Yes she did. She was after him, too. She lured him over to her condo and tried to seduce him. I saw it, and I couldn't let it happen after I saved him from Olivia."

I was still standing in the middle of the room, and I knew I had to do something soon. I started toward the table by the kitchen counter.

"I told you not to move," Charlotte said.

"You aren't going to shoot me here. There are too many neighbors around, and you won't be able to get away."

"Who cares. They'll think it's the thunder."

I was almost at the table. I reached toward the note she'd written.

"Oh, no, you don't. I'll take that."

She lunged for it, stretching out her arms to get it. I grabbed the coffee cup from the night before and threw it at her as hard as I could.

Cold coffee streamed down her face as the mug hit her in the forehead. I knew I hadn't hit her hard enough to stop her for long, but I took off. It was my only hope. We clattered down the stairs, but she grabbed me by the hair before I got to the front door and pushed me outside.

"Don't try any more smartass tricks." She pushed the gun in my back, just the way Ryan had done with the lighter.

"We'll go for a ride, after all. Turn left when you get to the sidewalk."

That was the way I wanted to go. Now, if only the panel truck was still there. I waved my hands, but not so Charlotte could see me.

Suddenly, Jason Hendrix and his cameraman burst out of the truck. The light on a videocam lit up my face, but I was prepared for it. The light must have blinded Charlotte, and she turned to flee. I swung around and tackled her with a move that would have made the Denver Broncos proud.

"She's the killer," I screamed as we both landed in a puddle of water.

"Keep it rolling," Jason yelled as Charlotte tried to slither away like a snake.

She was dragging me along behind her, and it was all I could do to hold on to her legs. "Damn it, will somebody help me?"

By the time Jason and his cohort managed to untangle us, someone had retrieved Charlotte's gun. I thought it was probably Jason, but when I looked up, I saw Stan bending over us putting Charlotte's hands behind her back. The person who'd grabbed the gun was Betty, and for the life of me, I couldn't think what the former bag lady was doing here.

I must be having a nightmare, a concussion, or worse—an out-of-body experience because—I could see that huddled behind Betty was my mother. She was yelling at the top of her lungs.

"Oh, be quiet, Cece," Betty said. "Me and Stan got this thing under control."

Meanwhile, the camera kept rolling, just the way Jason had ordered. News at eleven or the Denver equivalent, only it was too late to make tonight's broadcast.

"What are you doing here?" I finally asked as I staggered to my feet. It was a general question for anyone who cared to answer.

"We been out to dinner with Stan," Betty said as Mom

nodded her head. "We were telling him how I found that credit card receipt in the *Dumpster* out behind the lawyer lady's office up in Aspen after your ma was thrown in the slammer."

"Falsely arrested," Mom squeaked.

"In a Dumpster, huh?" I asked, picking up on the creative spin the menopausal madcaps had put on finding the receipt in Patricia's wastebasket.

By then, Stan was up and had grabbed the gun from Betty. That was a relief. I'd once seen the bag lady turn into a trigger-happy Ma Barker when she had a gun. Stan kept the gun turned on Charlotte as he asked me what the hell was going on. I started to tell him, but he insisted that Jason remove the mike that he'd thrust in my face. Thankfully, all of Denver wouldn't get to hear my hysterical account of the events that led up to the capture of Olivia and Karen's killer.

"It was like this," I said, "Charlotte admitted she killed Olivia and Karen, and she was planning to kill me, but meanwhile, she'd been up in my place looking for—" In the distance, just beyond Stan's left shoulder, I saw a bedraggled looking animal racing up the front steps of my building.

"It's Spot. I'll be back in a minute." Stan grabbed at my arm, but I yanked away and ran toward the front door.

It was a miracle, but the cat was alive. He must have landed in a bush that had broken his fall, or else he'd used up one of his nine lives. I gave the cat a loving pat on the head, and when I opened the door, he streaked into the building and up the stairs. That was all I could do for the moment.

I rushed back to where everyone was still circled around Charlotte, who was now in handcuffs.

Stan was calling for back-up, but as soon as he finished, I continued, "Charlotte was up in my place looking for a pile of newspapers where she'd planted some incriminating evidence against me, but I'd taken the bundles over to Betty's for her to *recycle* them."

I put the same emphasis on recycle that Betty had put on Dumpster. After all, I needed to put my own spin on the fact that I'd removed the newspaper, even if it made me start itching, and what better person to take them to than a former bag lady who used to collect old newspapers as a regular habit.

"Yeah," Betty said, picking up on what I said. "I was going to recycle them. You betcha. But we sure didn't know about no incriminatin' evidence."

CHAPTER 29

The next few hours were a blur. Charlotte was hauled off to jail, and then I was escorted downtown in the wee hours Sunday morning to make what I hoped was my final statement.

Before Mom and Betty were given rides back to wherever they came from, Mom asked if we could have one last dinner together that night before she headed back to Phoenix on Monday. Promises, promises.

Betty jumped at the invitation. "Great," she said. "I'll tell Artie it's a girls' night out."

As Mom left, she was giving dirty looks in Betty's direction. Apparently, she hadn't meant the offer as an open invitation.

And the last I saw of Stan, he promised to stop by later that day. Oh, sure, now that I didn't need him.

The person I needed to talk to was Mack, and I called him as soon as I got home from police headquarters. Filled with a fatherly concern, he came over right away and helped me haul a very irritated Spot to an animal clinic where a vet proclaimed that the cat wasn't any the worse for his bad experience.

I was, though. I was crashing fast, especially when Mack began to fuss.

"You should have come to me with that note last night, not gone to Stan's place," Mack said.

"I know. I know. I promise the next time something like this happens—" God forbid. "—I'll come to you first."

Mack was still at my place when Nat showed up, and Mack's irritation was nothing compared to the police reporter's.

"Damn it, Mandy, what's the idea of giving the big scoop to a TV station," Nat yelled. "I get up this morning and see all your daring-do on the Sunday morning news."

"Whoops," I said, "I was going to call you about it, but I figured the story wouldn't be on until tonight."

Nat kept ranting and raving.

"I can explain," I interrupted. "Jason Hendrix probably saved my life. If he hadn't been there, I'd probably be dead by now. Would you rather have a scoop or have me alive?"

He put his hand to his chin and considered the two options for a minute. "I'm thinking. I'm thinking."

"Jack Benny, right?" Mack was referring to the late comedian's famous response to "Your money or your life?"

Nat grinned at his own cleverness, and I knew the worst was over. It gave me a chance to ask him a question about Charlotte planting incriminating evidence in my stack of newspapers and the subsequent search warrant. "I'm sure she's the one who tipped off the cops about the newspapers, but what I can't figure out is why she came here that night and pretended to spot the evidence," I said, "when she already knew it was there."

"Oh, that's easy," Nat said. "She probably found out that it would take corroboration from another source before a search warrant could be generated on an anonymous tip. She had to figure out a way to give her name and make the whole thing look legitimate. Besides, she probably wanted to testify at your trial. I hear she went berserk when the police told her they couldn't find any evidence in your apartment, and she's down there singing like the fat lady right now."

Finally, after I gave him an exclusive interview and promised to buy him dinner for a week, he left. Mack departed, too, and I took a badly needed nap.

Stan awakened me out of a sound sleep a few hours later, and maybe that's why I said what I did when he apologized for dropping out of my life a few days before.

"But you could have dropped out of this case," I said. "In fact, Nat told me you had to get permission from the lead detective even to assist on it."

"I know, but I thought I could help you more if I were involved."

"I'm sorry, Stan, but I'm tired, and I'm confused about our relationship right now. I would rather have had you here, and I can't help thinking that you're always going to put your job ahead of our personal lives."

Stan looked hurt, but that's the way I'd felt when he said it was better if we didn't talk for awhile. He didn't even argue with me. He just left, and that hurt even more.

I couldn't get back to sleep after that, so after tossing and turning until five-thirty, I finally got ready and headed over to Betty's apartment to get her for our farewell dinner with Mom. I deliberately chose to pick her up first so I wouldn't have to hear Mom complain about her.

And complain Mom did, but only on the short trip from her hotel room to my car.

"The nerve of Betty to invite herself along," she said.

"Well, you could have said you didn't want her to come."

"Not as long as she knows about—well, you know."

I took the mismatched malcontents to Greta's, the German restaurant on Seventeenth, where my problems with Stan had begun. But that wasn't the reason I chose it. I selected it because it was one of those "theme" places that Mom likes and yet it had food hearty enough for Betty.

"Well, isn't this nice," Mom said, giving her approval once we were seated at a window table.

"Sure got a lot of clocks," Betty said, looking at the cuckoo clocks on the wall.

"Hello, fraulein," said the waitress with the blonde braids and Alpine attire who'd said men were scum. "I hope you dumped that guy you were in here with the other night."

"What guy?" Mom asked.

"Who cares," Betty said. "Let's eat."

"What guy?" Mom asked again.

"Well, if you must know, it was Stan."

"I like him," said Mom, always interested in any marital prospects for her daughter. She'd long since forgiven him for hauling Mack off for questioning in another murder investigation. "So how are you two lovebirds getting along?"

"Who cares," Betty said. "I'm hungry."

I decided I might as well get it over with right then. "As a matter of fact, I just broke up with him."

Mom gave a sad little gasp. "Oh, why did you do that, dear?"

How did I tell my eager mother and a disinterested ex-bag lady that I'd felt abandoned by him? Finally I said, "I think his job will always come first with him, and I need some time to deal with that."

"Oh, good, then you haven't closed the door completely," Mom said. "You should think twice before you let him get away." Thinking twice was something Mom had never done as she wed and shed four husbands after my father died, but she'd apparently found happiness with her current spouse, Herbie, down in Phoenix.

"Oh, for Christ's sakes, Cece, let the kid run her own life." This from Betty, who'd just played Thelma to Mom's Louise in an effort to help me out. "Besides, I agree with the boss lady. I never did like him much. He's a cop."

Mom compressed her lips and picked up the menu. "Perhaps we should decide what we want for dinner."

"It's all in some foreign language," Betty complained.

Eventually we ordered, and I returned to the subject of Stan. "Why did you happen to be outside my apartment with him last night?"

"We were comin' to get that Pat-person's credit card receipt," Betty said. " 'Course now we don't need it no more."

"And who cooked up that bit about the Dumpster?"

"It was me," Betty said. "See, I'd been doing some serious thinkin', and I was worried about you not having an alibi for when that Karen person was killed, especially since you was tryin' to protect us."

"We were sorry about that, Amanda," Mom piped in, patting my hand, "but we didn't know what to do about it under the circumstances."

"Then I had this idea, and I called Cece over the other night to talk about it."

"So it wasn't just a social call?" That certainly confirmed my suspicions that the two of them had been up to no good. "And you just made up that story about going to Black Hawk, huh, Mom?" How could I have fallen for the same trick twice?

"Oh, Evelyn and I did that, too," Mom said, "but we came home early so I could meet with Betty to discuss what we should do."

"And you decided on this plan to meet with Stan and tell him about your false arrest and Betty finding the credit card receipt in a Dumpster, not Patricia's wastebasket?"

Mom looked a little guilty, but Betty wasn't going to let me get away with anything. "Yeah, just like when the police came over to my place this morning and got those newspapers you'd given me to *recycle*."

What could I say? I itched all the way through dinner, but at least the real culprit was under arrest and Ryan was awaiting trial on the kidnapping and carnapping charges.

When I finally got home, Larry was waiting for me by my apartment door. "I came over to tell you how grateful I am that you found the killer and saved my life," he said. "Charlotte probably would have come after me next."

"I didn't do it for you, Larry," I said, unlocking the door and moving inside. "I did it for me and the rest of the women you've used."

I may have left the door open a crack for Stan, the way Mom said, but this was one door I planned to close permanently. I slammed it in Larry's face.

ABOUT THE AUTHOR

Dolores Johnson, a former newspaper journalist, is a field reporter for *American Drycleaner* magazine. She is the author of four other Mandy Dyer mysteries and lives in Aurora, Colorado, where she is at work on her next novel.

MANDY'S FAVORITE CLEANING TIP

Lipstick is a tough stain to remove because it's a dye in an oil-soluble wax base. Use a dry-cleaning solvent or laundry spot remover on the back of the fabric with a paper towel underneath to absorb the lipstick. Blot and repeat until stain is gone. Then dampen the stained area and rub with a bar of soap. For "dry clean only" fabrics, send the garment to a reliable dry cleaner (See Chapter 15).